Just So Stories

Do you know how the elephant got his trunk?
Or how the leopard got his spots?
Or how the rhinoceros got his wrinkly skin?
Or how the camel got his hump?
You don't?
Well, then this is just the book for you!

Rudyard Kipling answers all these questions and many more in this collection of some of the most delightful and nonsensical animal stories ever written for children.

RUDYARD KIPLING
Just So Stories

Illustrations by EARL MAYAN

Companion Library

Grosset & Dunlap

PUBLISHERS
NEW YORK

Contents

[v]

Illustrations

[vii]

Just So Stories

HOW
THE FIRST
LETTER WAS
WRITTEN

ONCE UPON A MOST EARLY TIME WAS A
Neolithic man. He was not a Jute or an
Angle, or even a Dravidian, which he might
well have been, Best Beloved, but never mind
why. He was a Primitive, and he lived cavily
in a Cave, and he wore very few clothes.
And he couldn't read and he couldn't write

and he didn't want to. And except when he was hungry he was quite happy.

His name was Tegumai Bopsulai, and that means, "Man-who-does-not-put-his-foot-forward-in-a-hurry." But we, O Best Beloved, will call him Tegumai, for short.

And his wife's name was Teshumai Tewindrow, and that means, "Lady-who-asks-a-very-many-questions." But we, O Best Beloved, will call her Teshumai, for short.

And his little girl-daughter's name was Taffimai Metallumai, and that means, "Small-person-without-any-manners-who-ought-to-be-spanked." But I'm going to call her Taffy. And she was Tegumai Bopsulai's Best Beloved and her own Mummy's Best Beloved, and she was not spanked half as much as was good for her.

And they were all three very happy.

As soon as Taffy could run about, she went everywhere with her Daddy Tegumai, and sometimes they would not come home to the Cave till they were hungry, and then Teshumai Tewindrow would say, "Where in the world have you two been to, to get so shocking dirty? Really, my Tegumai, you're no better than my Taffy!"

Now attend and listen!

One day Tegumai Bopsulai went down through the beaver-swamp to the Wagai River to spear carp-fish for dinner, and Taffy went, too. Tegumai's spear was made of wood with shark's teeth at the end, and before he had caught any fish at all, he accidentally broke it clean across by jabbing it down too hard on the bottom of the river.

They were miles and miles from home (of course they had their lunch with them in a little bag), and Tegumai had forgotten to bring any extra spears.

"Here's a pretty kettle of fish!" said Tegumai. "It will take me half the day to mend this."

"There's your big black spear at home," said Taffy. "Let me run back to the Cave and ask Mummy to give it me."

"It's too far for your little fat legs," said Tegumai. "Besides, you might fall into the beaver-swamp and be drowned. We must make the best of a bad job."

He sat down and took out a little leather mendy-bag, full of reindeer-sinews and strips of leather, and lumps of bee's-wax and resin, and began to mend the spear.

Taffy sat down, too, with her toes in the water and her chin in her hand, and thought very hard. Then she said—

"I say, Daddy, it's an awful nuisance that you and I don't know how to write, isn't it? If we did, we could send a message for the new spear."

"Taffy," said Tegumai, "how often have I told you not to use slang? 'Awful' isn't a pretty word—but it *would* be a convenience, now that you mention it, if we could write home."

Just then a Stranger-man came along the river. But he belonged to a far tribe, the Tewaras, and he did not understand one word of Tegumai's language. He stood on the bank and smiled at Taffy, because he had a little girl-daughter of his own at home. Tegumai drew a hank of deer-sinews from his mendy-bag and began to mend his spear.

"Come here," said Taffy. "Do you know where my Mummy lives?"

And the Stranger-man said "Um!"—being, as you know, a Tewara.

"Silly!" said Taffy. And she stamped her foot, because she saw a shoal of very big carp going up the river just when her Daddy couldn't use his spear.

"Don't bother grownups," said Tegumai, so busy with his spear-mending that he did not turn around.

"I aren't," said Taffy. "I only want him to do what I want him to do, and he won't understand."

"Then don't bother me," said Tegumai, and he went on pulling and straining at the deer-sinews with his mouth full of loose ends.

The Stranger-man—a genuine Tewara he was—sat down on the grass, and Taffy showed him what her Daddy was doing.

The Stranger-man thought, "This is a very wonderful child. She stamps her foot at me and she makes faces. She must be the daughter of that noble Chief who is so great that he won't take any notice of me."

So he smiled more politely than ever.

"Now," said Taffy, "I want you to go to my Mummy, because your legs are longer than mine, and you won't fall into the beaver-swamp, and ask for Daddy's other spear—the one with the black handle that hangs over our fireplace."

The Stranger-man (*and* he was a Tewara) thought, "This is a very, very wonderful child. She waves her arms and she shouts at me, but I don't understand a word of what she says. But if I don't do what she wants, I greatly fear that that haughty Chief, Man-who-turns-his-back-on-callers, will be angry."

He got up and twisted a big flat piece of bark off a birch tree and gave it to Taffy. He did this, Best Beloved, to show that his heart was as white as the birch-bark and that he meant no harm. But Taffy didn't quite understand.

"Oh!" said she. "Now I see! You want my Mummy's living address? Of course I can't write, but I can draw pictures if I've anything sharp to scratch with. Please lend me the shark's tooth off your necklace."

The Stranger-man (and *he* was a Tewara) didn't say anything, so Taffy put up her little hand and pulled at the beautiful bead and seed and shark-tooth necklace around his neck.

The Stranger-man (and he *was* a Tewara) thought, "This is a very, very, very wonderful child. The shark's tooth on my necklace is a magic shark's tooth, and I was always told that if anybody touched it without my leave they would immediately swell up or burst, but this child doesn't swell up or burst, and that important Chief, Man-who-attends-strictly-to-his-business, who has not yet taken any notice of me at all, doesn't seem to be afraid that she will swell up or burst. I had better be more polite."

So he gave Taffy the shark's tooth, and she lay down flat on her tummy with her legs in the air, like some people when they want to draw pictures, and she said, "Now I'll draw you some beautiful pictures! You can look over my shoulder, but you mustn't joggle. First I'll draw Daddy fishing. It isn't very like him, but Mummy will know, because I've drawn his spear all broken. Well, now I'll draw the other spear that he wants, the black-handled spear. It looks as if it was sticking in Daddy's back, but that's because the shark's tooth slipped and this piece of bark isn't big enough. That's the spear I want you to fetch, so I'll draw a picture of me myself 'splaining to you. My hair doesn't stand up like I've drawn, but it's easier to draw that way. Now I'll draw you. *I* think you're very nice, really, but I can't make you pretty in the picture, so you mustn't be 'fended. Are you 'fended?"

The Stranger-man (and he was *a* Tewara) smiled. He thought, "There must be a big battle going to be fought somewhere, and this extraordinary child, who takes my magic shark's tooth but who does not swell up or burst, is telling me to call all the great Chief's

"*Well, now I'll draw the other spear that he wants*"

tribe to help him. He *is* a great Chief, or he would have noticed me."

"Look," said Taffy, drawing very hard and rather scratchily, "now I've drawn you, and I've put the spear that Daddy wants into your hand, just to remind you that you're to bring it. Now I'll show you how to find my Mummy's living address. You go along till you come to two trees (those are trees), and then you go over a hill (that's a hill), and then you come into a beaver-swamp all full of beavers. I haven't put in all the beavers, because I can't draw beavers, but I've drawn their heads, and that's all you'll see of them when you cross the swamp. Mind you don't fall in! Then our Cave is just beyond the beaver-swamp. It isn't as high as the hills, really, but I can't draw things very small. That's my Mummy outside. She is beautiful. She is the most beautifulest Mummy there ever was, but she won't be 'fended when she sees I've drawn her so plain. She'll be pleased of me because I can draw. Now, in case you forget, I've drawn the spear that Daddy wants *outside* our Cave. It's *inside* really, but you show the picture to my Mummy and she'll give it you. I've made her holding up her hands, because I know she'll be so pleased to see you. Isn't it a beautiful picture? And do you quite understand, or shall I 'splain again?"

The Stranger-man (and he was a *Tewara*) looked at the picture and nodded very hard. He said to himself, "If I do not fetch this great Chief's tribe to help him, he will be slain by his enemies who are coming up on all sides with spears. Now I see why the great Chief pretended not to notice me! He feared that his enemies were hiding in the bushes and would see him deliver a message to me. Therefore, he turned his back, and let the wise and wonderful child draw the terrible picture showing me his difficulties. I will now go and get help for him from his tribe."

He did not even ask Taffy the road, but raced off into the bushes like the wind, with the birch-bark in his hand, and Taffy sat down most pleased.

"What have you been doing, Taffy?" said Tegumai. He had mended his spear and was carefully waving it to and fro.

"It's a little berangement of my own, Daddy dear," said Taffy. "If you won't ask me questions, you'll know all about it in a little time, and you'll be surprised. You don't know how surprised you'll be, Daddy! Promise you'll be surprised."

"Very well," said Tegumai, and went on fishing.

The Stranger-man—did you know he was a Tewara?—hurried away with the picture and ran for some miles, till quite by accident he found Teshumai Tewindrow at the door of her Cave, talking to some other Neolithic ladies who had come in to a Primitive lunch. Taffy was very like Teshumai, especially about the upper part of the face and the eyes, so the Stranger-man—always a pure Tewara —smiled politely and handed Teshumai the birch-bark. He had run hard, so that he panted, and his legs were scratched with brambles, but he still tried to be polite.

As soon as Teshumai saw the picture, she screamed like anything and flew at the Stranger-man. The other Neolithic ladies at once knocked him down and sat on him in a long line of six, while Teshumai pulled his hair.

"It's as plain as the nose on this Stranger-man's face," she said. "He has stuck my Tegumai all full of spears, and frightened poor Taffy so that her hair stands all on end—and not content with that, he brings me a horrid picture of how it was done. Look!" She showed the picture to all the Neolithic ladies sitting patiently on the Stranger-man. "Here is my Tegumai with his arm broken. Here is a spear sticking into his back. Here is a man with a spear ready to throw. Here is another man throwing a spear from a Cave, and here are a whole pack of people" (they were Taffy's beavers really, but they did look rather

like people) "coming up behind Tegumai.
Isn't it shocking!"

"Most shocking!" said the Neolithic ladies,
and they filled the Stranger-man's hair with
mud (at which he was surprised), and they
beat upon the Reverberating Tribal Drums,
and called together all the chiefs of the Tribe
of Tegumai, with their Hetmans and Dolmans, all Neguses, Woons, and Akhoonds of
the organization, in addition to the Warlocks,
Angekoks, Juju-men, Bonzes, and the rest,
who decided that before they chopped the
Stranger-man's head off, he should instantly
lead them down to the river and show them
where he had hidden poor Taffy.

By this time the Stranger-man (in spite of
being a Tewara) was really annoyed. They
had filled his hair with mud . . . they had
rolled him up and down on knobby pebbles . . . they had sat upon him in a long line
of six . . . they had thumped him and
bumped him till he could hardly breathe.
And though he did not understand their language, he was almost sure that the names the

Neolithic ladies called him were not ladylike.

However, he said nothing till all the Tribe of Tegumai were assembled, and then he led them back to the bank of the Wagai River, and there they found Taffy making daisy chains, and Tegumai carefully spearing small carp with his mended spear.

"Well, you *have* been quick!" said Taffy. "But why did you bring so many people? Daddy, dear, this is my surprise. *Are* you surprised, Daddy?"

"Very," said Tegumai, "but it has ruined all my fishing for the day. Why, the whole dear, kind, nice, clean, quiet Tribe is here, Taffy."

And so they were. First of all walked Teshumai Tewindrow and the Neolithic ladies, tightly holding on to the Stranger-man, whose hair was full of mud (although he was a Tewara). Behind them came the Head Chief, the Vice-Chief, the Deputy and Assistant Chiefs (all armed to the upper teeth), the Hetmans and Heads of Hundreds, Platoffs with their Platoons, and Dolmans with their Detachments; Woons, Neguses, and Akhoonds ranking in the rear (still armed to the teeth).

Behind them was the Tribe in hierarchical order, from owners of four caves (one for each season), a private reindeer-run, and two salmon-leaps, to feudal and prognathous Villeins, semi-entitled to half a bearskin of winter nights, seven yards from the fire, and adscript serfs, holding the reversion of a scraped marrow-bone under heriot. (Aren't those beautiful words, Best Beloved?)

They were all there, prancing and shouting, and they frightened every fish for twenty miles, and Tegumai thanked them in a fluid Neolithic oration.

Then Teshumai Tewindrow ran down and kissed and hugged Taffy very much. But the Head Chief of the Tribe of Tegumai took Tegumai by the top-knot feathers and shook him severely.

"Explain! Explain! Explain!" cried all the Tribe of Tegumai.

"Goodness' sakes alive!" said Tegumai.

"Let go of my top-knot! Can't a man break his carp-spear without the whole countryside descending on him? You're a very interfering people."

"I don't believe you've brought my Daddy's black-handled spear, after all," said Taffy. "And what *are* you doing to my nice Stranger-man?"

They were thumping him by twos and threes and tens till his eyes turned round and round. He could only gasp and point at Taffy.

"Where are the bad people who speared you, my darling?" said Teshumai Tewind-row.

"There weren't any," said Tegumai. "My only visitor this morning was the poor fellow that you are trying to choke. Aren't you well, or are you ill, O Tribe of Tegumai?"

"He came with a horrible picture," said the Head Chief, "a picture that showed you were full of spears."

"Er—um—pr'aps I'd better 'splain that I

[29]

gave him that picture," said Taffy, but she did not feel quite comfy.

"You!" said the Tribe of Tegumai all together. "Small-person-with-no-manners-who-ought-to-be-spanked! You?"

"Taffy dear, I'm afraid we're in for a little trouble," said her Daddy, and put his arm round her, so she didn't care.

"Explain! Explain! Explain!" said the Head Chief of the Tribe of Tegumai, and he hopped on one foot.

"I wanted the Stranger-man to fetch Daddy's spear, so I drawded it," said Taffy. "There wasn't lots of spears. There was only one spear. I drawded it three times to make sure. I couldn't help it looking as if it stuck into Daddy's head—there wasn't room on the birch-bark—and those things that Mummy called bad people are my beavers. I drawded them to show him the way through the swamp . . . and I drawded Mummy at the mouth of the Cave looking pleased because he is a nice Stranger-man. Why have you filled his hair with mud? Wash him!"

Nobody said anything at all for a long time, till the Head Chief laughed.

Then the Stranger-Man (who was at least a Tewara) laughed.

Then Tegumai laughed till he fell down flat on the bank.

Then all the Tribe laughed more and worse and louder.

The only people who did not laugh were Teshumai Tewindrow and all the Neolithic ladies. They were very polite to all their husbands, and said "Idiot!" ever so often.

Then the Head Chief of the Tribe of Tegumai cried and said and sang, "O Small-person-without-any-manners-who-ought-to-be-spanked, you've hit upon a great invention!"

"I didn't intend to. I only wanted Daddy's black-handled spear," said Taffy.

"Never mind. It *is* a great invention, and some day men will call it writing. At present it is only pictures, and, as we have seen today, pictures are not always properly understood. But a time will come, O Babe of Tegumai, when we shall make letters—all twenty-six of 'em—and when we shall be able to read as well as to write, and then we shall always say exactly what we mean without any mistakes. Let the Neolithic ladies wash the mud out of the stranger's hair."

"I shall be glad of that," said Taffy, "because, after all, though you've brought every single other spear in the Tribe of Tegumai, you've forgotten my Daddy's black-handled spear."

Then the Head Chief cried and said and sang, "Taffy dear, the next time you write a picture-letter, you'd better send a man who can talk our language with it, to explain what it means. I don't mind it, myself, because I am a Head Chief, but it's very bad for the rest of the Tribe of Tegumai, and, as you can see, it surprises the stranger."

Then they adopted the Stranger-man (a genuine Tewara of Tewar) into the Tribe of Tegumai, because he was a gentleman and did not make a fuss about the mud that the Neolithic ladies had put into his hair.

But from that day to this (and I suppose it is all Taffy's fault), very few little girls have ever liked learning to read or write. Most of them prefer to draw pictures and play with their Daddies—just like Taffy.

HOW
THE WHALE
GOT HIS TINY
THROAT

SOME STORIES ARE MEANT TO BE READ
quietly and some stories are meant to be told
aloud. Some stories are only proper for rainy
mornings, and some for long, hot afternoons
when one is lying in the open, and some stories
are bedtime stories.

All the Blue Skalallatoot stories are morning tales (I do not know why, but that is what Effie says). All the stories about Orvin Sylvester Woodsey, the leftover New England fairy who did not think it well-seen to fly, and who used patent labor-saving devices instead of charms, are afternoon stories, because they were generally told in the shade of the woods. You could alter and change these tales as much as you pleased, but in the evening there were stories meant to put Effie to sleep, and you were not allowed to alter those by one single little word. They had to be told just so, or Effie would wake up and put back the missing sentence.

So at last they came to be like charms, all three of them—the whale tale, the camel tale, and the rhinoceros tale. Of course little people are not alike, but I think if you catch some Effie rather tired and rather sleepy at the end of the day, and if you begin in a low voice and tell the tales precisely as I have written them down, you will find that Effie will presently curl up and go to sleep.

Now, this is the first tale, and it tells how the whale got his tiny throat:

Once upon a time there was a whale, and he lived in the sea and he ate fishes. He ate the starfish and the garfish, and the crab and the dab, and the plaice and the dace, and the skate and his mate, and the mackereel and the pickereel, and the really truly twirly-whirly eel. All the fishes he could find in all the sea he ate with his mouth—so!

At last there was only one little fish left in all the sea, and he was an astute fish, and he swam a little behind the whale's right ear so as to be out of harm's way. Then the whale stood up on his tail and said, "I'm hungry."

And the little 'stute fish said in a little 'stute voice, "Noble and generous Cetacean, have you ever tried Man?"

"No," said the whale. "What is it like?"

"Nice," said the little 'stute fish. "Nice, but nubbly."

"Then fetch me a dozen," said the whale, and he made the sea froth up with his tail.

"One at a time is enough," said the 'stute

fish. "If you swim to latitude 41.42, longitude 36.37 (that is magic), you will find sitting *on* a raft, *in* the middle of the sea, with nothing on but a pair of blue canvas breeches, a pair of suspenders (you must *not* forget the suspenders), and a jackknife, one shipwrecked mariner, who, it is only fair to tell you, is a man of infinite-resource-and-sagacity."

So the whale swam and swam to latitude 41.42, longitude 36.37, as fast as he could swim—and *on* a raft, *in* the middle of the sea, *with* nothing to wear except a pair of blue canvas breeches, a pair of suspenders (you must particularly remember the suspenders) and a jackknife, he found one single, solitary shipwrecked mariner trailing his toes in the

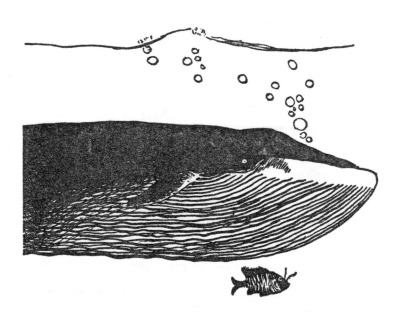

water.   (He had his mother's leave to paddle, or else he would never have done it, because he was a man of infinite-resource-and-sagacity.)

Then the whale opened his mouth back and back and back till it nearly touched his tail. And he swallowed the shipwrecked mariner, and the raft he was sitting on, and his blue canvas breeches, and the suspenders (which you *must* not forget), and the jackknife—he swallowed them all down into his warm, dark inside cupboards, and then he smacked his lips—so, and turned round three times on his tail.

But as soon as the mariner, who was a man of infinite-resource-and-sagacity, found himself in the whale's warm, dark inside cupboards, he hopped and he jumped and he thumped and he bumped, and he pranced and he danced, and he banged and he clanged, and he leaped and he creeped, and he prowled and he howled, and he cried and he sighed, and he crawled and he bawled, and he danced hornpipes where he shouldn't, and the whale felt very unhappy indeed. (*Have* you forgotten the suspenders?)

So he said to the 'stute fish, "This man is truly very nubbly, and, besides, he is making me hiccup. What shall I do?"

"Tell him to come out," said the 'stute fish. So the whale called down his own throat to the shipwrecked mariner, "Come out and behave yourself. I've got the hiccups."

"Nay—nay," said the mariner. "Not so, but far otherwise. Take me to my natal shore and the white-cliffs-of-Albion, and I'll think about it." And he began to dance again.

"You had better humor him," said the 'stute fish to the whale. "I ought to have warned you that he is a man of infinite-resource-and-sagacity."

So the whale swam and swam and swam, with both flippers and his tail, as hard as he could for the hiccups. And at last he saw the mariner's natal shore and the white-cliffs-of-Albion, and he rushed halfway up the beach, and opened his mouth wide and wide and wide, and said, "Change here for Winchester, Ashuelot, Nashua, Keene, and stations on the *Fitch*burg road." And just as he said "Fitch," the mariner walked out of his mouth.

But while the whale had been swimming, the mariner, who was indeed a person of infinite-resource-and-sagacity, had taken his jackknife and cut up the raft into a little square grating all running crisscross, and he had tied it firm with his suspenders (*now* you know why you were not to forget the suspenders), and he dragged that grating good and tight into the whale's throat, and there it stuck. Then he recited the following *Sloka*, which, as you have not heard it, I will now proceed to relate:

> *By means of a grating*
> *I have stopped your ating.*

For the mariner—he was also an Hi-ber-ni-an. And he stepped out on the shingle, and went home to his mother, who had given him leave to trail his toes in the water. And he married and lived happily ever afterward.

So did the whale, but from that day on, the grating in his throat, which he could neither cough up nor swallow down, prevented him eating anything except very, very small fish— and that is the reason why whales nowadays never eat men or boys or little girls.

The 'stute fish went and hid himself in the mud under the doorsills of the Equator. He was afraid the whale might be angry with him.

The sailor took the jackknife home. He was wearing the blue canvas breeches when he walked out on the shingle. The suspenders were left behind, you see, to tie the grating with. And that is the end of *that* tale.

HOW
THE CAMEL
GOT HIS HUMP

Now THIS IS THE SECOND TALE, AND IT tells how the camel got his big hump.

In the beginning of years, when the world was so new and all, and the animals were just beginning to work for Man, there was a Camel, and he lived in the middle of a Howling Desert because he did not want to work. And besides, he was a Howler himself. So he ate sticks and thorns and tamarisk and milkweed and prickles, most 'scruciating idle.

And when anybody spoke to him he said, "Humph!"—just "Humph!"—and no more.

Presently the Horse came to him one Monday morning, with a saddle on his back and a bit in his mouth, and said, "Camel, oh Camel, come out and trot like the rest of us."

"Humph!" said the Camel. And the Horse went away and told the Man.

Presently the Dog came to him with a stick in his mouth, and said, "Camel, oh Camel, come and fetch and carry like the rest of us."

"Humph!" said the Camel. And the Dog went away and told the Man.

Presently the Ox came to him, with a yoke on his neck, and said, "Camel, oh Camel, come and plow like the rest of us."

"Humph!" said the Camel. And the Ox went away and told the Man.

At the end of the day the Man called the Horse and the Dog and the Ox together, and said, "Three, oh Three, I'm very sorry for you, with the world so new and all. But that Humph-thing in the desert can't work or he

At the end of the day the Man called the Horse
and the Dog and the Ox together

would have been here by now, so I am going to leave him alone, and you must work double time to make up for it."

That made the Three very angry, with the world so new and all, and they held a palaver and a pow-wow on the edge of the desert. And the Camel came chewing milkweed *most* 'scruciating idle, and laughed at them. Then he said, "Humph!" and went away again.

Presently there came along the Djinn in charge of All Deserts, rolling in a cloud of dust (Djinns always travel that way because it is Magic), and he stopped to palaver and pow-wow with the Three.

"Djinn of All Deserts," said the Horse, "*is* it right for anyone to be idle, with the world so new and all?"

"Certainly not," said the Djinn.

"Well," said the Horse, "there's a thing in the middle of your Howling Desert with a long neck and long legs, and he hasn't done a stroke of work since Monday morning. He won't trot."

"Whew!" said the Djinn, whistling.

[52]

"That's my camel, for all the gold in Arabia! What does he say about it?"

"He says 'Humph,'" said the Dog. "And he won't fetch and carry."

"Did he say anything else?"

"Only 'Humph.' And he won't plow," said the Ox.

"Very good," said the Djinn. "I'll humph him if you will kindly wait a minute."

The Djinn rolled himself up in his dust-cloak, and took a bearing across the Desert, and found the Camel most 'scruciatingly idle, looking at his own reflection in a pool of water.

"Come hither, my tall friend," said the Djinn. "What's this I hear of your doing no work, with the world so new and all?"

"Humph!" said the Camel.

The Djinn sat down with his chin in his hand and began to think a Great Magic, while the Camel looked at his reflection in the pool of water.

"You've given the Three extra work ever since Monday morning, all on account of your 'scruciating idleness," said the Djinn. "Have you anything to say for yourself?"

"Humph!" said the Camel.

"You'll say that once too often," said the Djinn. And he went on thinking Magics, with his chin in his hand.

And the Camel said it again. But no sooner had he said it than he saw his back, that he was so proud of, puffing up and puffing up into a great big lollopping humph.

"Do you see that?" said the Djinn. "That's your very own humph that you've brought upon your very own self by not working. Today is Thursday, and you've done no work since Monday, when the work began. Now you are going to work."

"How can I," said the Camel, "with this humph on my back?"

"That's made a-purpose," said the Djinn, "all because you missed those three days. You will be able to work now for three days without eating, because you can live on your humph. And don't you ever say I never did anything for you. Come out of the desert and go to the Three, and behave. Humph, your-self!"

And the Camel humphed himself, humph and all, and went away to join the Three. And from that day to this, the Camel always wears a humph (they call it "hump" now, not to hurt his feelings)—but he has never yet caught up with the three days that he missed at the beginning of the world, and he has never yet learned how to behave.

HOW THE RHINOCEROS GOT HIS WRINKLY SKIN

ONCE UPON A TIME, ON AN UNINHABITED
island on the shores of the Red Sea, there
lived a Parsee from whose hat the rays of the
sun were reflected in more-than-oriental
splendor. And the Parsee lived by the Red
Sea with nothing but his hat and a kerosene

cooking stove of the kind that you must particularly never touch.

And one day he took flour and water and currants and plums and sugar and things, and made himself one cake which was two feet across and three feet thick. It was indeed a Superior Comestible (*that's* magic), and he put it on the stove because *he* was allowed to cook on that stove, and he baked it and he baked it till it was all done brown and smelled most sentimental.

But just as he was going to eat it, there came down to the beach from the altogether uninhabited interior one Rhinoceros with a horn on his nose, two piggy eyes, and no manners.

In those days the Rhinoceros' skin fitted him quite tight. There were no wrinkles in it anywhere. He looked exactly like a Noah's Ark Rhinoceros, but of course much bigger.

All the same, he had no manners then, and he has no manners now, and he never will have any manners. He said, "How!" and the Parsee left that cake and climbed to the top of a palm tree with nothing on but his hat from which the rays of the sun were always reflected in more-than-oriental splendor.

And the Rhinoceros upset the oil-stove with his nose, and the cake rolled on the sand, and he spiked that cake on the horn on his nose, and he ate it and he went away, waving his tail, to the desolate and exclusively uninhabited interior which abuts on the islands of Mazanderan, Socotra and the Promontories of the Larger Equinox.

Then the Parsee came down from his palm tree and put the stove on its legs and recited the following *Sloka* which as you have not heard I will now proceed to relate:

> *Them that take cakes*
> *Make dreadful mistakes.*

And there was a great deal more in that than would meet the Casual Eye!

Because, five weeks later, there was a heat wave in the Red Sea, and everybody took off all the clothes they had. The Parsee took off his hat, but the Rhinoceros took off his skin and carried it over his shoulder as he came down to the beach to bathe. In those days it buttoned up the back with three buttons and looked like a waterproof. He said nothing whatever about the cake because he had eaten it all, and he never had any manners, then, since, or henceforward. He waddled straight into the water and blew bubbles through his nose, leaving his skin on the beach.

Presently the Parsee came by and found the skin, and he smiled one smile that ran all round his face two times. Then he danced three times round the skin and rubbed his hands.

Then he went to his camp and filled his hat with cake crumbs—old, dry, stale, tickly cake crumbs, for the Parsee never ate anything but cake, and never swept out his camp. He took that skin, and he shook that skin, and he scrubbed that skin, and he rubbed that skin just as full of old, dry, stale, tickly cake crumbs and some burned currants as ever it could *possibly* hold.

Then he climbed to the top of his palm tree and waited for the Rhinoceros to come out of the water and put it on.

Then he climbed to the top of his palm tree and waited for the Rhinoceros to come out

And the Rhinoceros did. He buttoned it up the back with three buttons, and it tickled like cake crumbs in bed. Then he wanted to scratch, but that made it worse, and then he lay down on the sands and rolled and rolled and rolled, and every time he rolled, the cake crumbs tickled him worse and worse and worse.

Then he ran to the palm tree and rubbed and rubbed and rubbed himself against it. He rubbed so much and so hard that he rubbed his skin into a great fold over his shoulders, and another fold over his back where the buttons used to be (but he rubbed the buttons off), and he rubbed some more folds over his legs.

And it spoiled his temper, but it didn't make the least difference to the cake crumbs. They were inside his skin and they tickled.

So he went home, very angry indeed and horribly scratchy. And from that day to this every rhinoceros has great folds in his skin and a very bad temper, all on account of the cake crumbs inside.

But the Parsee came down from his palm

tree, under his hat from which the rays of the sun were reflected in more-than-oriental splendor, packed up the cooking-stove, and went away in the direction of Orotava, Amygdala, the upland meadows of Anantarivo and the marshes of Sonaput—where all small people, beginning to breathe slowly and evenly, must inevitably also accompany him —in order to arrive easily and unknowingly at the enormous battlements of the luxurious city of Uninterrupted Slumber.

THE
BEGINNING
OF THE
ARMADILLOS

THIS, OH, BEST BELOVED, IS ANOTHER STORY
of the High and Far-Off Times. In the very
middle of those times was a Stickly-Prickly
Hedgehog, and he lived on the banks of the
turbid Amazon, eating snails and things. And
he had a friend, a Slow Solid Tortoise, who
lived on the banks of the turbid Amazon, eat-

ing lettuces and things. And so that was all right, Best Beloved. Do you see?

But also, and at the same time, in those High and Far-Off Days, there was a Painted Jaguar, and he lived on the banks of the turbid Amazon, too. And he ate everything that he could catch. When he could not catch deer or monkeys, he would eat frogs and beetles. And when he could not catch frogs and beetles, he went to his mother and she told him how to eat hedgehogs and tortoises.

She said to him ever so many times, graciously waving her tail, "My son, when you find a hedgehog, you must drop him into the water, and then he will uncoil. And when you catch a tortoise, you must scoop him out of his shell with your paw." And so that was all right, Best Beloved.

One beautiful night on the banks of the turbid Amazon, Painted Jaguar found Stickly-Prickly Hedgehog and Slow-Solid Tortoise under the trunk of a fallen tree. They could not run away, and so Stickly-Prickly curled himself up into a ball, and Slow-Solid Tortoise drew in his head and feet into his shell as far as they would go.

"Now listen to me," said Painted Jaguar, "because this is very important. My mother said that when I meet a hedgehog, I am to drop him into the water and then he will uncoil. And when I meet a tortoise, I am to scoop him out of his shell with my paw. Now, which of you—"

"Are you sure?" said Stickly-Prickly Hedgehog. "Are you quite sure? Perhaps she said that when you uncoil a tortoise you must shell him out of the water with a scoop, and when you paw a hedgehog you must drop him."

"Are you sure?" said Slow-Solid Tortoise. "Are you quite sure? Perhaps she said that when you water a hedgehog you must drop him into your paw, and when you meet a tortoise you shell him till he uncoils."

"I don't think it was at all like that," said Painted Jaguar, but he felt a little puzzled. "Say it again more distinctly."

"When you scoop water with your paw,

you uncoil him with a hedgehog," said Stickly-Prickly. "Remember that, because it's important."

"But," said the Tortoise, "when you paw your meat, you drop it into a tortoise with a scoop. Why can't you understand?"

"You are making my head ache," said Painted Jaguar, "and besides, I didn't want your advice at all. I only wanted to know which of you is Hedgehog and which is Tortoise."

"I shan't tell you," said Stickly-Prickly. "But you can scoop me out of my shell if you like."

"Aha!" said Painted Jaguar. "Now I know you're Tortoise. You thought I wouldn't! Take that!"

Painted Jaguar darted out his paddy paw just as Stickly-Prickly curled himself up, and Jaguar's paw was filled with prickles. Worse than that, he knocked Stickly-Prickly away and away into the woods and the bushes where it was too dark to find him. Then he put his paddy paw into his mouth, and, of course, the prickles hurt him more than ever.

"Aha!" said the Painted Jaguar. *"Now I know
you're Tortoise!"*

As soon as he could speak he said, "Aha! Now I know he isn't Tortoise at all. But"—then he scratched his head—"how do I know that this other is Tortoise?"

"But I *am* Tortoise," said Slow-Solid. "Your mother was quite right. She said that you were to scoop me out of my shell with your paw. Begin."

"You didn't say she said that a minute ago," said Painted Jaguar, sucking the prickles out of his paddy paw. "You said she said something quite different."

"Well, suppose you say that I said that she said something quite different, I don't see that it makes any difference, because if she said what you said I said she said, it's just the same as if I said what she said she said. Of course, if you think she said that you were to uncoil me with a scoop, instead of pawing me into drops with a shell, I can't help that, can I?"

"But you said you wanted to be scooped out of your shell with my paw," said Painted Jaguar.

"If you'll think again, I didn't say anything

of the kind. I said that your mother said that you were to scoop me out of my shell."

"What will happen if I do?" said the Jaguar very cautiously.

"I don't know, because I've never been scooped out of my shell before. But I tell you, honestly, if you want to see me swim away, you've only got to drop me into the water."

"I don't believe it," said Painted Jaguar. "You've mixed up all the things my mother told me to do till I don't know whether I'm on my head or my painted tail, and now you come and tell me something I can understand, and I don't trust you one little bit. My mother told me that I was to drop one of you two into the water, and as you seem so anxious to be dropped, I think you don't want to be dropped. Now jump into the turbid Amazon, and be quick about it."

"I warn you, your mother won't be pleased. Don't say I didn't tell you," said Slow-Solid.

"If you say another word about what my mother said—" the Jaguar answered, but he had not finished the sentence before Slow-

Solid quietly dived into the turbid Amazon, swam under water for a long way and came out on the bank where Stickly-Prickly was waiting for him.

"That was a very narrow escape," said Stickly-Prickly. "I don't like Painted Jaguar. What did you tell him you were?"

"I told him I was a truthful Tortoise, but he wouldn't believe it. Now he's gone to tell his mother. Listen to him!"

They could hear Painted Jaguar roaring up and down among the trees and the bushes by the side of the turbid Amazon.

"Son, son!" said his mother ever so many times, graciously waving her tail. "What have you been doing that you shouldn't have done?"

"I tried to scoop something that said it was a Tortoise out of its shell with my paw, and my paw is full of per-rickles," said Painted Jaguar.

"Son, son!" said his mother ever so many times, graciously waving her tail. "By the prickles on your paddy paw I see that that must have been a Hedgehog. You should have dropped him into the water."

"I did that with another one, and he said he was a Tortoise, and I didn't believe him, and it was quite true, and he has dived, and he won't come up again, and I haven't anything at all to eat, and I think we had better find lodgings somewhere else. They are too clever on the turbid Amazon for poor me!"

"Son, son!" said his mother ever so many times, graciously waving her tail. "Now listen to me and remember what I say. A Hedgehog curls himself up into a ball and his prickles stick out every which way at once. By this you may know the Hedgehog."

"I don't like this old lady one little bit," said Stickly-Prickly, under the shadow of a large leaf. "I wonder what else she knows."

"A Tortoise can't curl himself up," Mother Jaguar went on, ever so many times, graciously waving her tail. "He only draws his head and legs into his shell. By this you may know the Tortoise."

"I don't like this old lady at all—at all," said

Slow-Solid Tortoise. "Even Speckly Jaguar can't forget those directions. It's a great pity that you can't swim, Stickly-Prickly."

"Don't talk to me," said Stickly-Prickly. "Just think how much better it would be if you could curl up. This *is* a mess! Listen to Painted Jaguar."

Painted Jaguar was sitting on the banks of the turbid Amazon, sucking prickles out of his paws and saying to himself:

> *"Can't curl, but can swim—*
> *Slow-Solid, that's him!*
> *Curls up, but can't swim,*
> *Stickly-Prickly, that's him!*

"He'll never forget that this month of Sundays," said Stickly-Prickly. "Hold up my chin, Slow-Solid. I'm going to try to learn to swim."

"Excellent!" said Slow-Solid, and he held up Stickly-Prickly's chin, while Stickly-Prickly kicked in the water of the turbid Amazon.

"You'll make a fine swimmer yet," said

Slow-Solid. "Now, not to be behindhand, if you can unlace my back-plates a little, I'll see what I can do toward curling up."

Stickly-Prickly helped to unlace Tortoise's back-plates, so that by twisting and straining, Slow-Solid actually managed to curl up a tiddy wee bit.

"Excellent!" said Stickly-Prickly. "But I wouldn't do any more just now. It's making you black in the face. Kindly lead me into the water once more and I'll practice that side stroke which you say is so easy."

"Excellent!" said Stickly-Prickly. "But more practice will make you a regular Gangetic Porpoise. Now, if I may trouble you to unlace my back- and front-plates, two holes, I'll try that fascinating bend that you say is so easy. Won't Painted Jaguar be surprised!"

"Excellent!" said Stickly-Prickly, all wet from the turbid Amazon. "I declare, I shouldn't know you from one of my own family. Two holes, I think you said. A little more expression, please, and don't grunt quite so much or Painted Jaguar may hear us. When you've finished, I want to try that long dive which you say is so easy. Won't Painted Jaguar be surprised?"

"Excellent!" said Slow-Solid. "A little more attention to holding your breath and you will be able to keep house at the bottom of the turbid Amazon. Now I'll try that exercise of wrapping my hind legs around my ears which you say is so peculiarly comfortable. Won't Painted Jaguar be surprised?"

"Excellent!" said Stickly-Prickly. "But it's straining your back-plates a little. They are all overlapping now instead of lying side by side."

"Oh, that's the result of exercise," said Slow-Solid. "I've noticed that your prickles seem to be melting one into another, and that you're growing to look rather more like a pine cone, and less like a chestnut burr, than you used to."

"Am I?" said Stickly-Prickly. "That's the effect of soaking in the water. Oh, won't Painted Jaguar be surprised!"

They continued their exercises, each helping the other, till morning came, and when the sun was high they rested and dried themselves, when they saw that they were both of them quite different from what they had been.

"Stickly-Prickly," said Tortoise after breakfast, "I am not what I was yesterday, but I think I may yet amuse Painted Jaguar."

"That was the very thing I was thinking just now," said Stickly-Prickly. "I think scales are a tremendous improvement on prickles—to say nothing of being able to swim. Oh, won't Painted Jaguar be surprised! Let's go and find him."

By and by, they found Painted Jaguar still nursing his paddy paw that had been hurt the night before. He was so astonished that he fell three times backward over his own painted tail without stopping.

"Good morning!" said Stickly-Prickly. "And how is your mamma this morning?"

"She is quite well, thank you," said Painted Jaguar, "but you must forgive me if I do not at this precise moment recall your name."

"That's unkind of you," said Stickly-Prickly, "seeing that this time yesterday you tried to scoop me out of my shell with your paw."

"But you hadn't any shell. It was all prickles," said Speckly Jaguar. "Just look at my paw."

"You told me to drop into the turbid Amazon and be drowned," said Slow-Solid. "Why are you so rude and forgetful today?"

"Don't you remember what your mother told you?" said Stickly-Prickly:

> *"Can't curl, but can swim—*
> *Stickly-Prickly, that's him!*
> *Curls up, but can't swim,*
> *Slow-Solid, that's him!"*

Then they both curled themselves up and rolled round and round Painted Jaguar till his eyes turned cartwheels in his head.

Then he went to fetch his mother.

"Mother," he said, "there are two new animals in the woods today, and the one that you said couldn't swim, swims. And the one that you said couldn't curl up, curls. And they've gone shares in their prickles, I think, because both of them are scaly all over, instead of one being smooth and the other very prickly. Besides that, they are rolling round and round in circles, and I don't feel comfy."

"Son, son!" said Mother Jaguar ever so many times, graciously waving her tail. "A hedgehog is a hedgehog, and can't be anything but a hedgehog. And a tortoise is a tortoise and can never be anything else."

"But it isn't a hedgehog, and it isn't a tortoise. It's a little bit of both, and I don't know its proper name."

"Nonsense!" said Mother Jaguar. "Everything has its proper name. I would call it 'armadillo' till I found out the real one. And I would leave it alone."

So Painted Jaguar did as he was told, especially about leaving them alone, but the curious thing is that from that day to this, oh, Best Beloved, no one on the banks of the turbid Amazon has ever called Stickly-Prickly and Slow-Solid anything except Armadillo.

There are hedgehogs and tortoises in other places, of course, but the real old and clever kind, with their scales lying lippety-lappety one over the other, like pine cone scales, that lived on the banks of the turbid Amazon in the High and Far-Off Days, are always called Armadillos because they were so clever.   So that's all right, Best Beloved.   Do you see?

THE CAT
THAT WALKED
BY HIMSELF

Hear and attend and listen . . . for this befell and behappened and became and was, O my Best Beloved, when the Tame animals were wild.

The Dog was wild, and the Horse was wild, and the Cow was wild, and the Sheep was wild, and the Pig was wild—as wild as wild could be—and they walked in the Wet Wild Woods by their wild lones.

But the wildest of all the wild animals was the Cat. He walked by himself, and all places were alike to him.

Of course, the Man was wild, too. He was dreadfully wild. He didn't even begin to be tame till he met the Woman, and she told him that she did not like living in his wild ways. She picked out a nice dry Cave, instead of a heap of wet leaves, to lie down in. And she strewed clean sand on the floor. And she lit a nice wood fire at the back of the Cave. And she hung a dried wild-horse skin, tail-down, across the opening of the Cave. And she said, "Wipe your feet, dear, when you come in, and now we'll keep house."

That night, Best Beloved, they ate wild sheep roasted on the hot stones, and flavored with wild garlic and wild pepper . . . and wild duck stuffed with wild rice and wild fenugreek and wild coriander . . . and marrow bone of wild oxen . . . and wild cherries . . . and wild grenadillas.

Then the Man went to sleep in front of the fire, ever so happy, but the Woman sat up, combing her hair. She took the bone of the shoulder of mutton—the big fat bladebone— and she looked at the wonderful marks on it, and she threw more wood on the fire, and she made a Magic. She made the First Singing Magic in the world.

Out in the Wet Wild Woods all the wild animals gathered together where they could see the light of the fire a long way off, and they wondered what it meant.

The Wild Horse stamped with his wild foot and said, "O my Friends and O my Enemies, why have the Man and the Woman made that great light in that great Cave, and what harm will it do us?"

Wild Dog lifted up his wild nose, smelled the smell of roast mutton, and said, "I will go up and look, and say, for I think it is good. Cat, come with me."

"Nenni!" said the Cat. "I am the Cat who walks by himself, and all places are alike to me. I will not come."

"Then we can never be friends again," said Wild Dog, and he trotted off to the Cave.

But when he had gone a little way, the Cat said to himself, "All places are alike to me. Why should I not go, too, and see and look and come away at my own liking?" So he slipped after Wild Dog softly, very softly, and hid himself where he could hear everything.

When Wild Dog reached the mouth of the Cave, he lifted up the dried horse-skin with his nose and sniffed the beautiful smell of the roast mutton, and the Woman, looking at the blade-bone, heard him, laughed, and said, "Here comes the first. Wild Thing out of the Wild Woods, what do you want?"

Wild Dog said, "O my Enemy and Wife of my Enemy, what is this that smells so good in the Wild Woods?"

Then the woman picked up a roasted mutton-bone and threw it to Wild Dog, and said, "Wild Thing out of the Wild Woods, taste and try."

Wild Dog gnawed the bone and it was more delicious than anything he had ever tasted, and he said, "O my Enemy and Wife of my Enemy, give me another."

The Woman said, "Wild Thing out of the Wild Woods, help my Man to hunt through the day and guard this Cave at night, and I will give you as many roast bones as you need."

"Ah!" said the Cat, listening. "This is a very wise Woman, but she is not so wise as I am."

Wild Dog crawled into the Cave and laid his head on the Woman's lap, and said, "O my Friend and Wife of my Friend, I will help your Man to hunt through the day, and at night I will guard your Cave."

"Ah!" said the Cat, listening. "That is a very foolish Dog." And he went back through the Wet Wild Woods, waving his wild tail and walking by his wild lone. But he never told anybody.

When the Man woke up, he said, "What is Wild Dog doing here?"

And the Woman said, "His name is not Wild Dog any more, but the First Friend, because he will be our friend for always and always and always. Take him with you when you go hunting."

Next night the Woman cut great green armfuls of fresh grass from the water-meadows, and dried it before the fire, so that it smelled like new-mown hay, and she sat at the mouth of the Cave and braided a halter out of horse-hide, and she looked at the shoulder of mutton-bone—at the big broad blade-bone—and she made a Magic. She made the Second Singing Magic in the world.

Out in the Wild Woods all the wild animals wondered what had happened to Wild Dog, and at last Wild Horse stamped with his foot and said, "I will go and see and say why Wild Dog has not returned. Cat, come with me."

"Nenni!" said the Cat. "I am the Cat who walks by himself, and all places are alike to me. I will not come." But all the same, he followed Wild Horse softly, very softly, and hid himself where he could hear everything.

When the Woman heard Wild Horse tripping and stumbling on his long mane, she laughed and said, "Here comes the second. Wild Thing out of the Wild Woods, what do you want?"

Wild Horse said, "O my Enemy and Wife of my Enemy, where is Wild Dog?"

The woman laughed, and picked up the blade-bone and looked at it, and said, "Wild Thing out of the Wild Woods, you did not come here for Wild Dog, but for the sake of this good grass."

And Wild Horse, tripping and stumbling on his long mane, said, "That is true—give it me to eat."

The Woman said, "Wild Thing out of the Wild Woods, bend your wild head and wear what I give you, and you shall eat the wonderful grass three times a day."

"Ah!" said the Cat, listening. "This is a clever Woman, but she is not so clever as I am."

Wild Horse bent his wild head, and the Woman slipped the braided hide halter over it, and Wild Horse breathed on the Woman's feet and said, "O my Mistress, and Wife of my Master, I will be your servant for the sake of the wonderful grass."

"Ah!" said the Cat, listening. "That is a

[93]

very foolish Horse." And he went back through the Wet Wild Woods, waving his wild tail and walking by his wild lone. But he never told anybody.

When the Man and the Dog came back from hunting, the Man said, "What is Wild Horse doing here?"

And the Woman said, "His name is not Wild Horse any more, but the First Servant, because he will carry us from place to place for always and always and always. Ride on his back when you go hunting."

Next day, holding her wild head high, so that her wild horns would not catch in the wild trees, Wild Cow came up to the Cave, and the Cat followed, and hid himself just the same as before. Everything happened just the same as before. The Cat said the same things as before. And when Wild Cow had promised to give her milk to the Woman every day in exchange for the wonderful grass, the Cat went back through the Wet Wild Woods waving his wild tail and walking by his wild lone, just the same as before. But he never told anybody. When the Man and the Horse and the Dog came home from hunting and asked the same questions same as before, the Woman said, "Her name is not Wild Cow any more, but the Giver of Good Food. She will give us the warm white milk for always and always and always, and I will take care of her while you and the First Friend and the First Servant go hunting."

Next day the Cat waited to see if any other Wild thing would go up to the Cave, but no one moved in the Wet Wild Woods, so the Cat walked there by himself. And he saw the Woman milking the Cow, and he saw the light of the fire in the Cave, and he smelled the smell of the warm white milk.

Cat said, "O my Enemy and wife of my Enemy, where did Wild Cow go?"

The Woman laughed and said, "Wild Thing out of the Wild Woods, go back to the woods again, for I have braided up my hair, and I have put away the magic blade-bone, and we have no more need of either friends or servants in our Cave."

Cat said, "I am not a friend, and I am not a servant. I am the Cat who walks by himself, and I wish to come into your cave."

Woman said, "Then why did you not come with First Friend on the first night?"

Cat grew very angry and said, "Has Wild Dog told tales of me?"

Then the Woman laughed and said, "You are the Cat who walks by himself, and all places are alike to you. You are neither a friend nor a servant. You have said it yourself. Go away and walk by yourself in all places alike."

Then Cat pretended to be sorry and said, "Must I never come into the Cave? Must I never sit by the warm fire? Must I never drink the warm white milk? You are very wise and very beautiful. You should not be cruel even to a Cat."

Woman said, "I knew I was wise, but I did not know I was beautiful. So I will make a bargain with you. If ever I say one word in your praise, you may come into the Cave."

"And if you say two words in my praise?" said the Cat.

"I never shall," said the Woman, "but if I say two words in your praise, you may sit by the fire in the Cave."

"And if you say three words?" said the Cat.

"I never shall," said the Woman, "but if I say three words in your praise, you may drink the warm white milk three times a day for always and always and always."

Then the Cat arched his back and said, "Now let the Curtain at the mouth of the Cave, and the Fire at the back of the Cave, and the Milk-pots that stand beside the Fire, remember what my Enemy and the Wife of my Enemy has said."

And he went away through the Wet Wild Woods, waving his wild tail and walking by his wild lone.

That night when the Man and the Horse and the Dog came home from hunting, the Woman did not tell them of the bargain that she had made with the Cat, because she was afraid that they might not like it.

Cat went far and far away and hid himself in the Wet Wild Woods by his wild lone for a long time till the Woman forgot all about him. Only the Bat—the little upside-down Bat— that hung inside the Cave, knew where Cat hid . . . and every evening Bat would fly to Cat with news of what was happening.

One evening Bat said, "There is a Baby in the Cave. He is new and pink and fat and small, and the Woman is very fond of him."

"Ah," said the Cat, listening, "but what is the Baby fond of?"

"He is fond of things that are soft and tickle," said the Bat. "He is fond of warm things to hold in his arms when he goes to sleep. He is fond of being played with. He is fond of all those things."

"Ah," said the Cat, listening, "then my time has come."

Next night Cat walked through the Wet Wild Woods and hid very near the Cave till morning-time, and Man and Dog and Horse went hunting. The Woman was busy cooking that morning, and the Baby cried and interrupted. So she carried him outside the Cave and gave him a handful of pebbles to play with. But still the Baby cried.

Then the Cat put out his paddy paw and patted the Baby on the cheek, and it cooed. And the Cat rubbed against its fat knees and tickled it under its fat chin with his tail. And the Baby laughed. And the Woman heard him and smiled.

Then the Bat—the little upside-down Bat—that hung in the mouth of the Cave, said, "O my Hostess and Wife of my Host and Mother of my Host's Son, a Wild Thing from the Wild Woods is most beautifully playing with your Baby."

"A blessing on that Wild Thing, whoever he may be," said the Woman, straightening her back, "for I was a busy woman this morning and he has done me a service."

That very minute and second, Best Beloved, the dried horse-skin Curtain that was stretched tail-down at the mouth of the Cave fell down—*woosh!*—because it remembered the bargain she had made with the Cat, and when the Woman went to pick it up—lo and behold!—the Cat was sitting quite comfy inside the Cave.

"O my Enemy and Wife of my Enemy and Mother of my Enemy," said the Cat, "it is I . . . for you have spoken a word in my praise, and now I can sit within the Cave for always and always and always. But still I am the Cat who walks by himself, and all places are alike to me."

The Woman was very angry, and shut her lips tight and took up her spinning-wheel and began to spin.

But the Baby cried because the Cat had gone away, and the Woman could not hush it, for it struggled and kicked and grew black in the face.

"O my Enemy and Wife of my Enemy and Mother of my Enemy," said the Cat, "take a strand of the wire that you are spinning and tie it to your spinning-whorl and drag it along the floor, and I will show you a magic that shall

*"But still I am the Cat who walks by himself,
and all places are alike to me"*

make your Baby laugh as loudly as he is now crying."

"I will do so," said the Woman, "because I am at my wits' end, but I will not thank you for it."

She tied the thread to the little clay spindle wheel and drew it across the floor, and the Cat ran after it and patted it with his paws and rolled head over heels, and tossed it backward over his shoulder and chased it between his hind legs and pretended to lose it, and pounced down upon it again, till the Baby laughed as loudly as it had been crying, and scrambled after the Cat and frolicked all over the Cave till it grew tired and settled down to sleep with the Cat in its arms.

"Now," said the Cat, "I will sing the Baby a song that shall keep him asleep for an hour." And he began to purr, loud and low, low and loud, till the Baby fell fast asleep.

The Woman smiled as she looked down upon the two of them and said, "That was wonderfully done. No question but you are very clever, O Cat."

That very minute and second, Best Beloved, the smoke of the fire at the back of the Cave came down in clouds from the roof—*puff!*—because it remembered the bargain she had made with the Cat, and when it had cleared away—lo and behold!—the Cat was sitting quite comfy close to the fire.

"O my Enemy and Wife of my Enemy and Mother of my Enemy," said the Cat, "it is I . . . for you have spoken a second word in my praise, and now I can sit by the warm fire at the back of the Cave for always and always and always. But still I am the Cat who walks by himself, and all places are alike to me."

Then the Woman was very, very angry, and let down her hair and put more wood on the fire and brought out the broad blade-bone of the shoulder of mutton and began to make a Magic that would prevent her from saying a third word in praise of the Cat. It was not a Singing Magic, Best Beloved, it was a Still Magic. And by and by the Cave grew so still that a little mouse crept out of a corner and ran across the floor.

[103]

"O my Enemy and Wife of my Enemy and Mother of my Enemy," said the Cat, "is that little mouse part of your magic?"

"Oh, no, indeed!" said the Woman, and she dropped the blade-bone and jumped upon the footstool in front of the fire and braided up her hair very quick for fear that the mouse would run up it.

"Ah," said the Cat, watching, "then the mouse will do me no harm if I eat it?"

"No," said the Woman, braiding up her hair. "Eat it quickly and I will ever be grateful to you."

Cat made one jump and caught the little mouse, and the Woman said, "A hundred thanks. Even the First Friend is not quick enough to catch little mice as you have done. You must be very wise."

That very moment and second, O Best Beloved, the Milk-pot that stood by the fire cracked in two pieces—*ffft*—because it remembered the bargain she had made with the Cat, and when the Woman jumped down from the footstool—lo and behold!—the Cat was lapping up the warm white milk that lay in one of the broken pieces.

"O my Enemy and Wife of my Enemy and Mother of my Enemy," said the Cat, "it is I . . . for you have spoken three words in my praise, and now I can drink the warm white milk three times a day for always and always and always. But *still* I am the Cat who walks by himself, and all places are alike to me."

Then the Woman laughed and set the Cat a bowl of the warm white milk and said, "O Cat, you are as clever as a man, but remember that your bargain was not made with the Man or the Dog, and I do not know what they will do when they come home."

"What is that to me?" said the Cat. "If I have my place in the Cave by the fire and my warm white milk three times a day, I do not care what the Man or the Dog can do."

That evening, when the Man and the Dog

came into the Cave, the Woman told them all the story of the bargain while the Cat sat by the fire and smiled.

Then the Man said, "Yes, but he has not made a bargain with me or with all proper Men after me."

Then he took off his two leather boots and he took up his little stone axe (that makes three) and he fetched a piece of wood and a hatchet (that is five altogether), and he set them out in a row and he said, "Now we will make *our* bargain. If you do not catch mice when you are in the Cave for always and always and always, I will throw these five things at you whenever I see you, and so shall all proper Men do after me."

"Ah," said the Woman, listening, "this is a very clever Cat, but he is not so clever as my Man."

The Cat counted the five things (and they looked very knobby) and he said, "I will catch mice when I am in the Cave for always and always and always—but *still* I am the Cat who walks by himself, and all places are alike to me."

"Not when I am near," said the Man. "If you had not said that last, I would have put all these things away for always and always and always; but I am now going to throw my two boots and my little stone axe (that makes three) at you whenever I meet you. And so shall all proper Men do after me!"

Then the Dog said, "Wait a minute. He has not made a bargain with *me* or with all proper Dogs after me." And he showed his teeth and said, "If you are not kind to the Baby while I am in the Cave for always and always and always, I will hunt you till I catch you, and when I catch you I will bite you. And so shall all proper Dogs do after me."

"Oh," said the Woman, listening, "this is a very clever Cat, but he is not so clever as the Dog."

Cat counted the Dog's teeth (and they looked very pointed) and he said, "I will be kind to the Baby while I am in the Cave, as long as he does not pull my tail too hard, for always and always and always. But *still* I am the Cat that walks by himself, and all places are alike to me."

"Not when I am near," said the Dog. "If you had not said that last, I would have shut my mouth for always and always and always. But *now* I am going to hunt you up a tree whenever I meet you. And so shall all proper Dogs do after me."

Then the Man threw his two boots and his little stone axe (that makes three) at the Cat, and the Cat ran out of the Cave and the Dog chased him up a tree. And from that day to this, Best Beloved, three proper Men out of five will always throw things at a Cat whenever they meet him, and all proper Dogs will chase him up a tree.

But the Cat keeps his side of the bargain, too. He will kill mice and he will be kind to Babies when he is in the house, just as long as they do not pull his tail too hard.

But when he has done that, and between

times, and when the moon gets up and night comes, he is the Cat that walks by himself, and all places are alike to him. Then he goes out to the Wet Wild Woods or up the Wet Wild Trees or on the Wet Wild Roofs, waving his wild tail and walking by his wild lone.

HOW
THE LEOPARD
GOT HIS
SPOTS

IN THE DAYS WHEN EVERYBODY STARTED
fair, Best Beloved, the Leopard lived in a place
called the High Veldt. 'Member it wasn't the
Low Veldt, or the Bush Veldt, or the Sour
Veldt, but the 'sclusively bare hot shiny High
Veldt, where there was sand and sandy-
colored rock and 'sclusively tufts of sandy-
yellowish grass.

The Giraffe and the Zebra and the Eland
and the Koodoo and the Hartebeest lived there
and they were 'sclusively sandy-yellow-
brownish all over. But the Leopard, he was
the 'sclusivest, sandiest-yellowest-brownest of
them all—a grayish-yellowish, catty-shaped
kind of beast, and he matched the 'sclusively
yellowish-grayish-brownish color of the High
Veldt to one hair.

That was very bad for the Giraffe and the
Zebra and the rest of them; for he would lie
down by a 'sclusively yellowish-grayish-
brownish stone or clump of grass, and when
the Giraffe or the Zebra or the Eland or the
Koodoo or the Bush-Buck or the Bonte Buck
came by, he would surprise them out of their
jumpsome lives.

Also, there was an Ethiopian with bows and
arrows (a 'sclusively grayish-brownish-
yellowish man he was then), who lived on the
High Veldt with the Leopard. The two used
to hunt together—the Ethiopian with his bows
and arrows, and the Leopard 'sclusively with

his teeth and claws—till the Giraffe and the Eland and the Koodoo and the Quagga and all the rest of them didn't know which way to jump, Best Beloved. They didn't, indeed.

After a long time—people lived for ever so long in those days—they learned to avoid anything that looked like a Leopard or an Ethiopian. And bit by bit—the Giraffe began it (his legs were longest)—they went away from the High Veldt.

They scuttled for days and days and days till they came to a great forest, 'sclusively full of trees and bushes and stripy, speckly, patchy shadows, and there they hid, and after another long time, what with standing half in the shade and half out of it, and what with the slippery-slidy shadows of the trees falling on them, the Giraffe grew blotchy and the Zebra grew stripy and the Eland and the Koodoo grew darker with little gray lines on their backs like bark on a tree trunk. And though you could hear them and smell them, you could very seldom see them—and then only when you knew precisely where to look.

They had a beautiful time in the 'sclusively speckly-spickly shadows of the forest, while the Leopard and the Ethiopian ran about all over the 'sclusively grayish-yellowish-reddish High Veldt wondering where all their breakfasts and their dinners and their teas had gone.

At last they were so hungry that they ate rats and beetles and rock rabbits, the Leopard and the Ethiopian, and then they had the big tummy-ache, both together; and then they met Baviaan—the dog-headed barking Baboon, who is quite the wisest animal in all South Africa.

Said Leopard to Baviaan (and it was a very hot day), "Where has all the game gone?"

And Baviaan winked. *He* knew.

Said the Ethiopian to Baviaan, "Can you tell me the present habitat of the aboriginal Fauna?"

And Baviaan winked. *He* knew.

Then said Baviaan, "The game has gone

into other spots, and my advice to you, Leopard, is to go into other spots as soon as you can."

And the Ethiopian said, "That is all very fine, but I wish to know whither the aboriginal Fauna has migrated."

Then said Baviaan, "The aboriginal Fauna has joined the aboriginal Flora because it was high time for a change. And my advice to you, Ethiopian, is to change as soon as you can."

That puzzled the Leopard and the Ethiopian, but they set off to look for the aboriginal Flora, and presently, after ever so many days, they saw a great, high, tall forest full of tree trunks, all 'sclusively speckled and dotted and splashed and slashed and hatched and cross-hatched with shadows.

"What is this," said the Leopard, "that is so 'sclusively dark and so full of little pieces of light?"

"I don't know," said the Ethiopian, "but it ought to be the aboriginal Flora. I can smell

Giraffe and I can hear Giraffe, but I can't see Giraffe."

"That's curious," said the Leopard. "I suppose it is because we have just come in out of the sunshine. I can smell Zebra and I can hear Zebra, but I can't see Zebra."

"Wait a bit," said the Ethiopian. "It's a long time since we've hunted 'em. Perhaps we've forgotten what they were like."

"Fiddle!" said the Leopard. "I remember them perfectly on the High Veldt, especially their marrowbones. Giraffe is about seventeen feet high, of a 'sclusively fulvous golden-yellow from head to heel—and Zebra is about four and a half feet high of a 'sclusively gray-fawn color from head to heel."

"Umm," said the Ethiopian, looking into the speckly-spickly shadows of the aboriginal Flora. "Then they ought to show up in this dark place like ripe bananas in a smokehouse."

But they didn't. The Leopard and the Ethiopian hunted all day, and though they could smell them and hear them, they never saw one of them.

"For goodness' sake," said the Leopard at tea time, "let us wait till it gets dark. This daylight hunting is a perfect scandal."

So they waited till dark, and then the Leopard heard something breathing sniffily in the starlight that fell all stripy through the branches, and he jumped in the direction of the noise. It smelled like Zebra and it felt like Zebra, and when he knocked it down, it kicked like Zebra. So he said, "Be quiet. This is much too serious for dumb-crambo. (He meant he wouldn't eat him up, Best Beloved.) I am going to sit on your head till morning, because there is something about you I don't understand."

Presently he heard a grunt and a crash and a scramble, and the Ethiopian called out, "I've caught a thing that I can't see. It smells like Giraffe and it kicks like Giraffe."

"Don't you trust it," said the Leopard. "Sit on its head till the morning—same as me."

So they sat down hard till morning-time and then Leopard said, "What have you at your end of the table, Brother?"

The Ethiopian scratched his head and said, "It ought to be 'sclusively a rich fulvous orange-tawny from head to heel, and it ought to be Giraffe, but it is covered all over with chestnut blotches. What have you at your end of the table, Brother?"

And the Leopard scratched his head and said, "It ought to be 'sclusively a delicate grayish fawn, and it ought to be Zebra, but it is covered all over with black and chestnut stripes. What in the world have you been doing to yourself, Zebra? Don't you know that if you were on the High Veldt I could see you ten miles off?"

"Yes," said the Zebra, "but this isn't the High Veldt. Can't you see?"

"I can now," said the Leopard. "But I couldn't all yesterday. How is it done?"

"Let us up," said the Zebra, "and we will show you."

They let the Zebra and the Giraffe get up. And the Zebra moved away to some little thorn-bushes where the sunlight fell all stripy, and the Giraffe moved off to some tallish trees where the shadows fell all blotchy.

"Now watch," said the Zebra and the Giraffe. "This is the way it's done. One—two—three! And where's your breakfast?"

Leopard stared and Ethiopian stared, but all they could see were stripy shadows and blotched shadows in the forest, but never a sign of Zebra or Giraffe. They had just walked off and hidden themselves in the shadowy forest.

"Hi!" said the Ethiopian. "That's a trick worth learning. Take a lesson by it, Leopard. You show up in this dark place like a bar of soap in a coal hod."

"Ho!" said the Leopard. "Would it surprise you very much to know that you show up in this dark place like a mustard-plaster on a sack of coals?"

"Well, calling names won't catch dinner," said the Ethiopian. "The long and the little of it is that we don't match our backgrounds. I'm going to take Baviaan's advice. He told

"*The long and the little of it is that we don't match our backgrounds,*" *said the Ethiopian*

me I ought to change, and as I've nothing to change except my skin, I'm going to change that."

"What to?" said the Leopard, tremendously excited.

"To a nice working blackish-brownish color, with a little purple in it and a touch of slaty-blue. It will be the very thing for hiding in hollows and behind trees."

So he changed his skin then and there, and the Leopard was more excited than ever. He had never seen a man change his skin before.

"But what about me?" he said when the Ethiopian had worked his last little finger into his fine new black skin.

"You take Baviaan's advice, too. He told you to go into spots."

"So I did," said the Leopard. "I went into other spots as fast as I could. I went into this spot with you, and a lot of good it has done me."

"Oh," said the Ethiopian, "Baviaan didn't mean spots in South Africa. He meant spots on your skin."

"What's the use of that?" said the Leopard.

"Think of Giraffe," said the Ethiopian. "Or if you prefer stripes, think of Zebra. They find their spots and stripes give them perfect satisfaction."

"Umm," said the Leopard. "I wouldn't look like Zebra—not for anything."

"Well, make up your mind," said the Ethiopian, "because I'd hate to go hunting without you, but I must if you insist on looking like a sunflower in a back parlor."

"I'll take spots, then," said the Leopard, "but don't make 'em too big. I wouldn't be like Giraffe—not for anything."

"I'll make 'em with the tips of my fingers," said the Ethiopian. "There's plenty black left on my skin still. Stand over!"

Then the Ethiopian put his five fingers close together. You can see them on any Leopard, and wherever the five fingers touched, they left five little black marks all close together. You can see them on any Leopard's skin you like, Best Beloved. Sometimes the fingers slipped and the marks got a little blurred, but if you look closely at any Leopard now, you will see that there are always five spots, off five fat, black fingertips.

"Now you *are* a beauty!" said the Ethiopian. "You can lie out on the bare ground and look like a heap of pebbles. You can lie out on the naked rocks and look like a piece of pudding-stone. You can lie out on a leafy branch and look like sunshine, through the leaves. And you can lie right across the center of a path and look like nothing in particular. Think of that and purr!"

"But if I'm all this," said the Leopard, "why didn't you go spotty, too?"

"Oh, plain black's best," said the Ethiopian. "Now come along and we'll see if we can't get even with Mr. One-Two-Three-Where's-your-Breakfast?"

So they went away and lived happily ever afterward, Best Beloved. That is all.

Oh, now and then you will hear grownups say, "Can the Ethiopian change his skin or the Leopard his spots?" I don't think grownups would keep on saying such an absurd thing if the Leopard and Ethiopian hadn't done it once—do you? But they will never do it again, Best Beloved. They are quite contented as they are.

HOW
THE ELEPHANT
GOT HIS
TRUNK

IN THE HIGH AND FAR-OFF TIMES THE ELE-
phant, oh, Best Beloved, had no trunk. He
had only a blackish, bulgy nose, as big as a
boot, that he could wriggle about from side to
side. But he could not pick up things with it.

But there was one Elephant—a new Elephant—an Elephant's Child—who was full of 'satiable curtiosity, and that means he asked ever so many questions. And he lived in Africa, and he filled all Africa with his 'satiable curtiosities.

He asked his aunt, the Ostrich, why her tail feathers grew just so, and she spanked him with her hard claw.

He asked his uncle, the Giraffe, what made his skin spotty, and his uncle, the Giraffe, spanked him with his hard, hard hoof.

And still he was full of 'satiable curtiosity.

He asked his other aunt, the Hippopotamus, why her eyes were red, and she spanked him with her hard, hard hoof.

And he asked his other uncle, the Baboon, why melons tasted just so, and his other uncle, the Baboon, spanked him with his hard, hard paw.

And still he was full of 'satiable curtiosity.

He asked questions about everything that he saw, or heard, or felt, or smelled, or touched, and all his uncles and his aunts spanked him.

And still he was full of 'satiable curtiosity.

One fine morning in the middle of the Precession of the Equinoxes, this 'satiable Elephant's Child asked a new fine question that he had never asked before. He asked, "What does the Crocodile have for dinner?" Then everybody said "Hush!" in a loud and dretful tone, and they spanked him immediately and directly.

By and by, when that was finished, he came upon Kolokolo Bird sitting in the middle of a wait-a-bit thorn and he said, "My father has spanked me and my mother has spanked me—all my aunts and uncles have spanked me for my 'satiable curtiosity—and still I want to know what the Crocodile has for dinner!"

Then Kolokolo Bird said, with a mournful cry, "Go to the banks of the great, gray-green, greasy Limpopo River, all set about with fever-trees, and find out."

That very next morning, when there was nothing left of the Equinoxes, because the Precession had gone by, this 'satiable Elephant's Child took a hundred pounds of bananas, and a hundred pounds of sugar cane, and seventeen melons, and said to all his families, "Good-by. I am going to the great, gray-green, greasy Limpopo River all set about with fever-trees to find out what the Crocodile has for dinner."

And they all spanked him once more for luck, though he requested them most politely to abstain.

Then he went away, a little warm, but not at all astonished, eating melons and throwing the rind about.

He went from Graham's town to Kimberley, and from Kimberley to Khama's Country, and from Khama's Country he went east by north, eating melons all the time, till at last he came to the banks of the great, gray-green, greasy Limpopo River all set about with fever-trees, precisely as Kolokolo Bird had said.

Now you must know and understand, oh, Best Beloved, that till that very week, and day, and hour, and minute, this 'satiable Elephant's Child had never seen a Crocodile and did not know what one was like.   It was all his 'satiable curtiosity.

The first thing he found was a Bi-Colored-Python-Rock-Snake curled round a rock.

" 'Scuse me," said the Elephant's Child, most politely, "but have you seen such a thing as a Crocodile in these promiscuous parts?"

"Have I seen a Crocodile?" said the Bi-Colored-Python-Rock-Snake, in a voice of dretful scorn.   "What will you ask me next?"

" 'Scuse me," said the Elephant's Child, "but could you kindly tell me what he has for dinner?"

Then the Bi-Colored-Python-Rock-Snake uncoiled himself from the rock and spanked the Elephant's Child with his hard, hard tail.

"That is odd," said the Elephant's Child, "because my father and my mother, and my uncle and my aunt, not to mention my other aunt, the Hippopotamus, and my other uncle, the Baboon, have all spanked me for my 'satiable curtiosity—and I suppose this is the same thing."

So he said good-by very politely to the Bi-Colored-Python-Rock-Snake, and helped to coil him up on the rock again, and went on, a little warm but not at all astonished, eating melons and throwing the rind about till he trod on what he thought was a log at the very edge of the great, gray-green, greasy Limpopo River all set about with fever-trees. But it was really the Crocodile, oh, Best Beloved, and the Crocodile winked one eye.

" 'Scuse me," said the Elephant's Child most politely, "but do you happen to have seen a Crocodile in these promiscuous parts?"

Then the Crocodile winked the other eye and lifted half his tail out of the mud. And the Elephant's Child stepped back most politely, because he did not wish to be spanked again.

"Come hither, Little One," said the Crocodile. "Why do you ask such things?"

" 'Scuse me," said the Elephant's Child most politely, "but my father has spanked me, my mother has spanked me—not to mention my aunt, the Ostrich, and my uncle, the Giraffe, who can kick ever so hard, as well as my other aunt, the Hippopotamus, and my other uncle, the Baboon, *and* including the Bi-Colored-Python-Rock-Snake just up the bank who spanks harder than any of them. And so, if it's quite all the same to you, I don't want to be spanked any more."

"Come hither, Little One," said the Crocodile, "for I am the Crocodile," and he wept Crocodile tears to show it was quite true.

Then the Elephant's Child grew all breathless, and panted and kneeled down on the bank and said, "You are the very person I have been looking for all these long days. Will you please tell me what you have for dinner?"

"Come hither, Little One," said the Crocodile, "and I'll whisper."

Then the Elephant's Child, very excited and breathing hard, put his head down close to the Crocodile's musky, tusky mouth, and the Crocodile caught him by his little nose, which up to that very week, day, hour, and minute, was no bigger than a boot, though much more useful.

"I think," said the Crocodile—and he said it

between his teeth like this—"I think today we will begin with Elephant's Child!"

At this, oh, Best Beloved, the Elephant's Child was much annoyed, and he said—speaking through his nose like this—"Led go! You are hurtig be!"

Then the Bi-Colored-Python-Rock-Snake scuffled down from the bank and said, "My young friend, if you do not now, immediately and instantly, pull as hard as ever you can, it is my opinion that your acquaintance in the large-pattern leather ulster (and by this he meant the Crocodile) will jerk you into yonder limpid stream before you can say Jack Robinson."

Bi-Colored-Python-Rock-Snakes always talk this way.

Then the Elephant's Child sat back on his little haunches, and pulled, and pulled, and pulled, and his nose began to stretch.

And the Crocodile floundered into the water, making it all creamy with great sweeps of his tail, and *he* pulled, and pulled, and pulled.

And the Elephant's Child's nose kept on

stretching, and the Elephant's Child spread all his little four legs and pulled, and pulled, and pulled. And his nose kept on stretching, and the Crocodile threshed his tail like an oar, and *he* pulled, and pulled, and pulled, and at each pull the Elephant's Child's nose grew longer and longer—and it hurt!

Then the Elephant's Child felt his legs slipping, and he said through his nose, which was now nearly five feet long, "This is too buch for be!"

Then the Bi-Colored-Python-Rock-Snake came down from the bank and knotted himself in a double clove-hitch round the Elephant's Child's hind legs and said, "Rash and inexperienced traveler, we will now seriously devote ourselves to a little hard pulling, because if we do not, it is my impression that yonder self-propelling man-of-war with the armor-plated upper deck (and by this, oh, Best Beloved, he meant the Crocodile) will permanently vitiate your future career."

That is the way all Bi-Colored-Python-Rock-Snakes talk.

So he pulled, and the Elephant's Child pulled, and the Crocodile pulled, but the Elephant's Child and the Bi-Colored-Python-Rock-Snake pulled hardest, and at last the Crocodile let go of the Elephant's Child's nose with a plop that you could hear all up and down the Limpopo.

Then the Elephant's Child sat down most hard and sudden, but first he was careful to say, "Thank you," to the Bi-Colored-Python-Rock-Snake, and next he was kind to his nose and wrapped it all up in cool banana leaves and hung it in the great, gray-green, greasy Limpopo to cool.

"What are you doing that for?" said the Bi-Colored-Python-Rock-Snake.

" 'Scuse me," said the Elephant's Child, "but my nose is out of shape and I am waiting for the swelling to go down."

"Then you will have to wait a long time," said the Bi-Colored-Python-Rock-Snake. "Some people do not know what is good for them."

The Elephant's Child sat there three days,

waiting for his nose to get well. But it never grew any shorter, and besides, it made him squint. For, oh, Best Beloved, you will see and understand that the Crocodile had pulled it out into a really truly trunk, same as all Elephants have today.

At the end of the third day a fly came and stung him on the shoulder, and instantly he lifted up his trunk and hit that fly dead with the end of it.

" 'Vantage number one!" said the Bi-Colored-Python-Rock-Snake. "You couldn't have done that with a mere-smear nose. Try and eat a little now."

Before he thought what he was doing, the Elephant's Child put out his trunk and plucked a large bundle of grass, dusted it clean against his forelegs and stuffed it into his own mouth.

" 'Vantage number two!" said the Bi-Colored-Python-Rock-Snake. "You couldn't have done that with a mere-smear nose. Don't you think the sun is hot here?"

"It is," said the Elephant's Child, and, before he thought what he was doing, he scooped up a lump of mud from the banks of the great, gray-green, greasy Limpopo and slapped it on his head where it made a cool mudcap, all trickly behind his ears.

" 'Vantage number three!" said the Bi-Colored-Python-Rock-Snake. "You couldn't have done that with a mere-smear nose. Now how do you feel about being spanked again?"

" 'Scuse me," said the Elephant's Child, "but I would not like it at all."

"How would you like to spank somebody?" said the Bi-Colored-Python-Rock-Snake.

"I would like it very much indeed," said the Elephant's Child.

"Well," said the Bi-Colored-Python-Rock-Snake, "you will find that new nose of yours very useful to spank people with."

"Thank you," said the Elephant's Child. "I'll remember that. And now I think I'll go home to my families, and try it."

So the Elephant's Child went home across Africa, frisking and whisking his trunk.

When he wanted fruit to eat, he pulled it down from a tree, instead of waiting for it to fall as he used to do. When he wanted grass, he plucked it up from the ground, instead of going on his knees as he used to do. When the flies bit him, he broke off the branch of a tree and used it as a fly-whisk. And he made himself a new, cool, slushy mudcap whenever the sun was hot. When he felt lonely walking through Africa, he sang to himself down his trunk, and the noise was louder than several brass bands. He went especially out of his way to find a Hippopotamus (she was no relation of his), and he spanked her very hard to make sure that the Bi-Colored-Python-Rock-Snake had spoken the truth about his new trunk. The rest of the time he picked up the melon rinds that he had dropped on his way to the Limpopo—for he was a Tidy Pachyderm.

One evening he came back to all his families and he coiled up his trunk and said, "How do you do?" They were glad to see him and immediately said, "Come here and be spanked for your 'satiable curtiosity."

"Pooh," said the Elephant's Child. "I don't think you peoples know anything about spanking, but *I* do and I'll show you."

Then he uncurled his trunk and knocked two of his brothers head over heels.

"Oh, Bananas!" said they. "Where did you learn that trick and what have you done to your nose?"

"I got a new one from the Crocodile on the bank of the great, gray-green, greasy Limpopo River," said the Elephant's Child. "I asked him what he had for dinner and he gave me this to keep."

"It looks very ugly," said the Baboon.

"It does," said the Elephant's Child. "But it's very useful." And he picked up his other uncle, the Baboon, by one leg and heaved him into a bees' nest.

Then that bad Elephant's Child spanked all his families for a long time till they were very warm and greatly astonished. He pulled out his Ostrich Aunt's tail feathers, and he caught his uncle, the Giraffe, by the hind leg and dragged him through a thorn bush. And he shouted at his other aunt, the Hippopotamus, and blew bubbles into her ear when she was sleeping in the water after meals. But he never let anyone touch Kolokolo Bird.

In the end, things grew so bad that all his families went off one by one to the banks of the great, gray-green, greasy Limpopo River to borrow new noses from the Crocodile. When they came back, everything started fair. And ever since that day, oh, Best Beloved, all the Elephants you will ever see, besides all those that you won't, have trunks precisely like the trunk of the 'satiable Elephant's Child.

THE
SING-SONG
OF OLD MAN
KANGAROO

NOT ALWAYS WAS THE KANGAROO AS WE
now behold him, but a different animal with
four short legs. He was gray and he was
woolly, and his pride was inordinate. He
danced in a desert in the middle of Australia
and he went to the Little God Nqa.

He went to Nqa at six before breakfast,
saying, "Make me different from all other
animals by five this afternoon."

Up jumped Nqa from his bath in the saltpan and shouted, "Go away!"

He was gray and he was woolly, and his pride was inordinate. He danced on a rockledge in the middle of Australia and he went to the Middle God Nquing.

He went to Nquing at eight after breakfast, saying, "Make me different from all other animals. Make me, also, wonderfully popular by five this afternoon."

Up jumped Nquing from his burrow in the spinifex and shouted, "Go away!"

He was gray and he was woolly, and his pride was inordinate. He danced on a sand-bank in the middle of Australia and he went to the Big God Nqung.

He went to Nqung at ten before dinner-time, saying, "Make me different from all other animals. Make me popular and wonderfully run after by five this afternoon."

Up jumped Nqung from his roost in the Blue Gums and shouted, "Yes, I will!"

Nqung called Dingo—Yellow-Dog Dingo

—always hungry, dusty in the sunshine, and showed him Kangaroo. Nqung said, "Dingo! Wake up, Dingo! Do you see that gentleman dancing on an ashpit? He wants to be different from all other animals. He wants to be popular and very truly run after. Dingo, make him so!"

Up jumped Dingo—Yellow-Dog Dingo— and said, "What, *that* cat-rabbit?"

Off ran Dingo—Yellow-Dog Dingo—always hungry, grinning like a coal scuttle, and ran after Kangaroo.

Off went the proud Kangaroo on his four little legs like a rabbit.

This, oh, Beloved of mine, ends the first part of the tale.

He ran through the desert.

He ran through the mountains.

He ran through the saltpans.

He ran through the reedbeds.

He ran through the Blue Gums.

He ran through the spinifex.

He ran till his front legs ached.

*Off ran Dingo—Yellow-Dog Dingo—always
hungry, grinning like a coal scuttle, and
ran after Kangaroo*

He had to!

Still ran Dingo—Yellow-Dog Dingo—always hungry, grinning like a rattrap, never getting nearer, never getting farther.

He had to!

Still ran Kangaroo—Old Man Kangaroo. He ran through the ti-trees.

He ran through the mulga.

He ran through the long grass.

He ran through the short grass.

He ran through the Tropics of Capricorn and Cancer.

He ran till his hind legs ached.

He had to!

Still ran Dingo—Yellow-Dog Dingo—hungrier and hungrier—grinning like a horse-collar, never getting nearer, never getting farther.

And they came to the Wollgong River.

Now there wasn't any bridge, and there wasn't any ferryboat, and Kangaroo didn't know how to get over, so he stood on his legs and hopped.

He had to!

He hopped through the Flinders.

He hopped through the cinders.

He hopped through the deserts in the middle of Australia.

He hopped like a Kangaroo.

First he hopped one yard.   Then he hopped three yards.   Then he hopped five yards, his legs growing stronger, his legs growing longer. He hadn't any time for rest or refreshment, and he wanted them very much.

Still ran Dingo—Yellow-Dog Dingo—a little bit bewildered, but always hungry, and wondering what in the world or out of it made Old Man Kangaroo hop.

For he hopped like a cricket, like a pea on a gridiron, or a new rubber ball on a nursery floor.

He had to!

He tucked up his front legs.

He hopped on his hind legs.

He stuck out his tail for a balance-weight behind him.

And he hopped through the Darling Downs.

He had to!

Still ran Dingo—Tired-Dog Dingo—hungrier and hungrier, very much bewildered, and wondering when in the world or out of it would Old Man Kangaroo stop.

Then came Nqung from his roost in the Blue Gums and said, "It's five o'clock."

Down sat Dingo—Poor-Dog Dingo—always hungry, dusty in the sunshine, and hung out his tongue and howled.

Down sat Kangaroo—Old Man Kangaroo—stuck out his tail like a milking-stool behind him, and said, "Thank goodness *that's* finished!"

Then said Nqung, who is always a gentleman, "Why aren't you grateful to Yellow-Dog Dingo? Why don't you thank him for all he has done for you?"

Then said Kangaroo—tired old Kangaroo—"He's chased me out of the homes of my childhood. He's chased me out of my regular

[153]

mealtimes. He's altered my shape so I'll never get it back, and he's played Old Scratch with my legs."

Then said Nqung, "Perhaps I'm mistaken, but didn't you ask me to make you different from all other animals, as well as to make you very truly sought after, by five this afternoon?"

"Yes," said Kangaroo. "I wish now I hadn't. I thought you would do it by charms and incantations, but this is a practical joke."

"Joke!" said Nqung from his roost in the Blue Gums. "Say that again and I'll whistle up Dingo and run your hind legs off."

"No," said the Kangaroo. "I must apologize. Legs are legs and you needn't alter 'em, so far as I am concerned. I only meant to explain to Your Lordliness that I've had nothing to eat since morning and I'm very empty, indeed."

"Yes," said Dingo—Yellow-Dog Dingo— "I am just in the same situation. I've made him different from all other animals, but what may I have for my tea?"

Then said Nqung from his roost in the Blue Gums, "Come and ask me about it tomorrow, because I'm going to bed."

So they were left in the middle of Australia, Old Man Kangaroo and Yellow-Dog Dingo, and each said, "That's *your* fault."

SAMUEL CLEMENS

The Prince
AND
The Pauper

COMPANION LIBRARY

Grosset & Dunlap

PUBLISHERS

NEW YORK

The quality of mercy . . .
                                is twice bless'd;
It blesseth him that gives, and him that takes;
'Tis mightiest in the mightiest: it becomes
The throned monarch better than his crown.

                                        MERCHANT OF VENICE

PREFACE

I will set down a tale as it was told to me by one who had it of his father, which latter had it of his father, this last having in like manner had it of his father, and so on, back and still back, three hundred years and more, the fathers transmitting it to the sons and so preserving it. It may be history, it may be only a legend, a tradition. It may have happened, it may not have happened; but it could have happened. It may be that the wise and the learned believed it in the old days; it may be that only the unlearned and the simple loved it and credited it.

CONTENTS

Illustrations

1

The Birth of the Prince and the Pauper

In the ancient city of London, on a certain autumn day in the second quarter of the sixteenth century, a boy was born to a poor family of the name of Canty, who did not want him. On the same day another English child was born to a rich family of the name of Tudor, who did want him. All England wanted him too. England had so longed for him, and hoped for him, and prayed God for him that now that he was really come, the people went nearly mad for joy. Mere acquaintances hugged and kissed each other and cried. Everybody took a holiday, and high and low, rich and poor, feasted and danced and sang, and got very mellow; and they kept this up for days and nights together. By day London was a sight to see, with gay banners waving from every balcony and housetop and splendid pageants marching along. By night it was again a sight to see, with its great bonfires at every corner and its troops of revelers making merry around them. There was no talk in all of England but of the new baby, Edward Tudor,

Prince of Wales, who lay lapped in silks and satins, unconscious of all this fuss, and not knowing that great lords and ladies were tending him and watching over him—and not caring either. But there was no talk about the other baby, Tom Canty, lapped in his poor rags, except among the family of paupers whom he had just come to trouble with his presence.

2

Tom's Early Life

Let us skip a number of years.

London was fifteen hundred years old, and was a great town—for that day. It had a hundred thousand inhabitants—some think double as many. The streets were very narrow, and crooked, and dirty, especially in that part where Tom Canty lived, which was not far from London Bridge. The houses were of wood, with the second story projecting over the first, and the third sticking its elbows out beyond the second. The higher the houses grew, the broader they grew. They were skeletons of strong crisscross beams, with solid material between coated with plaster. The beams were painted red or blue or black, according to the owner's taste, and this gave the houses a very picturesque look. The windows were small, glazed with little diamond-shaped panes, and they opened outward on hinges like doors.

The house which Tom's father lived in was up a foul little pocket called Offal Court, out of Pudding Lane. It was small, decayed, and rickety, but it was packed full of wretchedly poor families. Canty's tribe occupied a room on the third floor. The mother and father had a sort of bedstead in the corner; but Tom, his grand-mother, and his two sisters, Bet and Nan, were not restricted—they had all the floor to themselves and might sleep where they chose. There were the remains of a blanket or two and some bundles of ancient and dirty straw, but these could not rightly be called beds, for they were not organized; they were kicked into a general pile mornings, and selections made from the mass at night for service.

Bet and Nan were fifteen years old—twins. They were goodhearted girls, unclean, clothed in rags, and profoundly ignorant. Their mother was like them. But the father and the grandmother were a couple of fiends. They got drunk whenever they could; then they fought each other or anybody else who came in the way; they cursed and swore always, drunk or sober; John Canty was a thief, and his mother a beggar. They made beggars of the children but failed to make thieves of them. Among, but not of, the dreadful rabble that inhabited the house was a good old priest whom the king had turned out of house and home with a pension of a few farthings, and he used to get the children aside and teach them right ways secretly. Father Andrew also taught Tom a little Latin and how to read and write, and would have done the same with the girls, but they were afraid of the jeers of their friends, who could not have endured such a queer accomplishment in them.

All Offal Court was just such another hive as Canty's house. Drunkenness, riot, and brawling were the order there every night and nearly all night long. Broken heads were as common as hunger in that place. Yet little Tom was not unhappy. He had a hard time of it, but did not know it. It was the sort of time that all the Offal Court boys had; therefore he supposed it was the correct and comfortable thing. When he came home empty-handed at night, he knew his father would curse him and thrash him first, and that when he was done the awful grandmother would do it all over again and improve on it, and that away in the night his starving mother would slip to him stealthily with any miserable scrap or crust she had been able to save for him by going hungry herself, notwithstanding she was often caught in that sort of treason and soundly beaten for it by her husband.

No, Tom's life went along well enough, especially in summer. He only begged just enough to save himself, for the laws against mendicancy were stringent and the penalties heavy; so he put in a good deal of his time listening to good Father Andrew's charming old tales and legends about giants and fairies, dwarfs and genii, and enchanted castles, and gorgeous kings and princes. His head grew to be full of these wonderful things, and many a night as he lay in the dark on his scant and offensive straw, tired, hungry, and smarting from a thrashing, he unleashed his imagination and soon forgot his aches and pains in delicious picturings to himself of the charmed life of a petted prince in a regal palace. One desire came in time to haunt him day and night: it was to see a real prince, with his own eyes. He spoke of it once to some of his Offal Court comrades, but they jeered him and scoffed him so unmercifully that he was glad to keep his dream to himself after that.

He often read the priest's old books and got him to explain and enlarge upon them. His dreamings and readings worked certain changes in him by and by. His dream people were so fine that he grew to lament his shabby clothing and his dirt and to wish to be clean and better clad. He went on playing in the mud just the same, and enjoying it too; but instead of splashing around in the Thames solely for the fun of it, he began to find an added value in it because of the washings and cleansings it afforded.

Tom could always find something going on around the Maypole in Cheapside and at the fairs; and now and then he and the rest of London had a chance to see a military parade when some famous unfortunate was carried prisoner to the Tower by land or boat. One summer's day he saw poor Anne Askew and three men burned at the stake in Smithfield and heard an exbishop preach a sermon to them which did not interest him. Yes, Tom's life was varied and pleasant enough on the whole.

By and by Tom's reading and dreaming about princely life wrought such a strong effect upon him that he began to *act* the prince, unconsciously. His speech and manners became curiously ceremonious and courtly, to the vast admiration and amusement of his intimates. But Tom's influence among these young people began to grow now day by day, and in time he came to be looked up to by them, with a sort of wondering awe, as a superior being. He seemed to know so much! And he could do and say such marvelous things! And withal, he was so deep and wise! Tom's remarks and Tom's performances were reported by the boys to their elders; and these also presently began to discuss Tom Canty and to regard him as a most gifted and extraordinary creature. Full-grown people brought their perplexities to Tom for solution and were often astonished at the wit and wisdom of his decisions. In fact he was become a hero to all who knew him except his own family—these only saw nothing in him.

Privately, after a while, Tom organized a royal court! He was the prince; his special comrades were guards, chamberlains, equerries, lords- and ladies-in-waiting, and the royal family. Daily the mock prince was received with elaborate ceremonials borrowed by Tom from his romantic readings; daily the great affairs of the mimic kingdom were discussed in the royal council; and daily his mimic highness issued decrees to his imaginary armies, navies, and viceroyalties.

After which, he would go forth in his rags and beg a few farthings, eat his poor crust, take his customary cuffs and abuse, and then stretch himself upon his handful of foul straw and resume his empty grandeurs in his dreams.

And still his desire to look just once upon a real prince in the flesh grew upon him, day by day, and week by week, until at last it absorbed all other desires and became the one passion of his life.

One January day, on his usual begging tour, he tramped despondently up and down the region round about Mincing Lane and Little East Cheap, hour after hour, barefooted and cold, looking in at cookshop windows and longing for the dreadful pork pies and other deadly inventions displayed there; for to him these were dainties fit for the angels; that is, judging by the smell they were, for it had never been his good luck to own and eat one. There was a cold drizzle of rain; the atmosphere was murky; it was a melancholy day. At night Tom reached home so wet and tired and hungry that it was not possible for his father and grandmother to observe his forlorn condition and not be moved—after their fashion; wherefore they gave him a brisk cuffing at once and sent him to bed. For a long time his pain and hunger and the swearing and fighting going on in the building kept him awake; but at last his thoughts drifted away to far, romantic lands, and he fell asleep in the company of jeweled and gilded princelings who lived in vast palaces and had servants salaaming before them or flying to execute their orders. And then as usual, he dreamed that *he* was a princeling himself.

All night long the glories of his royal estate shone upon him: he moved among great lords and ladies in a blaze of light, breathing perfumes, drinking in delicious music, and answering the reverent obeisances of the glittering throng as it parted to make way for him, with here a smile and there a nod of his princely head.

And when he awoke in the morning and looked upon the wretchedness about him, his dream had had its usual effect: it had intensified the sordidness of his surroundings a thousandfold. Then came bitterness, and heartbreak, and tears.

3

Tom's Meeting
with the Prince

Tom got up hungry, and sauntered hungry away, but with his thoughts busy with the shadowy splendors of his night's dreams. He wandered here and there in the city, hardly noticing where he was going or what was happening around him. People jostled him, and some gave him rough speech; but it was all lost on the musing boy. By and by he found himself at Temple Bar, the farthest from home he had ever traveled in that direction. He stopped and considered a moment, then fell into his imaginings again, and passed on outside the walls of London. The Strand had ceased to be a country road then and regarded itself as a street, but by a strained construction; for though there was a tolerably compact row of houses on one side of it, there were only some scattering great buildings on the other, these being palaces of rich nobles, with ample and beautiful grounds stretching to the river—grounds that are now closely packed with grim acres of brick and stone.

Tom discovered Charing Village presently and rested

himself at the beautiful cross built there by a bereaved king of earlier days; then idled down a quiet, lovely road past the great cardinal's stately palace, toward a far more mighty and majestic palace beyond—Westminster. Tom stared in glad wonder at the vast pile of masonry, the wide-spreading wings, the frowning bastions and turrets, the huge stone gateway, with its gilded bars and its magnificent array of colossal granite lions, and the other signs and symbols of English royalty. Was the desire of his soul to be satisfied at last? Here indeed was a king's palace. Might he not hope to see a prince now, a prince of flesh and blood, if heaven were willing?

At each side of the gilded gate stood a living statue, that is to say, an erect and stately and motionless man-at-arms clad from head to heel in shining steel armor. At a respectful distance were many country folk and people from the city waiting for any chance glimpse of royalty that might offer. Splendid carriages with splendid people in them and splendid servants outside were arriving and departing by several other noble gateways that pierced the royal enclosure.

Poor little Tom, in his rags, approached and was moving slow and timidly past the sentinels, with a beating heart and a rising hope, when all at once he caught sight through the golden bars of a spectacle that almost made him shout for joy. Within was a comely boy, tanned and brown with sturdy outdoor sports and exercises, whose clothing was all of lovely silks and satins, shining with jewels—at his hip a little jeweled sword and dagger, dainty buskins on his feet, with red heels, and on his head a jaunty crimson cap with drooping plumes fastened with a great sparkling gem. Several gorgeous gentlemen stood near—his servants, without a doubt. Oh! He was a prince—a prince, a living prince, a real prince—without the shadow of a question; and the prayer of the pauper-boy's heart was answered at last.

Tom's breath came quick and short with excitement, and his eyes grew big with wonder and delight. Everything gave way in his mind instantly to one desire: that was to get close to the prince and have a good, devouring look at him. Before he knew what he was about, he had his face against the gate bars. The next instant one of the soldiers snatched him rudely away and sent him spinning among the gaping crowd of country gawks and London idlers.

The soldier said, "Mind thy manners, thou young beggar!"

The crowd jeered and laughed, but the young prince sprang to the gate with his face flushed and his eyes flashing with indignation and cried out, "How darst thou use a poor lad like that! How darst thou use the king my father's meanest subject so! Open the gates and let him in!"

You should have seen that fickle crowd snatch off their hats then. You should have heard them cheer and shout, "Long live the Prince of Wales!"

The soldiers presented arms with their halberds, opened the gates, and presented again as the little Prince of Poverty passed in, in his fluttering rags, to join hands with the Prince of Limitless Plenty.

Edward Tudor said, "Thou lookest tired and hungry: thou'st been treated ill. Come with me."

Half a dozen attendants sprang forward to—I don't know what; interfere, no doubt. But they were waved aside with a right royal gesture, and they stopped stock-still where they were, like so many statues. Edward took Tom to a rich apartment in the palace, which he called his cabinet. By his command a repast was brought such as Tom had never encountered before except in books. The prince, with princely delicacy and breeding, sent away the servants so that his humble guest might not be embarrassed by their critical presence; then he sat nearby and asked questions while Tom ate.

"What is thy name, lad?"

"Tom Canty, an' it please thee, sir."

" 'Tis an odd one. Where dost live?"

"In the city, please thee, sir. Offal Court, out of Pudding Lane."

"Offal Court! Truly 'tis another odd one. Hast parents?"

"Parents have I, sir, and a grandam likewise that is but indifferently precious to me—God forgive me if it be offense to say it—also twin sisters, Nan and Bet."

"Then is thy grandam not over kind to thee, I take it."

"Neither to any other is she, so please your Worship. She hath a wicked heart and worketh evil all her days."

"Doth she mistreat thee?"

"There be times that she stayeth her hand, being asleep or overcome with drink; but when she hath her judgment clear again, she maketh it up to me with goodly beatings."

A fierce look came into the little prince's eyes, and he cried out, "What! Beatings?"

"Oh, indeed, yes, please you, sir."

"*Beatings!* And thou so frail and little. Hark ye; before the night come she shall hie her to the Tower. The king my father—"

"In sooth, you forget, sir, her low degree. The Tower is for the great alone."

"True, indeed. I had not thought of that. I will

consider of her punishment. Is thy father kind to
thee?"

"Not more than Grammer Canty, sir."

"Fathers be alike, mayhap. Mine hath not a doll's
temper. He smiteth with a heavy hand, yet spareth me;
he spareth me not always with his tongue, though, sooth
to say. How doth thy mother use thee?"

"She is good, sir, and giveth me neither sorrow nor
pain of any sort. And Nan and Bet are like to her in
this."

"How old be these?"

"Fifteen, an' it please you, sir."

"The lady Elizabeth, my sister, is fourteen, and the
lady Jane Grey, my cousin, is of mine own age, and
comely and gracious withal; but my sister the lady Mary,
with her gloomy mien and—Look you; do thy sisters
forbid their servants to smile, lest the sin destroy their
souls?"

"They? Oh, dost think, sir, that *they* have servants?"

The little prince contemplated the little pauper
gravely a moment, then said, "And prithee, why not?
Who helpeth them undress at night? Who attireth
them when they rise?"

"None, sir. Wouldst have them take off their garment and sleep without—like beasts?"

"Their garment! Have they but one?"

"Ah, good your Worship, what would they do with
more? Truly they have not two bodies each."

"It is a quaint and marvelous thought! Thy pardon,
I had not meant to laugh. But thy good Nan and thy
Bet shall have raiment and lackeys enow, and that soon
too; my cofferer shall look to it. No, thank me not; 'tis
nothing. Thou speakest well; thou hast an easy grace in
it. Art learned?"

"I know not if I am or not, sir. The good priest that is called Father Andrew taught me, of his kindness, from his books."

"Knowst thou the Latin?"

"But scantly, sir, I doubt."

"Learn it, lad; 'tis hard only at first. The Greek is harder; but neither these nor any tongues else, I think, are hard to the lady Elizabeth and my cousin. Thou shouldst hear those damsels at it! But tell me of thy Offal Court. Hast thou a pleasant life there?"

"In truth, yes, so please you, sir, save when one is hungry. There be Punch-and-Judy shows, and monkeys—oh, such antic creatures, and so bravely dressed!— and there be plays wherein they that play do shout and fight till all are slain, and 'tis so fine to see, and costeth but a farthing, albeit 'tis main hard to get the farthing, please your Worship."

"Tell me more."

"We lads of Offal Court do strive against each other with the cudgel, like to the fashion of the 'prentices, sometimes."

The prince's eyes flashed. Said he, "Marry, that would not I mislike. Tell me more."

"We strive in races, sir, to see who of us shall be fleetest."

"That I would like also. Speak on."

"In summer, sir, we wade and swim in the canals and in the river, and each doth duck his neighbor, and spatter him with water, and dive and shout and tumble and—"

" 'Twould be worth my father's kingdom but to enjoy it once! Prithee go on."

"We dance and sing about the Maypole in Cheapside; we play in the sand, each covering his neighbor up; and times we make mud pastry—oh, the lovely mud, it hath not its like for delightfulness in all the world!—we do fairly wallow in the mud, sir, saving your Worship's presence."

"Oh, prithee say no more; 'tis glorious! If that I could but clothe me in raiment like to thine, and strip my feet, and revel in the mud once, just once, with none to rebuke me or forbid, meseemeth I could forgo the crown!"

"And if that I could clothe me once, sweet sir, as thou art clad, just once—"

"Oho, wouldst like it? Then so shall it be. Doff thy rags and don these splendors, lad! It is a brief happiness, but will be not less keen for that. We will have it while we may, and change again before any come to molest."

A few minutes later the little Prince of Wales was garlanded with Tom's fluttering odds and ends, and the little Prince of Pauperdom was tricked out in the gaudy plumage of royalty. The two went and stood side by side before a great mirror, and lo, a miracle: there did not seem to have been any change made! They stared at each other, then at the glass, then at each other again. At last the puzzled princeling said, "What dost thou make of this?"

"Ah, good your Worship, require me not to answer. It is not meet that one of my degree should utter the thing."

"Then will *I* utter it. Thou hast the same hair, the same eyes, the same voice and manner, the same form and stature, the same face and countenance that I bear. Fared we forth naked, there is none could say which was you, and which the Prince of Wales. And now that I am clothed as thou wert clothed, it seemeth I should be able the more nearly to feel as thou didst when the brute soldier—Hark ye, is not this a bruise upon your hand?"

"Yes; but it is a slight thing, and your Worship knoweth that the poor man-at-arms—"

"Peace! It was a shameful thing and a cruel!" cried the little prince, stamping his bare foot. "If the king— Stir not a step till I come again! It is a command!"

In a moment he had snatched up and put away an article of national importance that lay upon a table, and was out at the door and flying through the palace grounds in his bannered rags, with a hot face and glowing eyes. As soon as he reached the great gate, he seized the bars and tried to shake them, shouting, "Open! Unbar the gates!"

The soldier that had maltreated Tom obeyed promptly; and as the prince burst through the portal, half smothered with royal wrath, the soldier fetched him a sounding box on the ear that sent him whirling to the roadway and said, "Take that, thou beggar's spawn, for what thou got'st me from his Highness!"

The crowd roared with laughter. The prince picked himself out of the mud and made fiercely at the sentry, shouting, "I am the Prince of Wales, my person is sacred; and thou shalt hang for laying thy hand upon me!"

The soldier brought his halberd to a present arms and said mockingly, "I salute your gracious Highness." Then angrily, "Be off, thou crazy rubbish!"

Here the jeering crowd closed around the poor little prince and hustled him far down the road, hooting him and shouting, "Way for his royal Highness! Way for the Prince of Wales!"

4

The Prince's Troubles Begin

After hours of persistent pursuit and persecution, the little prince was at last deserted by the rabble and left to himself. As long as he had been able to rage against the mob, and threaten it royally, and royally utter commands that were good stuff to laugh at, he was very entertaining; but when weariness finally forced him to be silent, he was no longer of use to his tormentors and they sought amusement elsewhere. He looked about him now but could not recognize the locality. He was within the city of London—that was all he knew. He moved on aimlessly, and in a little while the houses thinned and the passersby were infrequent. He bathed his bleeding feet in the brook which flowed then where Farrington Street now is, rested a few moments, then passed on, and presently came upon a great space with only a few scattered houses in it and a prodigious church. He recognized this church. Scaffoldings were about everywhere, and swarms of workmen, for it was undergoing elaborate repairs. The prince took heart at once;

he felt that his troubles were at an end now. He said to himself, "It is the ancient Grey Friars' Church, which the king my father hath taken from the monks and given for a home forever for poor and forsaken children, and new-named it Christ's Church. Right gladly will they serve the son of him who hath done so generously by them, and the more that that son is himself as poor and as forlorn as any that be sheltered here this day, or ever shall be."

He was soon in the midst of a crowd of boys who were running, jumping, playing at ball and leapfrog, and otherwise disporting themselves, and right noisily too. They were all dressed alike, and in the fashion which in that day prevailed among servingmen and 'prentices—that is to say, each had on the crown of his head a flat black cap about the size of a saucer, which was not useful as a covering, it being of such scanty dimensions; neither was it ornamental; from beneath it the hair fell, unparted, to the middle of the forehead, and was cropped straight around; a clerical band at the neck; a blue gown that fitted closely and hung as low as the knees or lower; full sleeves; a broad red belt; bright-yellow stockings, gartered above the knees; low shoes with large metal buckles. It was a sufficiently ugly costume.

The boys stopped their play and flocked about the prince, who said with native dignity, "Good lads, say to your master that Edward, Prince of Wales, desireth speech with him."

A great shout went up at this, and one rude fellow said, "Marry, art thou his Grace's messenger, beggar?"

The prince's face flushed with anger, and his ready hand flew to his hip, but there was nothing there. There was a storm of laughter, and one boy said, "Didst mark that? He fancied he had a sword—belike he is the prince himself."

This sally brought more laughter. Poor Edward drew himself up proudly and said, "I am the prince, and it ill beseemeth you that feed upon the king my father's bounty to use me so."

This was vastly enjoyed, as the laughter testified. The youth who had first spoken shouted to his comrades, "Ho, swine, slaves, pensioners of his Grace's princely father, where be your manners? Down on your marrowbones, all of ye, and do reverence to his kingly port and royal rags!"

With boisterous mirth they dropped upon their knees in a body and did mock homage to their prey. The prince spurned the nearest boy with his foot and said fiercely, "Take thou that till the morrow come and I build thee a gibbet!"

Ah, but this was not a joke; this was going beyond fun. The laughter ceased on the instant, and fury took its place. A dozen shouted, "Hale him forth! To the horsepond, to the horsepond! Where be the dogs? Ho, there, Lion! Ho, Fangs!"

Then followed such a thing as England had never seen before—the sacred person of the heir to the throne rudely buffeted by plebeian hands and set upon and torn by dogs.

As night drew to a close that day, the prince found himself far down in the close-built portion of the city. His body was bruised, his hands were bleeding, and his rags were all besmirched with mud. He wandered on and on, and grew more and more bewildered, and so tired and faint he could hardly drag one foot after the other. He had ceased to ask questions of anyone, since they brought him only insult instead of information. He kept muttering to himself, "Offal Court—that is the name; if I can but find it before my strength is wholly spent and I drop, then am I saved, for his people will take me to the palace and prove that I am none of theirs, but the true prince, and I shall have mine own again." And now and then his mind reverted to his treatment by those rude Christ's Hospital boys, and he said, "When I am king, they shall not have bread and shelter only, but also teachings out of books, for a full belly is little worth where the mind is starved, and the heart. I will keep this diligently in my remembrance, that this day's lesson be not lost upon me, and my people suffer thereby; for learning softeneth the heart and breedeth gentleness and charity."

The lights began to twinkle, it came on to rain, the wind rose, and a raw and gusty night set in. The houseless prince, the homeless heir to the throne of England, still moved on, drifting deeper into the maze of squalid alleys where the swarming hives of poverty and misery were massed together.

Suddenly a great drunken ruffian collared him and said, "Out to this time of night again, and hast not brought a farthing home, I warrant me! If it be so, an' I do not break all the bones in thy lean body, then am I not John Canty, but some other."

The prince twisted himself loose, unconsciously brushed his profaned shoulder, and eagerly said, "Oh, art *his* father, truly? Sweet heaven grant it be so; then wilt thou fetch him away and restore me!"

"*His* father? I know not what thou meanst; I but know I am *thy* father, as thou shalt soon have cause to—"

"Oh, jest not, palter not, delay not! I am worn, I am wounded, I can bear no more. Take me to the king my father, and he will make thee rich beyond thy wildest dreams. Believe me, man, believe me! I speak no lie, but only the truth! Put forth thy hand and save me! I am indeed the Prince of Wales!"

The man stared down, stupefied, upon the lad, then shook his head and muttered, "Gone stark mad as any Tom o' Bedlam!"—then collared him once more and said with a coarse laugh and an oath, "But mad or no mad, I and thy Grammer Canty will soon find where the soft places in thy bones lie, or I'm no true man!"

With this he dragged the frantic and struggling prince away and disappeared up a front court followed by a delighted and noisy swarm of human vermin.

5

Tom as a Patrician

Tom Canty, left alone in the prince's cabinet, made good use of his opportunity. He turned himself this way and that before the great mirror, admiring his finery; then walked away, imitating the prince's high-bred carriage, and still observing results in the glass. Next he drew the beautiful sword and bowed, kissing the blade and laying it across his breast as he had seen a noble knight do, by way of salute to the lieutenant of the Tower, five or six weeks before, when delivering the great lords of Norfolk and Surrey into his hands for captivity. Tom played with the jeweled dagger that hung upon his thigh; he examined the costly and exquisite ornaments of the room; he tried each of the sumptuous chairs and thought how proud he would be if the Offal Court herd could only peep in and see him in his grandeur. He wondered if they would believe the marvelous tale he should tell when he got home or if they would shake their heads and say his overtaxed imagination had at last upset his reason.

At the end of half an hour it suddenly occurred to him that the prince was gone a long time; then right away he began to feel lonely; very soon he fell to listening and longing, and ceased to toy with the pretty things about him; he grew uneasy, then restless, then distressed. Suppose someone should come and catch him in the prince's clothes, and the prince not there to explain. Might they not hang him at once and inquire into his case afterward? He had heard that the great were prompt about small matters. His fears rose higher and higher, and trembling, he softly opened the door to the antechamber, resolved to fly and seek the prince, and through him, protection and release. Six gorgeous gentlemen servants and two young pages of high degree, clothed like butterflies, sprung to their feet and bowed low before him. He stepped quickly back and shut the door. He said, "Oh, they mock at me! They will go and tell. Oh! Why came I here to cast away my life?"

He walked up and down the floor, filled with nameless fears, listening, starting at every trifling sound. Presently the door swung open and a silken page said, "The lady Jane Grey."

The door closed, and a sweet young girl, richly clad, bounded toward him. But she stopped suddenly and said in a distressed voice, "Oh, what aileth thee, my lord?"

Tom's breath was nearly failing him, but he made shift to stammer out, "Ah, be merciful, thou! In sooth I am no lord, but only poor Tom Canty of Offal Court in the city. Prithee let me see the prince, and he will of his grace restore to me my rags and let me hence unhurt. Oh, be thou merciful and save me!"

By this time the boy was on his knees and supplicating with his eyes and uplifted hands as well as with his tongue. The young girl seemed horror-striken. She cried out, "Oh, my lord, on thy knees? And to *me!*"

Then she fled away in fright; and Tom, smitten with despair, sank down, murmuring, "There is no help, there is no hope. Now will they come and take me."

Whilst he lay there benumbed with terror, dreadful tidings were speeding through the palace. The whisper, for it was whispered always, flew from menial to menial, from lord to lady, down all the long corridors, from story to story, from saloon to saloon, "The prince hath gone mad, the prince hath gone mad!" Soon every saloon, every marble hall, had its group of glittering lords and ladies and other groups of dazzling lesser folk, talking earnestly together in whispers, and every face had in it dismay. Presently a splendid official came marching by these groups, making solemn proclamation, "In the name of the king! Let none list to this false and foolish matter, upon pain of death, nor discuss the same, nor carry it abroad. In the name of the king!"

The whisperings ceased as suddenly as if the whisperers had been stricken dumb.

Soon there was a general buzz along the corridors of, "The prince! See, the prince comes!"

Poor Tom came slowly walking past the low-bowing groups, trying to bow in return, and meekly gazing upon his strange surroundings with bewildered and pathetic eyes. Great nobles walked upon each side of him, making him lean upon them, and so steady his steps. Behind him followed the court physicians and some servants.

Presently Tom found himself in a noble apartment of the palace and heard the door close behind him. Around him stood those who had come with him. Before him, at a little distance, reclined a very large and very fat man with a wide, pulpy face and a stern expression. His large head was very gray; and his whiskers, which he wore only around his face, like a frame, were gray also. His clothing was of rich stuff, but old and slightly frayed in places. One of his swollen legs had a pillow under it and was wrapped in bandages.

There was silence now, and there was no head there but was bent in reverence, except this man's. This stern-countenanced invalid was the dread Henry VIII. He said—and his face grew gentle as he began to speak— "How now, my lord Edward, my prince? Hast been minded to cozen me, the good king thy father, who loveth thee and kindly useth thee, with a sorry jest?"

Poor Tom was listening, as well as his dazed faculties would let him, to the beginning of this speech; but when the words "me, the good king" fell upon his ear, his face blanched and he dropped as instantly upon his knees as if a shot had brought him there. Lifting up his hands, he exclaimed, "Thou the *king?* Then am I undone indeed!"

This speech seemed to stun the king. His eyes wandered from face to face aimlessly, then rested, bewildered, upon the boy before him. Then he said in a tone of deep disappointment, "Alack, I had believed the rumor disproportioned to the truth, but I fear me 'tis not so." He breathed a heavy sigh and said in a gentle voice, "Come to thy father, child; thou are not well."

Tom was assisted to his feet, and approached the Majesty of England, humble and trembling. The king took the frightened face between his hands and gazed earnestly and lovingly into it awhile, as if seeking some grateful sign of returning reason there, then pressed the curly head against his breast and patted it tenderly. Presently he said, "Dost not know thy father, child? Break not mine old heart; say thou knowst me. Thou *dost* know me, dost thou not?"

"Yea, thou art my dread lord the king, whom God preserve!"

"True, true—that is well—be comforted, tremble not so; there is none here would hurt thee; there is none here but loves thee. Thou art better now; thy ill dream passeth; is't not so? And thou knowest thyself now also; is't not so? Thou wilt not miscall thyself again, as they say thou didst a little while agone?"

"I pray thee of thy Grace believe me, I did but speak the truth, most dread lord, for I am the meanest among thy subjects, being a pauper born, and 'tis by a sore mischance and accident I am here, albeit I was therein nothing blameful. I am but young to die, and thou canst save me with one little word. Oh, speak it, sir!"

"Die? Talk not so, sweet prince; peace, peace, to thy troubled heart; thou shalt not die!"

Tom dropped upon his knees with a glad cry, "God requite thy mercy, O my king, and save thee long to bless thy land!" Then springing up, he turned a joyful face toward the two lords-in-waiting and exclaimed, "Thou heardst it! I am not to die; the king hath said it!" There was no movement, save that all bowed with grave respect; but no one spoke. He hesitated, a little confused, then turned timidly toward the king, saying, "I may go now?"

"Go? Surely, if thou desirest. But why not tarry yet a little? Whither wouldst go?"

Tom dropped his eyes and answered humbly, "Peradventure I mistook; but I did think me free, and so was I moved to seek again the kennel where I was born and bred to misery, yet which harboreth my mother and my sisters, and so is home to me; whereas these pomps and splendors whereunto I am not used—Oh, please you, sir, to let me go!"

The king was silent and thoughtful awhile, and his face betrayed a growing distress and uneasiness. Presently he said, with something of hope in his voice, "Perchance he is but mad upon this one strain and hath

his wits unmarred as toucheth other matter. God send
it may be so! We will make trial."

Then he asked Tom a question in Latin, and Tom
answered him lamely in the same tongue. The king was
delighted, and showed it. The lords and doctors manifested their gratification also. The king said, " 'Twas
not according to his schooling and ability, but sheweth
that his mind is but diseased, not stricken fatally. How
say you, sir?"

The physician addressed bowed low and replied, "It
jumpeth with mine own conviction, sire, that thou hast
divined aright."

The king looked pleased with this encouragement,
coming as it did from so excellent authority, and
continued with good heart, "Now mark ye all; we will
try him further."

He put a question to Tom in French. Tom stood
silent a moment, embarrassed by having so many eyes
centered upon him, then said diffidently, "I have no
knowledge of this tongue, so please your majesty."

The king fell back upon his couch. The attendants
flew to his assistance; but he put them aside and said,
"Trouble me not—it is nothing but a scurvy faintness.
Raise me! There, 'tis sufficient. Come hither, child;
there, rest thy poor troubled head upon thy father's
heart and be at peace. Thou'lt soon be well; 'tis but a
passing fantasy. Fear thou not; thou'lt soon be well."
Then he turned toward the company; his gentle manner
changed, and baleful lightnings began to play from his
eyes. He said, "List ye all! This my son is mad, but it
is not permanent. Overstudy hath done this, and
somewhat too much of confinement. Away with his
books and teachers! See ye to it. Pleasure him with
sports, beguile him in wholesome ways, so that his health
come again." He raised himself higher still and went on

with energy, "He is mad, but he is my son and England's heir, and mad or sane, still shall he reign! And hear ye further, and proclaim it: whoso speaketh of this his distemper worketh against the peace and order of these realms and shall to the gallows! Give me to drink—I burn: this sorrow sappeth my strength. There, take away the cup. Support me. There, that is well. Mad, is he? Were he a thousand times mad, yet is he Prince of Wales, and I the king will confirm it. This very morrow shall he be installed in his princely dignity in due and ancient form. Take instant order for it, my lord Hertford."

One of the nobles knelt at the royal couch and said, "The king's majesty knoweth that the Hereditary Great Marshall of England lieth attainted in the Tower. It were not meet that one attainted—"

"Peace! Insult not mine ears with his hated name. Is this man to live forever? Am I to be balked of my will? Is the prince to tarry uninstalled because, forsooth, the realm lacketh an earl marshal free of treasonable taint to invest him with his honors? No, by the splendor of God! Warn my Parliament to bring me Norfolk's doom before the sun rise again, else shall they answer for it grievously!"

Lord Hertford said, "The king's will is law," and rising, returned to his former place.

Gradually the wrath faded out of the old king's face, and he said, "Kiss me, my prince. There. What fearest thou? Am I not thy loving father?"

"Thou art good to me that am unworthy, O mighty and gracious lord; that in truth I know. But—but—it grieveth me to think of him that is to die, and—"

"Ah, 'tis like thee, 'tis like thee! I know thy heart is still the same, even though thy mind hath suffered hurt, for thou wert ever of a gentle spirit. But this duke standeth between thee and thine honors; I will have another in his stead that shall bring no taint to his great office. Comfort thee, my prince; trouble not thy poor head with this matter."

"But is it not I that speed him hence, my liege? How long might he not live, but for me?"

"Take no thought of him, my prince; he is not worthy. Kiss me once again and go to thy trifles and amusements, for my malady distresseth me. I am aweary and would rest. Go with thine uncle Hertford and thy people, and come again when my body is refreshed."

Tom, heavyhearted, was conducted from the presence, for this last sentence was a deathblow to the hope he had cherished that now he would be set free. Once more he heard the buzz of low voices exclaiming, "The prince, the prince comes!"

His spirits sank lower and lower as he moved between the glittering files of bowing courtiers, for he recognized that he was indeed a captive now and might remain forever shut up in this gilded cage, a forlorn and friendless prince, except God in his mercy take pity on him and set him free.

And turn where he would, he seemed to see floating in the air the severed head and the remembered face of the great Duke of Norfolk, the eyes fixed on him reproachfully.

His old dreams had been so pleasant, but this reality was so dreary!

6

Tom Receives Instructions

Tom was conducted to the principal apartment of a noble suite and made to sit down, a thing which he was loath to do, since there were elderly men and men of high degree about him. He begged them to be seated also, but they only bowed their thanks or murmured them and remained standing. He would have insisted, but his "uncle" the Earl of Hertford whispered in his ear, "Prithee, insist not, my lord; it is not meet that they sit in thy presence."

The lord St. John was announced, and after making obeisance to Tom, he said, "I come upon the king's errand, concerning a matter which requireth privacy. Will it please your royal Highness to dismiss all that attend you here, save my lord the Earl of Hertford?"

Observing that Tom did not seem to know how to proceed, Hertford whispered him to make a sign with his hand and not trouble himself to speak unless he chose. When the waiting gentlemen had retired, Lord St. John said, "His Majesty commandeth that for due and weighty reasons of state, the prince's grace shall hide his infirmity in all ways that be within his power till it be passed and he be as he was before. To wit, that he shall deny to none that he is the true prince and heir to England's greatness; that he shall uphold his princely dignity and shall receive, without word or sign of protest, that reverence and observance which unto it do appertain of right and ancient usage; that he shall cease to speak to any of that lowly birth and life his malady hath conjured out of the unwholesome imaginings of o'erwrought fancy; that he shall strive with diligence to bring unto his memory again those faces which he was wont to know—and where he faileth he shall hold his peace, neither betraying by semblance of surprise or other sign that he hath forgot; that upon occasions of state, whensoever any matter shall perplex him as to the thing he should do or the utterance he should make, he shall show nought of unrest to the curious that look on, but take advice in that matter of the lord Hertford or my humble self, which are commanded of the king to be upon this service and close at call till this commandment be dissolved. Thus saith the king's majesty, who sendeth greeting to your royal Highness and prayeth that God will of his mercy quickly heal you and have you now and ever in his holy keeping."

The lord St. John made reverence and stood aside. Tom replied resignedly, "The king hath said it. None may palter with the king's command or fit it to his ease, where it doth chafe, with deft evasions. The king shall be obeyed."

Lord Hertford said, "Touching the king's majesty's ordainment concerning books and such like serious matters, it may peradventure please your Highness to ease your time with lightsome entertainment, lest you go wearied to the banquet and suffer harm thereby."

Tom's face showed inquiring surprise, and a blush followed when he saw Lord St. John's eyes bent sorrowfully upon him. His lordship said, "Thy memory still wrongeth thee, and thou hast shown surprise; but suffer it not to trouble thee, for 'tis a matter that will not bide, but depart with thy mending malady. My lord of Hertford speaketh of the city's banquet which the king's majesty did promise, some two months flown, your Highness should attend. Thou recallest it now?"

"It grieves me to confess it had indeed escaped me," said Tom in a hesitating voice, and blushed again.

At this moment the lady Elizabeth and the lady Jane Grey were announced. The two lords exchanged significant glances, and Hertford stepped quickly toward the door. As the young girls passed him, he said in a low voice, "I pray ye, ladies, seem not to observe his humors nor show surprise when his memory doth lapse, it will grieve you to note how it doth stick at every trifle."

Meantime Lord St. John was saying in Tom's ear, "Please you, sir, keep diligently in mind his Majesty's desire. Remember all thou canst, *seem* to remember all else. Let them not perceive that thou are much changed from thy wont, for thou knowest how tenderly thy old play-fellows bear thee in their hearts and how 'twould grieve them. Art willing, sir, that I remain? And thine uncle?"

Tom signified assent with a gesture and a murmured word, for he was already learning, and in his simple heart was resolved to acquit himself as best he might, according to the king's command.

In spite of every precaution, the conversation among the young people became a little embarrassing at times. More than once, in truth, Tom was near to breaking down and confessing himself unequal to his tremendous part; but the tact of the princess Elizabeth saved him, or a word from one or the other of the vigilant lords, thrown in apparently by chance, had the same happy effect. Once the little lady Jane turned to Tom and dismayed him with this question, "Hast paid thy duty to the queen's majesty today, my lord?"

Tom hesitated, looked distressed, and was about to stammer out something at hazard when Lord St. John took the word and answered for him with the easy grace of a courtier accustomed to encounter delicate difficulties and to be ready for them, "He hath indeed, madam, and she did greatly hearten him, as touching his Majesty's condition; is it not so, your Highness?"

Tom mumbled something that stood for assent, but felt that he was getting upon dangerous ground. Somewhat later it was mentioned that Tom was to study no more at present, whereupon her little ladyship exclaimed, " 'Tis a pity, 'tis such a pity! Thou wert proceeding bravely. But bide thy time in patience; it will not be for long. Thou'lt yet be graced with learning like thy father, and make thy tongue master of as many languages as his, good my prince."

"My father!" cried Tom, off his guard for the moment. "I trow he cannot speak his own so that any but the swine that wallow in the sties may tell his meaning; and as for learning of any sort soever—"

He looked up and encountered a solemn warning in my lord St. John's eyes.

He stopped, blushed, then continued low and sadly, "Ah, my malady persecuteth me again, and my mind wandereth. I meant the king's grace no irreverence."

"We know it, sir," said the princess Elizabeth, taking her "brother's" hand between her two palms, respectfully but caressingly; "trouble not thyself as to that. The fault is none of thine, but thy distemper's."

"Thou'rt a gentle comforter, sweet lady," said Tom gratefully, "and my heart moveth me to thank thee for't."

Once the giddy little lady Jane fired a simple Greek phrase at Tom. The princess Elizabeth's quick eye saw by the serene blankness of the target's front that the shaft was overshot, so she tranquilly delivered a return volley of sounding Greek on Tom's behalf and then straightway changed the talk to other matters.

Time wore on pleasantly, and likewise smoothly, on the whole. Snags and sandbars grew less and less frequent, and Tom grew more and more at his ease, seeing that all were so lovingly bent upon helping him and overlooking his mistakes. When it came out that the little ladies were to accompany him to the Lord Mayor's banquet in the evening, his heart gave a bound of relief and delight, for he felt that he should not be friendless now among that multitude of strangers, whereas an hour earlier the idea of their going with him would have been an insupportable terror to him.

Tom's guardian angels, the two lords, had had less comfort in the interview than the other parties to it. They felt much as if they were piloting a great ship through a dangerous channel; they were on the alert constantly, and found their office no child's play. Wherefore, at last, when the ladies' visit was drawing to a close and the lord Guilford Dudley was announced, they not only felt that their charge had been sufficiently taxed for the present, but also that they themselves were not in the best condition to take their ship back and make their anxious voyage all over again. So they respectfully advised Tom to excuse himself, which he was very glad to do, although a slight shade of disappointment might have been observed upon my lady Jane's face when she heard the splendid stripling denied admittance.

There was a pause now, a sort of waiting silence which Tom could not understand. He glanced at Lord Hert-

There was a pause now, a sort of waiting silence which Tom could not understand

ford, who gave him a sign, but he failed to understand that also. The ready Elizabeth came to the rescue with her usual easy grace. She made reverence and said, "Have we leave of the prince's grace my brother to go?"

Tom said, "Indeed your ladyships can have whatsoever of me they will for the asking; yet would I rather give them any other thing that in my poor power lieth than leave to take the light and blessing of their presence hence. Give ye good den, and God be with ye!" Then he smiled inwardly at the thought; " 'Tis not for nought I have dwelt but among princes in my reading and taught my tongue some slight trick of their broidered and gracious speech withal!"

When the illustrious maidens were gone, Tom turned wearily to his keepers and said, "May it please your lordships to grant me leave to go into some corner and rest me?"

Lord Hertford said, "So please your Highness, it is for you to command, it is for us to obey. That thou shouldst rest is indeed a needful thing, since thou must journey to the city presently."

He touched a bell, and a page appeared, who was ordered to desire the presence of Sir William Herbert. This gentleman came straightway and conducted Tom to an inner apartment. Tom's first movement there was to reach for a cup of water; but a silk-and-velvet servitor seized it, dropped upon one knee, and offered it to him on a golden salver.

Next the tired captive sat down and was going to take off his buskins, timidly asking leave with his eye, but another silk-and-velvet discomforter went down upon his knees and took the office from him. He made two or three further efforts to help himself, but being promptly forestalled each time, he finally gave up with a sigh of resignation and a murmured, "Beshrew me but I marvel they do not require to breathe for me also!" Slippered and wrapped in a sumptuous robe, he laid himself down at last to rest, but not to sleep, for his head was too full of thoughts and the room too full of people. He could not dismiss the former, so they stayed; he did not know enough to dismiss the latter, so they stayed also, to his vast regret—and theirs.

Tom's departure had left his two noble guardians alone. They mused awhile, with much headshaking and walking the floor; then Lord St. John said, "Plainly, what dost thou think?"

"Plainly, then, this. The king is near his end, my nephew is mad, mad will mount the throne, and mad remain. God protect England, since she will need it!"

"Verily it promiseth so, indeed. But—have you no misgivings as to—as to—"

The speaker hesitated and finally stopped. He evidently felt that he was upon delicate ground. Lord Hertford stopped before him, looked into his face with a clear, frank eye, and said, "Speak on; there is none to hear but me. Misgivings as to what?"

"I am full loath to word the thing that is in my mind, and thou so near to him in blood, my lord. But craving pardon if I do offend, seemeth it not strange that madness could so change his port and manner! Not but that his port and speech are princely still, but that they *differ* in one unweighty trifle or another from what his custom was aforetime. Seemeth it not strange that madness should filch from his memory his father's very lineaments; the customs and observances that are his due from such as be about him; and, leaving him his Latin, strip him of his Greek and French? My lord, be not

offended, but ease my mind of its disquiet and receive
my grateful thanks.   It haunteth me, his saying he was
not the prince, and so—"

"Peace, my lord, thou utterest treason!   Hast forgot
the king's command?   Remember I am party to thy
crime if I but listen."

St. John paled and hastened to say, "I was in fault, I do
confess it.   Betray me not, grant me this grace out of
thy courtesy, and I will neither think nor speak of this
thing more.   Deal not hardly with me, sir, else am I
ruined."

"I am content, my lord.   So thou offend not again,
here or in the ears of others, it shall be as though thou
hadst not spoken.   But thou needst not have misgivings.
He is my sister's son; are not his voice, his face, his form,
familiar to me from his cradle?   Madness can do all the
odd conflicting things thou seest in him, and more.
Dost not recall how that the old baron Marley, being
mad, forgot the favor of his own countenance that he
had known for sixty years, and held it was another's; nay,
even claimed he was the son of Mary Magdalene and
that his head was made of Spanish glass; and sooth to say,
he suffered none to touch it, lest by mischance some
heedless hand might shiver it.   Give thy misgivings
easement, good my lord.   This is the very prince, I know
him well—and soon will be thy king; it may advantage
thee to bear this in mind and more dwell upon it than
the other."

After some further talk, in which the lord St. John
covered up his mistake as well as he could by repeated
protests that his faith was thoroughly grounded now and
could not be assailed by doubts again, the lord Hertford
relieved his fellow keeper and sat down to keep watch
and ward alone.   He was soon deep in meditation.   And
evidently the   longer he   thought,   the   more   he   was

bothered. By and by he began to pace the floor and mutter.

"Tush, he *must* be the prince! Will any he in all the land maintain there can be two, not of one blood and birth, so marvelously twinned? And even were it so, 'twere yet a stranger miracle that chance should cast the one into the other's place. Nay, 'tis folly, folly, folly!"

Presently he said, "Now were he impostor and called himself prince, look you *that* would be natural; that would be reasonable. But lived ever an impostor yet who, being called prince by the king, prince by the court, prince by all, *denied* his dignity and pleaded against his exaltation? *No!* By the soul of St. Swithin, no! This is the true prince, gone mad!"

7

Tom's First Royal Dinner

Somewhat after one in the afternoon, Tom resignedly underwent the ordeal of being dressed for dinner. He found himself as finely clothed as before, but everything different, everything changed, from his ruff to his stockings. He was presently conducted with much state to a spacious and ornate apartment, where a table was already set for one. Its furniture was all of massy gold, and beautified with designs which well-nigh made it priceless, since they were the work of Benvenuto. The room was half filled with noble servitors. A chaplain said grace, and Tom was about to fall to, for hunger had long been constitutional with him, but was interrupted by my lord the Earl of Berkeley, who fastened a napkin about his neck, for the great post of Diaperers to the Princes of Wales was hereditary in this nobleman's family. Tom's cupbearer was present and forestalled all his attempts to help himself to wine. The Taster to his Highness the Prince of Wales was there also, prepared to taste any suspicious dish upon requirement and run the risk of being poisoned. He was only an ornamental appendage at this time and was seldom called upon to exercise his function; but there had been times, not many generations past, when the office of taster had its perils and was not a grandeur to be desired. Why they did not use a dog or a plumber seems strange, but all the ways of royalty are strange. My lord D'Arcy, First Groom of the Chamber, was there to do goodness knows what; but there he was—let that suffice. The Lord Chief Butler was there and stood behind Tom's chair, overseeing the solemnities under command of the Lord Great Steward and the Lord Head Cook, who stood near. Tom had three hundred and eighty-four servants beside these, but they were not all in that room, of course, nor the quarter of them; neither was Tom aware yet that they existed.

All those that were present had been well drilled within the hour to remember that the prince was temporarily out of his head and to be careful to show no surprise at his vagaries. These "vagaries" were soon on exhibition before them, but they only moved their compassion and their sorrow, not their mirth. It was a heavy affliction to them to see the beloved prince so stricken.

Poor Tom ate with his fingers mainly, but no one smiled at it or even seemed to observe it. He inspected his napkin curiously and with deep interest, for it was of a very dainty and beautiful fabric; then said with simplicity, "Prithee take it away, lest in mine unheedfulness it be soiled."

The Hereditary Diaperer took it away with reverent manner and without word or protest of any sort.

Tom examined the turnips and the lettuce with interest, and asked what they were and if they were to be eaten, for it was only recently that men had begun to raise these things in England in place of importing them as luxuries from Holland. His question was answered with grave respect, and no surprise manifested. When he had finished his dessert, he filled his pockets with nuts; but nobody appeared to be aware of it or disturbed by it. But the next moment he was himself disturbed by it and showed discomposure, for this was the only service he had been permitted to do with his own hands during the meal, and he did not doubt that he had done a most improper and unprincely thing. At that moment the muscles of his nose began to twitch, and the end of that organ to lift and wrinkle. This continued, and Tom began to evince a growing distress. He looked appealingly, first at one and then another of the lords about him, and tears came into his eyes. They sprang forward with dismay in their faces and begged to know his trouble. Tom said with genuine anguish, "I crave your indulgence; my nose itcheth cruelly. What is the custom and usage in this emergence? Prithee speed, for 'tis but a little time that I can bear it."

None smiled, but all were sore perplexed and looked one to the other in deep tribulation for counsel. But behold, here was a dead wall, and nothing in English history to tell how to get over it. The Master of Ceremonies was not present; there was no one who felt safe to venture upon this uncharted sea or risk the attempt to solve this solemn problem. Alas! There was no Hereditary Scratcher. Meantime the tears had overflowed their banks and begun to trickle down Tom's cheeks. His twitching nose was pleading more urgently than ever for relief. At last nature broke down the barriers of etiquette: Tom lifted up an inward prayer for pardon if he was doing wrong and brought relief to the burdened hearts of his court by scratching his nose himself.

His meal being ended, a lord came and held before him a broad, shallow, golden dish with fragrant rose water in it to cleanse his mouth and fingers with; and my lord the Hereditary Diaperer stood by with a napkin for his use. Tom gazed at the dish a puzzled moment or two, then raised it to his lips and gravely took a draft.

Then he returned it to the waiting lord and said, "Nay, it likes me not, my lord; it hath a pretty flavor, but it wanteth strength."

This new eccentricity of the prince's ruined mind made all the hearts about him ache, but the sad sight moved none to merriment.

Tom's next unconscious blunder was to get up and leave the table just when the chaplain had taken his stand behind his chair, and with uplifted hands and closed, uplifted eyes was in the act of beginning the blessing. Still nobody seemed to perceive that the prince had done a thing unusual.

By his own request, our small friend was now conducted to his private cabinet and left there alone to his own devices. Hanging upon hooks in the oaken wainscoting were the several pieces of a suit of shining steel armor, covered all over with beautiful designs exquisitely inlaid in gold. This martial panoply belonged to the true prince, a recent present from Madam Parr, the queen. Tom put on the greaves, the gauntlets, the plumed helmet, and such other pieces as he could don without assistance, and for a while was minded to call for help and complete the matter, but bethought him of the nuts he had brought away from dinner and the joy it would be to eat them with no crowd to eye him and no Grand Hereditaries to pester him with undesired services; so he restored the pretty things to their several places and soon was cracking nuts and feeling almost naturally happy for the first time since God for his sins had made him a prince. When the nuts were all gone, he stumbled upon some inviting books in a closet, among them one about the etiquette of the English court. This was a prize. He lay down upon a sumptuous divan and proceeded to instruct himself with honest zeal. Let us leave him there for the present.

8

The Question of the Seal

About five o'clock Henry VIII awoke out of an unrefreshing nap and muttered to himself, "Troublous dreams, troublous dreams! Mine end is now at hand; so say these warnings, and my failing pulses do confirm it." Presently a wicked light flamed up in his eye, and he muttered, "Yet will not I die till *he* go before."

His attendants perceiving that he was awake, one of them asked his pleasure concerning the Lord Chancellor, who was waiting without.

"Admit him, admit him!" exclaimed the king eagerly.

The Lord Chancellor entered and knelt by the king's couch, saying, "I have given order, and according to the king's command, the peers of the realm, in their robes, do now stand at the bar of the House, where, having confirmed the Duke of Norfolk's doom, they humbly wait his Majesty's further pleasure in the matter."

The king's face lit up with a fierce joy. Said he, "Lift me up! In mine own person will I go before my Parliament, and with mine own hand will I seal the warrant that rids me of—"

His voice failed, an ashen pallor swept the flush from his cheeks, and the attendants eased him back upon his

pillows and hurriedly assisted him with restoratives.
Presently he said sorrowfully, "Alack, how have I longed
for this sweet hour! And lo, too late it cometh, and I am
robbed of this so coveted chance. But speed ye, speed
ye! Let others do this happy office sith 'tis denied to me.
I put my Great Seal in commission; choose thou the
lords that shall compose it, and get ye to your work.
Speed ye, man! Before the sun shall rise and set again,
bring me his head, that I may see it."

"According to the king's command, so shall it be.
Will't please your Majesty to order that the Seal be now
restored to me, so that I may forth upon the business?"

"The Seal? Who keepeth the Seal but thou?"

"Please your Majesty, you did take it from me two
days since, saying it should no more do its office till your
own royal hand should use it upon the Duke of Norfolk's warrant."

"Why, so in sooth I did; I do remember it. What did
I with it? I am very feeble. So oft these days doth my
memory play the traitor with me. 'Tis strange,
strange—"

The king dropped into inarticulate mumblings, shaking his gray head weakly from time to time and grop-
ingly trying to recollect what he had done with the
Seal.

At last my lord Hertford ventured to kneel and offer
information, "Sire, if that I may be so bold, here be
several that do remember with me how that you gave the
Great Seal into the hands of his Highness the Prince of
Wales to keep against the day that—"

"True, most true!" interrupted the king. "Fetch it!
Go; time flieth!"

Lord Hertford flew to Tom, but returned to the king
before very long troubled and empty-handed. He delivered himself to this effect: "It grieveth me, my lord

the king, to bear so heavy and unwelcome tidings; but it is the will of God that the prince's affliction abideth still, and he cannot recall to mind that he received the Seal. So came I quickly to report, thinking it were waste of precious time and little worth withal that any should attempt to search the long array of chambers and saloons that belong unto his royal High—"

A groan from the king interrupted my lord at this point. After a little while his Majesty said, with a deep sadness in his tone, "Trouble him no more, poor child. The hand of God lieth heavy upon him, and my heart goeth out in loving compassion for him, and sorrow that I may not bear his burden on mine own old trouble-weighted shoulders, and so bring him peace."

He closed his eyes, fell to mumbling, and presently was silent. After a time he opened his eyes again and gazed vacantly around until his glance rested upon the kneeling Lord Chancellor. Instantly his face flushed with wrath: "What, thou here yet! By the glory of God, an' thou gettest not about that traitor's business, thy miter shall have holiday the morrow for lack of a head to grace withal!"

The trembling Chancellor answered, "Good your Majesty, I cry you mercy! I but waited for the Seal."

"Man, hast lost thy wits? The small Seal which aforetime I was wont to take with me abroad lieth in my treasury. And since the Great Seal hath flown away, shall not it suffice? Hast lost thy wits? Begone! And hark ye; come no more till thou do bring his head."

The poor Chancellor was not long in removing himself from this dangerous vicinity, nor did the commission waste time in giving the royal assent to the work of the slavish Parliament and appointing the morrow for the beheading of the premier peer of England, the luckless Duke of Norfolk.

9

The River Pageant

At nine in the evening the whole vast riverfront of the palace was blazing with light. The river itself, as far as the eye could reach citywards, was so thickly covered with watermen's boats and with pleasure barges, all fringed with colored lanterns and gently agitated by the waves, that it resembled a glowing and limitless garden of flowers stirred to soft motion by summer winds. The grand terrace of stone steps leading down to the water, spacious enough to mass the army of a German principality upon, was a picture to see, with its ranks of royal halberdiers in polished armor and its troops of brilliantly costumed servitors flitting up and down, and to and fro, in the hurry of preparation.

Presently a command was given, and immediately all living creatures vanished from the steps. Now the air was heavy with the hush of suspense and expectancy. As far as one's vision could carry, he might see the myriads of people in the boats rise up, and shade their eyes from the glare of lanterns and torches, and gaze toward the palace.

A file of forty or fifty state barges drew up to the steps. They were richly gilt, and their lofty prows and sterns were elaborately carved. Some of them were decorated with banners and streamers, some with cloth of gold and arras embroidered with coats of arms, others with silken flags that had numberless little silver bells fastened to them which shook out tiny showers of joyous music whenever the breezes fluttered them; others of yet higher pretensions, since they belonged to nobles in the prince's immediate service, had their sides picturesquely fenced with shields gorgeously emblazoned with armorial bearings. Each state barge was towed by a tender. Besides the rowers, these tenders carried each a number of men-at-arms in glossy helmet and breastplate, and a company of musicians.

The advance guard of the expected procession now appeared in the great gateway, a troop of halberdiers. They were dressed in striped hose of black and tawny, velvet caps graced at the sides with silver roses, and doublets of murrey-and-blue cloth embroidered on the front and back with the three feathers, the prince's blazon, woven in gold. Their halberd staves were covered with crimson velvet, fastened with gilt nails, and ornamented with gold tassels. Filing off on the right and left, they formed two long lines, extending from the gateway of the palace to the water's edge. A thick, rayed cloth, or carpet, was then unfolded and laid down between them by attendants in the gold-and-crimson liveries of the prince. This done, a flourish of trumpets resounded from within. A lively prelude arose from the musicians on the water, and two ushers with white wands marched with a slow and stately pace from the portal. They were followed by an officer bearing the civic mace, after whom came another carrying the city's sword; then several sergeants of the city guard, in their full accouterments and with badges on their sleeves; then the garter king-at-arms, in his tabard; then several knights of the bath, each with a white lace on his sleeve; then their esquires; then the judges, in their robes of scarlet and coifs; then the lord High Chancellor of England, in a robe of scarlet, open before and purfled with miniver; then a deputation of aldermen, in their scarlet cloaks; and then the heads of the different civic companies, in their robes of state. Now came twelve French gentlemen, in splendid habiliments, consisting of pourpoints of white damask barred with gold, short mantles of crimson velvet lined with violet taffeta, and carnation-colored *hauts-de-chausses,* and took their way down the steps. They were of the suite of the French ambassador, and were followed by twelve cavaliers of the suite of the Spanish ambassador, clothed in black velvet unrelieved by any ornament. Following these came several great English nobles with their attendants.

There was a flourish of trumpets within; and the prince's uncle, the future great Duke of Somerset, emerged from the gateway arrayed in a doublet of black cloth of gold and a cloak of crimson satin flowered with gold and ribanded with nets of silver. He turned, doffed his plumed cap, bent his body in a low reverence, and began to step backward, bowing at each step. A prolonged trumpet blast followed, and a proclamation, "Way for the high and mighty, the lord Edward, Prince of Wales!" High aloft on the palace walls a long line of red tongues of flame leaped forth with a thundercrash; the massed world on the river burst into a mighty roar of welcome; and Tom Canty, the cause and hero of it all, stepped into view and slightly bowed his princely head.

He was magnificently habited in a doublet of white satin, with a frontpiece of purple cloth of tissue, powdered with diamonds, and edged with ermine. Over this he wore a mantle of white cloth of gold pounced with the triple-feather crest, lined with blue satin, set with pearls and precious stones, and fastened with a clasp of brilliants. About his neck hung the Order of the Garter and several princely foreign orders, and wherever light fell upon him jewels responded with a blinding flash. O Tom Canty, born in a hovel, bred in the gutters of London, familiar with rags and dirt and misery, what a spectacle is this!

10

The Prince in the Toils

We left John Canty dragging the rightful prince into Offal Court, with a noisy and delighted mob at his heels. There was but one person in it who offered a pleading word for the captive, and he was not heeded; he was hardly even heard, so great was the turmoil. The prince continued to struggle for freedom and to rage against the treatment he was suffering, until John Canty lost what little patience was left in him and raised his oaken cudgel in a sudden fury over the prince's head. The single pleader for the lad sprang to stop the man's arm, and the blow descended upon his own wrist. Canty roared out, "Thou'lt meddle, wilt thou? Then have thy reward."

His cudgel crashed down upon the meddler's head; there was a groan, a dim form sank to the ground among the feet of the crowd, and the next moment it lay there in the dark alone. The mob pressed on, their enjoyment nothing disturbed by this episode.

Presently the prince found himself in John Canty's abode, with the door closed against the outsiders. By the vague light of a tallow candle which was thrust into a bottle he made out the main features of the loathsome den and also the occupants of it. Two frowzy girls and a middle-aged woman cowered against the wall in one corner with the aspect of animals habituated to harsh usage and expecting and dreading it now. From another corner stole a withered hag with streaming gray hair and malignant eyes. John Canty said to this one, "Tarry! There's fine mummeries here. Mar them not till thou'st enjoyed them; then let thy hand be heavy as thou wilt. Stand forth, lad. Now say thy foolery again, an' thou'st not forgot it. Name thy name. Who art thou?"

The insulted blood mounted to the little prince's cheek once more, and he lifted a steady and indignant gaze to the man's face and said, " 'Tis but ill breeding in such as thou to command me to speak. I tell thee now, as I told thee before, I am Edward, Prince of Wales, and none other."

The stunning surprise of this reply nailed the hag's feet to the floor where she stood, and almost took her breath. She stared at the prince in stupid amazement, which so amused her ruffianly son that he burst into a roar of laughter. But the effect upon Tom Canty's mother and sisters was different. Their dread of bodily injury gave way at once to distress of a different sort. They ran forward with woe and dismay in their faces, exclaiming, "O poor Tom, poor lad!"

The mother fell on her knees before the prince, put her hands upon his shoulders, and gazed yearningly into his face through her rising tears. Then she said, "O my poor boy! Thy foolish reading hath wrought its woeful work at last and ta'en thy wit away. Ah! Why didst thou cleave to it when I so warned thee 'gainst it? Thou'st broke thy mother's heart."

The prince looked into her face and said gently, "Thy

son is well and hath not lost his wits, good dame. Comfort thee; let me to the palace where he is, and straightway will the king my father restore him to thee."

"The king thy father! O my child! Unsay these words that be freighted with death for thee and ruin for all that be near to thee. Shake off this gruesome dream. Call back thy poor wandering memory. Look upon me. Am not I thy mother that bore thee and loveth thee?"

The prince shook his head and reluctantly said, "God knoweth I am loath to grieve thy heart, but truly have I never looked upon thy face before."

The woman sank back to a sitting posture on the floor, and covering her eyes with her hands, gave way to heartbroken sobs and wailings.

"Let the show go on!" shouted Canty. "What, Nan! What, Bet! Mannerless wenches! Will ye stand in the prince's presence? Upon your knees, ye pauper scum, and do him reverence!"

He followed this with another horselaugh. The girls began to plead timidly for their brother, and Nan said, "An' thou wilt but let him to bed, Father, rest and sleep will heal his madness; prithee, do."

"Do, Father," said Bet; "he is more worn than is his wont. Tomorrow will he be himself again, and will beg with diligence, and come not empty home again."

This remark sobered the father's joviality and brought his mind to business. He turned angrily upon the prince and said, "The morrow must we pay two pennies to him that owns this hole; two pennies, mark ye—all this money for a half year's rent, else out of this we go. Show what thou'st gathered with thy lazy begging."

The prince said, "Offend me not with thy sordid matters. I tell thee again I am the king's son."

A sounding blow upon the prince's shoulder from Canty's broad palm sent him staggering into goodwife Canty's arms, who clasped him to her breast and sheltered him from a pelting rain of cuffs and slaps by interposing her own person. The frightened girls retreated to their corner, but the grandmother stepped eagerly forward to assist her son. The prince sprang away from Mrs. Canty, exclaiming, "Thou shalt not suffer for me, madam. Let these swine do their will upon me alone."

This speech infuriated the swine to such a degree that they set about their work without waste of time. Between them they belabored the boy right soundly, and then gave the girls and their mother a beating for showing sympathy for the victim.

"Now," said Canty, "to bed, all of ye. The entertainment has tired me."

The light was put out, and the family retired. As soon as the snorings of the head of the house and his mother showed that they were asleep, the young girls crept to where the prince lay and covered him tenderly from the cold with straw and rags; and their mother crept to him also, and stroked his hair, and cried over him, whispering broken words of comfort and compassion in his ear the while. She had saved a morsel for him to eat also, but the boy's pains had swept away all appetite, at least for black and tasteless crusts. He was touched by her brave and costly defense of him and by her commiseration, and he thanked her in very noble and princely words, and begged her to go to her sleep and try to forget her sorrows. And he added that the king his father would not let her loyal kindness and devotion go unrewarded. This return to his "madness" broke her heart anew, and she strained him to her breast again and again and then went back, drowned in tears, to her bed.

As she lay thinking and mourning, the suggestion began to creep into her mind that there was an undefinable something about this boy that was lacking in Tom Canty, mad or sane. She could not describe it, she could not tell just what it was, and yet her sharp mother instinct seemed to detect it and perceive it. What if the boy were really not her son after all? Oh, absurd! She almost smiled at the idea, spite of her griefs and troubles. No matter, she found that it was an idea that would not "down," but persisted in haunting her. It pursued her, it harassed her, it clung to her, and refused to be put away or ignored. At last she perceived that there was not going to be any peace for her until she should devise a test that should prove, clearly and without question, whether this lad was her son or not, and so banish these wearing and worrying doubts. Ah yes, this was plainly the right way out of the difficulty; therefore she set her wits to work at once to contrive that test. But it was an easier thing to propose than to accomplish. She turned over in her mind one promising test after another, but was obliged to relinquish them all: none of them were absolutely sure, absolutely perfect; and an imperfect one could not satisfy her. Evidently she was racking her head in vain; it seemed manifest that she must give the matter up. While this depressing thought was passing through her mind, her ear caught the regular breathing of the boy, and she knew he had fallen asleep. And while she listened, the measured breathing was broken by a soft, startled cry, such as one utters in a troubled dream. This chance occurrence furnished her instantly with a plan worth all her labored tests combined. She at once set herself, feverishly but noiselessly to work to relight her candle, muttering to herself, "Had I but seen him *then*, I should have known! Since that day, when he was little, that the powder burst in his face, he hath never been startled of a sudden out of his dreams or out of his thinkings, but he hath cast his hand before his eyes, even as he did that day; and not as others would do it, with the palm inward, but always with the palm turned outward. I have seen it a hundred times, and it hath never varied nor ever failed. Yes, I shall soon know now!"

By this time she had crept to the slumbering boy's side with the candle, shaded, in her hand. She bent heedfully and warily over him, scarcely breathing in her suppressed excitement, and suddenly flashed the light in his face and struck the floor by his ear with her knuckles. The sleeper's eyes sprung wide open, and he cast a startled stare about him, but he made no special movement with his hands.

The poor woman was smitten almost helpless with surprise and grief, but she contrived to hide her emotions and to soothe the boy to sleep again; then she crept apart and communed miserably with herself upon the disastrous result of her experiment. She tried to believe that her Tom's madness had banished this habitual gesture of his, but she could not do it. "No," she said, "his *hands* are not mad; they could not unlearn so old a habit in so brief a time. Oh, this is a heavy day for me!"

Still, hope was as stubborn now as doubt had been before; she could not bring herself to accept the verdict of the test; she must try the thing again: the failure must have been only an accident; so she startled the boy out of his sleep a second and a third time, at intervals, with the same result which had marked the first test; then she dragged herself to bed and fell sorrowfully asleep, saying, "But I cannot give him up. Oh, no, I cannot, I cannot; he *must* be my boy!"

The poor mother's interruptions having ceased and the prince's pains having gradually lost their power to disturb him, utter weariness at last sealed his eyes in a profound and restful sleep. Hour after hour slipped away, and still he slept like the dead. Thus four or five hours passed. Then his stupor began to lighten. Presently while half asleep and half awake, he murmured, "Sir William!"

After a moment, "Ho, Sir William Herbert! Hie thee hither, and list to the strangest dream that ever. Sir William! Dost hear? Man, I did think me changed to a pauper, and—Ho there! Guards! Sir William! What! Is there no groom of the chamber in waiting? Alack, it shall go hard with—"

"What aileth thee?" asked a whisper near him. "Who art thou calling?"

"Sir William Herbert. Who art thou?"

"I? Who should I be but thy sister Nan? Oh, Tom, I had forgot! Thou'rt mad yet; poor lad thou'rt mad yet; would I had never woke to know it again! But prithee master thy tongue, lest we be all beaten till we die!"

The startled prince sprang partly up, but a sharp reminder from his stiffened bruises brought him to himself, and he sunk back among his foul straw with a moan and the ejaculation, "Alas, it was no dream then!"

In a moment all the heavy sorrow and misery which sleep had banished were upon him again, and he realized that he was no longer a petted prince in a palace with the adoring eyes of a nation upon him, but a pauper, an outcast, clothed in rags, prisoner in a den fit only for beasts, and consorting with beggars and thieves.

In the midst of his grief he began to be conscious of hilarious noises and shoutings, apparently but a block or two away. The next moment there were several sharp raps at the door; John Canty ceased from snoring and said, "Who knocketh? What wilt thou?"

A voice answered, "Knowst thou who it was thou laid thy cudgel on?"

"No. Neither know I, nor care."

"Belike thou'lt change thy note eftsoons. An' thou would save thy neck, nothing but flight may stead thee. The man is this moment delivering up the ghost. 'Tis the priest Father Andrew!"

"God-a-mercy!" exclaimed Canty. He roused his family and hoarsely commanded, "Up with ye all and fly, or bide where ye are and perish!"

Scarcely five minutes later the Canty household were in the street and flying for their lives. John Canty held the prince by the wrist and hurried him along the dark way, giving him this caution in a low voice, "Mind thy tongue, thou mad fool, and speak not our name. I will choose me a new name speedily to throw the law's dogs off the scent. Mind thy tongue, I tell thee!" He growled these words to the rest of the family: "If it so chance that we be separated, let each make for London Bridge; whoso findeth himself as far as the last linen-draper's shop on the bridge, let him tarry there till the others be come; then will we flee into Southwark together."

At this moment the party burst suddenly out of darkness into light, and not only into light, but into the midst of a multitude of singing, dancing, and shouting people massed together on the river frontage. There was a line of bonfires stretching as far as one could see, up and down the Thames; London Bridge was illuminated; Southwark Bridge likewise; the entire river was

aglow with the flash and sheen of colored lights; and
constant explosions of fireworks filled the skies with an
intricate commingling of shooting splendors and a thick
rain of dazzling sparks that almost turned night into
day; everywhere were crowds of revelers; all London
seemed to be at large.

John Canty delivered himself of a furious curse and
commanded a retreat, but it was too late. He and his
tribe were swallowed up in that swarming hive of
humanity and hopelessly separated from each other in
an instant. We are not considering that the prince was
one of his tribe; Canty still kept his grip upon him.
The prince's heart was beating high with hopes of escape
now. A burly waterman, considerably exalted with
liquor, found himself rudely shoved by Canty in his
efforts to plow through the crowd; he laid his great hand
on Canty's shoulder and said, "Nay, whither so fast,
friend? Dost canker thy soul with sordid business when
all that be leal men and true make holiday?"

"Mine affairs are mine own; they concern thee not,"
answered Canty roughly; "take away thy hand and let
me pass."

"Sith that is thy humor, thou'lt *not* pass till thou'st
drunk to the Prince of Wales, I tell thee that," said the
waterman, barring the way resolutely.

"Give me the cup, then, and make speed, make
speed!"

Other revelers were interested by this time. They
cried out, "The loving cup, the loving cup! Make the
sour knave drink the loving cup, else will we feed him to
the fishes."

So a huge loving cup was brought; the waterman,
grasping it by one of its handles, and with his other hand
bearing up the end of an imaginary napkin, presented it
in due and ancient form to Canty, who had to grasp the

opposite handle with one of his hands and take off the lid with the other, according to ancient custom. This left the prince hand-free for a second, of course. He wasted no time, but dived among the forest of legs about him and disappeared. In another moment he could not have been harder to find under that tossing sea of life if its billows had been the Atlantic's and he a lost sixpence.

He very soon realized this fact and straightway busied himself about his own affairs without further thought of John Canty. He quickly realized another thing too. To wit, that a spurious Prince of Wales was being feasted by the city in his stead. He easily concluded that the pauper lad, Tom Canty, had deliberately taken advantage of his stupendous opportunity and become a usurper.

Therefore there was but one course to pursue—find his way to the Guildhall, make himself known, and denounce the impostor. He also made up his mind that Tom should be allowed a reasonable time for spiritual preparation and then be hanged, drawn, and quartered according to the law and usage of the day in cases of high treason.

11

At Guildhall

The royal barge, attended by its gorgeous fleet, took its stately way down the Thames through the wilderness of illuminated boats. The air was laden with music; the river banks were beruffled with joy flames; the distant city lay in a soft luminous glow from its countless invisible bonfires; above it rose many a slender spire into the sky, encrusted with sparkling lights, wherefore in their remoteness they seemed like jeweled lances thrust aloft; as the fleet swept along, it was greeted from the banks with a continuous hoarse roar of cheers and the ceaseless flash and boom of artillery.

To Tom Canty, half buried in his silken cushions, these sounds and this spectacle were a wonder unspeakably sublime and astonishing. To his little friends at his side, the princess Elizabeth and the lady Jane Grey, they were nothing.

Arrived at the Dowgate, the fleet was towed up the limpid Walbrook (whose channel has now been for two centuries buried out of sight under acres of buildings) to Bucklersbury, past houses and under bridges populous with merrymakers and brilliantly lighted, and at last came to a halt in a basin where now is Barge Yard, in the center of the ancient city of London. Tom disembarked, and he and his gallant procession crossed Cheapside and made a short march through the Old Jewry and Basinghall street to the Guildhall.

Tom and his little ladies were received with due ceremony by the Lord Mayor and the Fathers of the City, in their gold chains and scarlet robes of state, and conducted to a rich canopy of estate at the head of the great hall, preceded by heralds making proclamation, and by the mace and the city sword. The lords and ladies who were to attend upon Tom and his two small friends took their places behind their chairs.

At a lower table the court grandees and other guests of noble degree were seated with the magnates of the city; the commoners took places at a multitude of tables on the main floor of the hall. From their lofty vantage ground the giants Gog and Magog, the ancient guardians of the city, contemplated the spectacle below them with eyes grown familiar to it in forgotten generations. There was a bugle blast and a proclamation, and a fat butler appeared in a high perch in the leftward wall, followed by his servitors bearing with impressive solemnity a royal Baron of Beef, smoking hot and ready for the knife.

After grace, Tom (being instructed) rose—and the whole house with him—and drank from a portly golden loving cup with the princess Elizabeth; from her it passed to the lady Jane and then traversed the general assemblage. So the banquet began.

By midnight the revelry was at its height. Now came one of those picturesque spectacles so admired in that old day. A description of it is still extant in the quaint wording of a chronicler who witnessed it:

"Space being made, presently entered a baron and an

earl appareled after the Turkish fashion in long robes of bawdkin powdered with gold, hats on their heads of crimson velvet, with great rolls of gold, girded with two swords called scimitars hanging by great bawdricks of gold. Next came yet another baron and another earl, in two long gowns of yellow satin, traversed with white satin, and in every bend of white was a bend of crimson satin, after the fashion of Russia, with furred hats of gray on their heads, either of them having an hatchet in their hands and boots with pikes" (points a foot long), "turned up. And after them came a knight, then the Lord High Admiral, and with him five nobles, in doublets of crimson velvet, voyded low on the back and before to the cannell-bone, laced on the breasts with chains of silver; and over that, short cloaks of crimson satin, and on their heads hats after the dancers' fashion, with pheasants' feathers in them. These were appareled after the fashion of Prussia. The torchbearers, which were about an hundred, were appareled in crimson satin and green, like Moors, their faces black. Next came in a *mommarye*. Then the minstrels, which were disguised, danced; and the lords and ladies did wildly dance also, that it was a pleasure to behold."

And while Tom, in his high seat, was gazing upon this "wild" dancing, lost in admiration of the dazzling commingling of kaleidoscopic colors which the whirling turmoil of gaudy figures below him presented, the ragged but real little Prince of Wales was proclaiming his rights and his wrongs, denouncing the impostor, and clamoring for admission at the gates of Guildhall! The crowd enjoyed this episode prodigiously and pressed forward and craned their necks to see the small rioter. Presently they began to taunt him and mock at him, purposely to goad him to a higher and still more entertaining fury. Tears of mortification sprung to his eyes, but he stood his ground and defied the mob right royally. Other taunts followed, added mockings stung him, and he exclaimed, "I tell ye again, you pack of unmannerly curs, I am the Prince of Wales! And all forlorn and friendless as I be, with none to give me word of grace or help me in my need, yet will not I be driven from my ground, but will maintain it!"

"Though thou be prince or no prince, 'tis all one; thou be'st a gallant lad, and not friendless neither! Here stand I by thy side to prove it; and mind I tell thee thou mightst have a worser friend than Miles Hendon and yet not tire thy legs with seeking. Rest thy small jaw, my child; I talk the language of these base kennel-rats like to a very native."

The speaker was a sort of Don Caesar de Bazan in dress, aspect, and bearing. He was tall, trim-built, muscular. His doublet and trunks were of rich material, but faded and threadbare, and their gold-lace adornments were sadly tarnished; his ruff was rumpled and damaged; the plume in his slouched hat was broken and had a bedraggled and disreputable look; at his side he wore a long rapier in a rusty iron sheath; his swaggering carriage marked him at once as a ruffler of the camp. The speech of this fantastic figure was received with an explosion of jeers and laughter. Some cried, " 'Tis another prince in disguise!" " 'Ware thy tongue, friend; belike he is dangerous!" "Marry, he looketh it; mark his eye!" "Pluck the lad from him; to the horsepond wi' the cub!"

Instantly a hand was laid upon the prince, under the impulse of this happy thought; as instantly the stranger's long sword was out and the meddler went to the earth under a sounding thump with the flat of it. The next moment a score of voices shouted, "Kill the dog! Kill him! Kill him!" And the mob closed in on the warrior, who backed himself against a wall and began to lay about him with his long weapon like a madman. His victims sprawled this way and that, but the mobtide poured over their prostrate forms and dashed itself against the champion with undiminished fury. His moments seemed numbered, his destruction certain, when suddenly a trumpet blast sounded, a voice shouted, "Way for the king's messenger!" and a troop of horsemen came charging down upon the mob, who fled out of harm's reach as fast as their legs could carry them. The bold stranger caught up the prince in his arms and was soon far away from danger and the multitude.

Return we within the Guildhall. Suddenly, high above the jubilant roar and thunder of the revel, broke the clear peal of a bugle note. There was instant silence, a deep hush; then a single voice rose—that of the messenger from the palace—and began to pipe forth a proclamation, the whole multitude standing, listening.

The closing words, solemnly pronounced, were, "The king is dead!"

The great assemblage bent their heads upon their breasts with one accord, remained so in profound silence a few moments; then all sunk upon their knees in a body, stretched out their hands toward Tom; and a mighty shout burst forth that seemed to shake the building, "Long live the king!"

Poor Tom's dazed eyes wandered abroad over this stupefying spectacle and finally rested dreamily upon the kneeling princesses beside him a moment, then upon the Earl of Hertford. A sudden purpose dawned in his face. He said in a low tone at Lord Hertford's ear, "Answer me truly, on thy faith and honor! Uttered I here a command, the which none but a king might hold privilege and prerogative to utter, would such commandment be obeyed, and none rise up to say me nay?"

"None, my liege, in all these realms. In thy person bides the majesty of England. Thou art the king; thy word is law."

Tom responded in a strong, earnest voice, and with great animation, "Then shall the king's law be law of mercy from this day, and never more be law of blood! Up from thy knees and away! To the Tower and say the king decrees the Duke of Norfolk shall not die!"

The words were caught up and carried eagerly from lip to lip far and wide over the hall, and as Hertford hurried from the presence, another prodigious shout burst forth, "The reign of blood is ended! Long live Edward, King of England!"

12

The Prince and His Deliverer

As soon as Miles Hendon and the little prince were clear of the mob, they struck down through back lanes and alleys toward the river. Their way was unobstructed until they approached London Bridge; then they plowed into the multitude again, Hendon keeping a fast grip upon the prince's—no, the king's— wrist. The tremendous news was already abroad, and the boy learned it from a thousand voices at once— "The king is dead!" The tidings struck a chill to the heart of the poor little waif and sent a shudder through his frame. He realized the greatness of his loss and was filled with a bitter grief, for the grim tyrant who had been such a terror to others had always been gentle with him. The tears sprung to his eyes and blurred all objects. For an instant he felt himself the most forlorn, outcast, and forsaken of God's creatures; then another cry shook the night with its far-reaching thunder, "Long live King Edward the Sixth!" And this made his eyes kindle and thrilled him with pride to his finger's ends.

"Ah," he thought, "how grand and strange it seems—I AM KING!"

Our friends threaded their way slowly through the throngs upon the bridge. This structure, which had stood for six hundred years and had been a noisy and populous thoroughfare all that time, was a curious affair, for a closely packed rank of stores and shops, with family quarters overhead, stretched along both sides of it, from one bank of the river to the other. The bridge was a sort of town to itself; it had its inn, its beer houses, its bakeries, its haberdasheries, its food markets, its manufacturing industries, and even its church. It looked upon the two neighbors which it linked together—London and Southwark—as being well enough as suburbs, but not otherwise particularly important. It was a close corporation, so to speak; it was a narrow town, of a single street a fifth of a mile long; its population was but a village population, and everybody in it knew all his fellow townsmen intimately and had known their fathers and mothers before them—and all their little family affairs into the bargain. It had its aristocracy, of course—its fine old families of butchers, and bakers, and what-not, who had occupied the same old premises for five or six hundred years and knew the great history of the bridge from beginning to end, and all its strange legends, and who always talked bridgy talk, and thought bridgy thoughts, and lied in a long, level, direct, substantial bridgy way. It was just the sort of population to be narrow and ignorant and self-conceited. Children were born on the bridge, were reared there, grew to old age and finally died without ever having set a foot upon any part of the world but London Bridge alone. Such people would naturally imagine that the mighty and interminable procession which moved through its street night and day, with its confused roar of shouts and cries, its neighings and bellowings and bleatings and its muffled thunder-tramp, was the one great thing in this world, and themselves somehow the proprietors of it. And so they were, in effect; at least they could exhibit it from their windows, and did—for a consideration— whenever a returning king or hero gave it a fleeting splendor, for there was no place like it for affording a long, straight, uninterrupted view of marching columns.

Men born and reared upon the bridge found life unendurably dull and inane elsewhere. History tells of one of these who left the bridge at the age of seventy-one and retired to the country. But he could only fret and toss in his bed; he could not go to sleep, the deep stillness was so painful, so awful, so oppressive. When he was worn out with it at last, he fled back to his old home, a lean and haggard specter, and fell peacefully to rest and pleasant dreams under the lulling music of the lashing waters and the boom and crash and thunder of London Bridge.

In the times of which we are writing, the bridge furnished "object lessons" in English history for its children, namely, the livid and decaying heads of renowned men impaled upon iron spikes atop of its gateways. But we digress.

Hendon's lodgings were in the little inn on the bridge. As he neared the door with his small friend, a rough voice said, "So, thou'rt come at last! Thou'lt not escape again, I warrant thee; and if pounding thy bones to a pudding can teach thee somewhat, thou'lt not keep us waiting another time, mayhap." And John Canty put out his hand to seize the boy.

Miles Hendon stepped in the way and said, "Not too fast, friend. Thou art needlessly rough, methinks. What is the lad to thee?"

"If it be any business of thine to make and meddle in others' affairs, he is my son."

" 'Tis a lie!" cried the little king hotly.

"Boldly said, and I believe thee, whether thy small headpiece be sound or cracked, my boy. But whether this scurvy ruffian be thy father or no, 'tis all one; he shall not have thee to beat thee and abuse, according to his threat, so thou prefer to bide with me."

"I do, I do—I know him not, I loathe him, and will die before I will go with him."

"Then 'tis settled, and there is nought more to say."

"We will see as to that!" exclaimed John Canty, striding past Hendon to get at the boy. "By force shall he—"

"If thou do but touch him, thou animated offal, I will spit thee like a goose!" said Hendon, barring the way and laying his hand upon his sword hilt. Canty drew back. "Now mark ye," continued Hendon, "I took this lad under my protection when a mob of such as thou would have mishandled him, mayhap killed him; dost imagine I will desert him now to a worser fate? For whether thou art his father or no—and sooth to say, I think it is a lie—a decent swift death were better for such a lad than life in such brute hands as thine. So go thy ways, and set quick about it, for I like not much bandying of words, being not overpatient in my nature."

John Canty moved off, muttering threats and curses, and was swallowed from sight in the crowd. Hendon ascended three flights of stairs to his room, with his charge, after ordering a meal to be sent thither. It was a poor apartment, with a shabby bed and some odds and ends of old furniture in it, and was vaguely lighted by a couple of sickly candles. The little king dragged himself to the bed and lay down upon it, almost exhausted with hunger and fatigue. He had been on his feet a good part of a day and a night, for it was now two or three o'clock in the morning, and had eaten nothing meantime. He murmured drowsily, "Prithee call me when the table is spread," and sunk into a deep sleep immediately.

A smile twinkled in Hendon's eye, and he said to himself, "By the mass, the little beggar takes to one's quarters and usurps one's bed with as natural and easy a grace as if he owned them—with never a by-your-leave or so-please-it-you, or anything of the sort. In his diseased ravings he called himself the Prince of Wales, and bravely doth he keep up the character. Poor little friendless rat, doubtless his mind has been disordered with ill usage. Well, I will be his friend; I have saved him, and it draweth me strongly to him; already I love the bold-tongued little rascal. How soldierlike he faced the smutty rabble and flung back his high defiance! And what a comely, sweet, and gentle face he hath, now that sleep hath conjured away its troubles and its griefs. I will teach him, I will cure his malady; yea, I will be his elder brother, and care for him and watch over him; and whoso would shame him or do him hurt may order his shroud, for though I be burnt for it he shall need it!"

He bent over the boy and contemplated him with kind and pitying interest, tapping the young cheek tenderly and smoothing back the tangled curls with his great brown hand. A slight shiver passed over the boy's form. Hendon muttered, "See, now, how like a man it was to let him lie here uncovered and fill his body with deadly rheums. Now what shall I do? 'Twill wake him to take him up and put him within the bed, and he sorely needeth sleep."

*The little king dragged himself to the bed
and lay down upon it*

He looked about for extra covering, but finding none, doffed his doublet and wrapped the lad in it, saying, "I am used to nipping air and scant apparel; 'tis little I shall mind the cold"; then walked up and down the room to keep his blood in motion, soliloquizing as before. "His injured mind persuades him he is Prince of Wales; 'twill be odd to have a Prince of Wales still with us, now that he that *was* the prince is prince no more, but king—for this poor mind is set upon the one fantasy and will not reason out that now it should cast by the prince and call itself the king. If my father liveth still, after these seven years that I have heard nought from home in my foreign dungeon, he will welcome the poor lad and give him generous shelter for my sake; so will my good elder brother, Arthur; my other brother, Hugh—but I will crack his crown, an' *he* interfere, the fox-hearted, ill-conditioned animal! Yes, thither will we fare—and straightway too."

A servant entered with a smoking meal, disposed it upon a small deal table, placed the chairs, and took his departure, leaving such cheap lodgers as these to wait upon themselves. The door slammed after him, and the noise woke the boy, who sprung to a sitting posture and shot a glad glance about him; then a grieved look came into his face and he murmured to himself with a deep sigh, "Alack, it was but a dream, woe is me." Next he noticed Miles Hendon's doublet—glanced from that to Hendon, comprehended the sacrifice that had been made for him, and said gently, "Thou art good to me; yes, thou art very good to me. Take it and put it on; I shall not need it more."

Then he got up and walked to the washstand in the corner, and stood there, waiting. Hendon said in a cheery voice, "We'll have a right hearty sup and bite now, for everything is savory and smoking hot, and that and thy nap together will make thee a little man again, never fear!"

The boy made no answer, but bent a steady look that was filled with grave surprise and also somewhat touched with impatience upon the tall knight of the sword. Hendon was puzzled and said, "What's amiss?"

"Good sir, I would wash me."

"Oh, is that all! Ask no permission of Miles Hendon for aught thou cravest. Make thyself perfectly free here, and welcome, with all that are his belongings."

Still the boy stood, and moved not; more, he tapped the floor once or twice with his small impatient foot. Hendon was wholly perplexed. Said he, "Bless us, what is it?"

"Prithee pour the water, and make not so many words!"

Hendon, suppressing a horselaugh and saying to himself, "By all the saints, but this is admirable!" stepped briskly forward and did the small insolent's bidding; then stood by in a sort of stupefaction until the command, "Come, the towel!" woke him sharply up. He took up a towel from under the boy's nose and handed it to him without comment. He now proceeded to comfort his own face with a wash, and while he was at it his adopted child seated himself at the table and prepared to fall to. Hendon dispatched his ablutions with alacrity, then drew back the other chair and was about to place himself at table when the boy said indignantly, "Forbear! Wouldst sit in the presence of the king?"

This blow staggered Hendon to his foundations. He muttered to himself, "Lo, the poor thing's madness is up with the time! It hath changed with the great change that is come to the realm, and now in fancy is he *king!* Good lack, I must humor the conceit too—there is no other way—faith, he would order me to the Tower, else!"

And pleased with this jest, he removed the chair from the table, took his stand behind the king, and proceeded to wait upon him in the courtliest way he was capable of.

While the king ate, the rigor of his royal dignity relaxed a little, and with his growing contentment came a desire to talk. He said, "I think thou callest thyself Miles Hendon, if I heard thee aright?"

"Yes, sire," Miles replied; then observed to himself, "If I *must* humor the poor lad's madness, I must sire him, I must majesty him, I must not go by halves, I must stick at nothing that belongeth to the part I play, else shall I play it ill and work evil to this charitable and kindly cause."

The king warmed his heart with a second glass of wine and said, "I would know thee—tell me thy story. Thou has a gallant way with thee, and a noble—art nobly born?"

"We are of the tail of the nobility, good your Majesty. My father is a baronet—one of the smaller lords, by knight service—Sir Richard Hendon, of Hendon Hall, by Monk's Holm, in Kent."

"The name has escaped my memory. Go on—tell me thy story."

" 'Tis not much, your Majesty, yet perchance it may beguile a short half hour for want of a better. My father, Sir Richard, is very rich and of a most generous nature. My mother died whilst I was yet a boy. I have two brothers: Arthur, my elder, with a soul like to his father's; and Hugh, younger than I, a mean spirit, covetous, treacherous, vicious, underhanded—a reptile. Such was he from the cradle; such was he ten years past, when I last saw him—a ripe rascal at nineteen, I being twenty then and Arthur twenty-two.   There is none other of us but the lady Edith, my cousin—she was sixteen then—beautiful, gentle, good, the daughter of an earl, the last of her race, heiress of a great fortune and a lapsed title.   My father was her guardian.   I loved her and she loved me, but she was betrothed to Arthur from the cradle, and Sir Richard would not suffer the contract to be broken.   Arthur loved another maid and bade us be of good cheer and hold fast to the hope that delay and luck together would some day give success to our several causes.   Hugh loved the lady Edith's fortune, though in truth he said it was herself he loved; but then 'twas his way, alway, to say the one thing and mean the other. But he lost his arts upon the girl; he could deceive my father, but none else.   My father loved him best of us all and trusted and believed him, for he was the youngest child and others hated him—these qualities being in all ages sufficient to win a parent's dearest love; and he had a smooth persuasive tongue, with an admirable gift of lying—and these be qualities which do mightily assist a blind affection to cozen itself.   I was wild—in troth I might go yet farther and say *very* wild, though 'twas a wildness of an innocent sort, since it hurt none but me, brought shame to none, nor loss, nor had in it any taint of crime or baseness or what might not beseem mine honorable degree.

"Yet did my brother Hugh turn these faults to good account, he seeing that our brother Arthur's health was but indifferent, and hoping the worst might work him profit were I swept out of the path— But 'twere a long tale, good my liege, and little worth the telling.   Briefly, then, this brother did deftly magnify my faults and make them crimes, ending his base work with finding a silken ladder in mine apartments—conveyed thither by his own means—and did convince my father by this and suborned evidence of servants and other lying knaves that I was minded to carry off my Edith and marry her in rank defiance of his will.

"Three years of banishment from home and England might make a soldier and a man of me, my father said, and teach me some degree of wisdom. I fought out my long probation in the continental wars, tasting sumptuously of hard knocks, privation, and adventure; but in my last battle I was taken captive, and during the seven years that have waxed and waned since then, a foreign dungeon hath harbored me. Through wit and courage I won to the free air at last and fled hither straight, and am but just arrived, right poor in purse and raiment, and poorer still in knowledge of what these dull seven years have wrought at Hendon Hall, its people and belongings. So please you, sir, my meager tale is told."

"Thou hast been shamefully abused!" said the little king with a flashing eye. "But I will right thee—by the cross will I! The king hath said it."

Then, fired by the story of Miles's wrongs, he loosed his tongue and poured the history of his own recent misfortunes into the ears of his astonished listener.

When he had finished, Miles said to himself, "Lo, what an imagination he hath! Verily this is no common mind, else, crazed or sane, it could not weave so straight and gaudy a tale as this out of the airy nothings wherewith it hath wrought this curious romaunt. Poor ruined little head, it shall not lack friend or shelter whilst I bide with the living. He shall never leave my side; he shall be my pet, my little comrade. And he shall be cured! Aye, made whole and sound; then will he make himself a name; and proud shall I be to say, 'Yes, he is mine—I took him, a homeless little ragamuffin, but I saw what was in him, and I said his name would be heard some day—behold him, observe him—was I right?' "

The king spoke in a thoughtful, measured voice, "Thou didst save me injury and shame, perchance my life, and so my crown. Such service demandeth rich reward. Name thy desire, and so it be within the compass of my royal power, it is thine."

This fantastic suggestion startled Hendon out of his reverie. He was about to thank the king and put the matter aside with saying he had only done his duty and desired no reward, but a wiser thought came into his head, and he asked leave to be silent a few moments and consider the gracious offer—an idea which the king gravely approved, remarking that it was best to be not too hasty with a thing of such great import.

Miles reflected during some moments, then said to himself, "Yes, that is the thing to do; by any other means it were impossible to get at it, and certes, this hour's experience has taught me 'twould be most wearing and inconvenient to continue as it is. Yes, I will propose it; 'twas a happy accident that I did not throw the chance away." Then he dropped upon one knee and said, "My poor service went not beyond the limit of a subject's simple duty and therefore hath no merit, but since your Majesty is pleased to hold it worthy some reward, I take heart of grace to make petition to this effect. Near four hundred years ago, as your Grace knoweth, there being ill blood betwixt John, king of England, and the king of France, it was decreed that two champions should fight together in the lists and so settle the dispute by what is called the arbitrament of God. These two kings, and the Spanish king, being assembled to witness and judge the conflict, the French champion appeared; but so redoubtable was he that our English knights refused to measure weapons with him. So the matter, which was a weighty one, was like to go against the English monarch by default. Now in the Tower lay the lord De Courcy, the mightiest arm in England, stripped of his honors and possessions, and wasting with long captivity. Appeal was made to him; he gave assent and came forth arrayed for battle; but no sooner did the Frenchman glimpse his huge frame and hear his famous name but he fled away, and the French king's cause was lost. King John restored De Courcy's titles and possessions and said, 'Name thy wish and thou shalt have it, though it cost me half my kingdom'; whereat De Courcy, kneeling, as I do now, made answer, 'This, then, I ask, my liege; that I and my successors may have and hold the privilege of remaining covered in the presence of the kings of England, henceforth while the throne shall last.' The boon was granted, as your Majesty knoweth; and there hath been no time these four hundred years that that line has failed of an heir; and so, even unto this day, the head of that ancient house still weareth his hat or helm before the king's majesty, without let or hindrance, and this none other may do. Invoking this precedent in aid of my prayer, I beseech the king to grant to me but this one grace and privilege—to my more than sufficient reward—and none other, to wit: that I and my heirs forever may *sit* in the presence of the Majesty of England!"

"Rise, Sir Miles Hendon, knight," said the king gravely, giving the accolade with Hendon's sword; "rise, and seat thyself. Thy petition is granted. Whilst England remains, and the crown continues, the privilege shall not lapse."

His Majesty walked apart, musing, and Hendon dropped into a chair at table, observing to himself, " 'Twas a brave thought and hath wrought me a mighty deliverance; my legs are grievously wearied. An' I had not thought of that, I must have had to stand for weeks, till my poor lad's wits are cured."   After a little, he went on, "And so I am become a knight of the Kingdom of Dreams and Shadows! A most odd and strange position truly for one so matter-of-fact as I.   I will not laugh—no, God forbid, for this thing which is so substanceless to me is *real* to him.   And to me also, in one way, it is not a falsity, for it reflects with truth the sweet and generous spirit that is in him."   After a pause: "Ah, what if he should call me by my fine title before folk! There'd be a merry contrast betwixt my glory and my raiment! But no matter; let him call me what he will, so it please him, I shall be content."

13

The Disappearance of the Prince

A heavy drowsiness presently fell upon the two comrades. The king said, "Remove these rags," meaning his clothing.

Hendon disappareled the boy without dissent or remark, tucked him up in bed, then glanced about the room, saying to himself ruefully, "He hath taken my bed again, as before; marry, what shall *I* do?"

The little king observed his perplexity and dissipated it with a word. He said sleepily, "Thou wilt sleep athwart the door and guard it." In a moment more he was out of his troubles, in a deep slumber.

"Dear heart, he should have been born a king!" muttered Hendon admiringly. "He playeth the part to a marvel."

Then he stretched himself across the door, on the floor, saying contentedly, "I have lodged worse for seven years; 'twould be but ill gratitude to Him above to find fault with this."

He dropped asleep as the dawn appeared. Toward noon he rose, uncovered his unconscious ward—a section at a time—and took his measure with a string. The king awoke just as he had completed his work, complained of the cold, and asked what he was doing.

" 'Tis done now, my liege," said Hendon; "I have a bit of business outside, but will presently return; sleep thou again—thou needest it. There—let me cover thy head also—thou'lt be warm the sooner."

The king was back in dreamland before this speech was ended. Miles slipped softly out and slipped as softly in again in the course of thirty or forty minutes, with a complete secondhand suit of boy's clothing, of cheap material and showing signs of wear, but tidy and suited to the season of the year. He seated himself and began to overhaul his purchase, mumbling to himself, "A longer purse would have got a better sort, but when one has not the long purse one must be content with what a short one may do:

> " 'There was a woman in our town
> In our town did dwell—'

"He stirred, methinks. I must sing in a less thunderous key; 'tis not good to mar his sleep, with this journey before him and he so wearied out, poor chap. This garment—'tis well enough—a stitch here and another there will set it aright. This other is better, albeit a stitch or two will not come amiss in it likewise. *These* be very good and sound, and will keep his small feet warm and dry—and odd new thing to him, belike, since he has doubtless been used to foot it bare, winters and summers the same. Would thread were bread, seeing one getteth a year's sufficiently for a farthing, and such a brave big needle without cost, for mere love. Now shall I have the demon's own time to thread it!"

And so he had. He did as men have always done, and probably always will do, to the end of time—held the needle still and tried to thrust the thread through the eye, which is the opposite of a woman's way. Time and time again the thread missed the mark, going sometimes on one side of the needle, sometimes on the other, sometimes doubling up against the shaft; but he was patient, having been through these experiences before when he was soldiering. He succeeded at last and took up the garment that had lain waiting meantime across his lap and began his work.

"The inn is paid—the breakfast that is to come, included—and there is wherewithal left to buy a couple of donkeys and meet our little costs for the two or three days betwixt this and the plenty that awaits us at Hendon Hall:

" *'She loved her hus—'*

"Body o' me! I have driven the needle under my nail! It matters little—'tis not a novelty—yet 'tis not a convenience neither. We shall be merry there, little one, never doubt it! Thy troubles will vanish, there, and likewise thy sad distemper:

" *'She loved her husband dearilee,*
But another man—'

"These be noble large stitches!"—holding the garment up and viewing it admiringly. "They have a grandeur and a majesty that do cause these small stingy ones of the tailorman to look mightily paltry and plebeian:

" *'She loved her husband dearilee,*
But another man he loved she—'

"Marry, 'tis done—a goodly piece of work, too, and wrought with expedition. Now will I wake him, apparel him, pour for him, feed him, and then will we hie us to the mart by the Tabard Inn in Southwark and—be pleased to rise, my liege!—he answereth not—what ho, my liege!—of a truth must I profane his sacred person with a touch, sith his slumber is deaf to speech. What!"

He threw back the covers; the boy was gone!

He stared about him in speechless astonishment for a moment, noticed for the first time that his ward's ragged raiment was also missing; then he began to rage and storm and shout for the innkeeper. At that moment a servant entered with the breakfast.

"Explain, thou limb of Satan, or thy time is come!" roared the man of war, and made so savage a spring toward the waiter that this latter could not find his tongue for the instant, for fright and surprise. "Where is the boy?"

In disjointed and trembling syllables the man gave the information desired.

"You were hardly gone from the place, your worship, when a youth came running and said it was your worship's will that the boy come to you straight, at the bridge end on the Southwark side. I brought him hither, and when he woke the lad and gave his message, the lad did grumble some little for being disturbed 'so early,' as he called it, but straightway trussed on his rags and went with the youth, only saying it had been better manners that your worship came yourself, not sent a stranger; and so—"

"And so thou'rt a fool: a fool, and easily cozened; hang all thy breed! Yet mayhap no hurt is done. Possibly no harm is meant the boy. I will go fetch him. Make the table ready. Stay! The coverings of the bed were disposed as if one lay beneath them; happened that by accident?"

"I know not, good your worship. I saw the youth meddle with them—he that came for the boy."

"Thousand deaths! 'Twas done to deceive me—'tis plain 'twas done to gain time. Hark ye! Was that youth alone?"

"All alone, your worship."

"Art sure?"

"Sure, your worship."

"Collect thy scattered wits—bethink thee—take time, man."

After a moment's thought the servant said, "When he came, none came with him; but now I remember me that as the two stepped into the throng of the bridge, a ruffian-looking man plunged out from some near place; and just as he was joining them—"

"What *then?* Out with it!" thundered the impatient Hendon, interrupting.

"Just then the crowd lapped them up and closed them in, and I saw no more, being called by my master, who was in a rage because a joint that the scrivener had ordered was forgot, though I take all the saints to witness that to blame *me* for that miscarriage were like holding the unborn babe to judgment for sins com—"

"Out of my sight, idiot! Thy prating drives me mad! Hold! Whither art flying? Canst not bide still an instant? Went they toward Southwark?"

"Even so, your worship; for, as I said before, as to the detestable joint, the babe unborn is no whit more blameless than—"

"Art here *yet!* And prating still? Vanish, lest I throttle thee!" The servitor vanished. Hendon followed after him, passed him, and plunged down the stairs two steps at a stride, muttering, " 'Tis that scurvy villain that claimed he was his son. I have lost thee, my poor little mad master—it is a bitter thought—and I had come to love thee so! No! By book and bell, *not* lost! Not lost, for I will ransack the land till I find thee again. Poor child, yonder is his breakfast and mine, but I have no hunger now; so let the rats have it. Speed, speed! That is the word!" As he wormed his swift way through the noisy multitudes upon the bridge, he several times said to himself, clinging to the thought, as if it were a particularly pleasing one, "He grumbled, but he *went*—he went, yes, because he thought Miles Hendon asked it, sweet lad—he would ne'er have done it for another, I know it well."

14

"Le Roi Est Mort—
Vive le Roi"

Toward daylight of the same morning, Tom Canty stirred out of a heavy sleep and opened his eyes in the dark. He lay silent a few moments, trying to analyze his confused thoughts and impressions and get some sort of meaning out of them; then suddenly he burst out in a rapturous but guarded voice, "I see it all, I see it all! Now God be thanked, I am indeed awake at last! Come, joy! Vanish, sorrow! Ho, Nan! Bet! Kick off your straw and hie ye hither to my side, till I do pour into your unbelieving ears the wildest madcap dream that ever the spirits of night did conjure up to astonish the soul of man withal! Ho, Nan, I say! Bet!"

A dim form appeared at his side, and a voice said, "Wilt deign to deliver thy commands?"

"Commands? Oh, woe is me, I know thy voice! Speak, thou—who am I?"

"Thou? In sooth, yesternight wert thou the Prince of Wales; today art thou my most gracious liege, Edward, King of England."

Tom buried his head among his pillows, murmuring plaintively, "Alack, it was no dream! Go to thy rest, sweet sir; leave me to my sorrows."

Tom slept again, and after a time he had this pleasant dream. He thought it was summer and he was playing all alone in the fair meadow called Goodman's Fields, when a dwarf only a foot high, with long red whiskers and a humped back, appeared to him suddenly and said, "Dig, by that stump." He did so and found twelve bright new pennies—wonderful riches! Yet this was not the best of it, for the dwarf said, "I know thee. Thou are a good lad and a deserving; thy distresses shall end, for the day of thy reward is come. Dig here every seventh day, and thou shalt find always the same treasure, twelve bright new pennies. Tell none—keep the secret." Then the dwarf vanished, and Tom flew to Offal Court with his prize, saying to himself, "Every night will I give my father a penny; he will think I begged it, it will glad his heart, and I shall no more be beaten. One penny every week the good priest that teacheth me shall have; Mother, Nan, and Bet the other four. We be done with hunger and rags now, done with fears and frets and savage usage."

In his dream he reached his sordid home all out of breath, but with eyes dancing with grateful enthusiasm, cast four of his pennies into his mother's lap, and cried out, "They are for thee! All of them, every one! For thee and Nan and Bet—and honestly come by, not begged nor stolen!"

The happy and astonished mother strained him to her breast and exclaimed, "It waxeth late; may it please your Majesty to rise?"

Ah, that was not the answer he was expecting. The dream had snapped asunder—he was awake.

He opened his eyes; the richly clad First Lord of the

Bedchamber was kneeling by his couch. The gladness of the lying dream faded away; the poor boy recognized that he was still a captive and a king. The room was filled with courtiers clothed in purple mantles—the mourning color—and with noble servants of the monarch. Tom sat up in bed and gazed out from the heavy silken curtains upon this fine company.

The weighty business of dressing began, and one courtier after another knelt and paid his court and offered to the little king his condolences upon his heavy loss whilst the dressing proceeded. In the beginning, a shirt was taken up by the Chief Equerry-in-Waiting, who passed it to the First Lord of the Buckhounds, who passed it to the Second Gentleman of the Bedchamber, who passed it to the Head Ranger of Windsor Forest, who passed it to the Third Groom of the Stole, who passed it to the Chancellor Royal of the Duchy of Lancaster, who passed it to the Master of the Wardrobe, who passed it to Norroy King-at-Arms, who passed it to the Constable of the Tower, who passed it to the Chief Steward of the Household, who passed it to the Hereditary Grand Diaperer, who passed it to the Lord High Admiral of England, who passed it to the Archbishop of Canterbury, who passed it to the First Lord of the Bedchamber, who took what was left of it and put it on Tom. Poor little wondering chap, it reminded him of passing buckets at a fire.

Each garment in its turn had to go through this slow and solemn process; consequently Tom grew very weary of the ceremony, so weary that he felt an almost gushing gratefulness when he at last saw his long silken hose begin the journey down the line and knew that the end of the matter was drawing near. But he exulted too soon. The First Lord of the Bedchamber received the hose and was about to encase Tom's legs in them when a sudden flush invaded his face and he hurriedly hustled the things back into the hands of the Archbishop of Canterbury with an astounded look and a whispered, "See, my lord!"—pointing to a something connected with the hose. The Archbishop paled, then flushed, and passed the hose to the Lord High Admiral, whispering, "See, my lord!" The admiral passed the hose to the Hereditary Grand Diaperer and had hardly breath enough in his body to ejaculate, "See, my lord!" The hose drifted backward along the line, to the Chief Steward of the Household, the Constable of the Tower, Norroy King-at-Arms, the Master of the Wardrobe, the Chancellor Royal of the Duchy of Lancaster, the Third Groom of the Stole, the Head Ranger of Windsor Forest, the Second Gentleman of the Bedchamber, the First Lord of the Buckhounds, accompanied always with that amazed and frightened "See! see!"—till they finally reached the hands of the Chief Equerry-in-Waiting, who gazed a moment, then hoarsely whispered, "Body of my life, a tag gone from a trusspoint! To the Tower with the Head Keeper of the King's Hose!"—after which he leaned upon the shoulder of the First Lord of the Buckhounds to regather his vanished strength whilst fresh hose, without any damaged strings to them, were brought.

But all things must have an end, and so in time Tom Canty was in a condition to get out of the bed. The proper official poured water, the proper official engineered the washing, the proper official stood by with a towel, and by and by Tom got safely through the purifying stage and was ready for the services of the Hairdresser Royal. When he at length emerged from this master's hands, he was a gracious figure and as pretty as a girl in his mantle and trunks of purple satin and purple-plumed cap. He now moved in state toward his breakfast room through the midst of the courtly assemblage; and as he passed, these fell back, leaving his way free, and dropped upon their knees.

After breakfast he was conducted, with regal ceremony, attended by his great officers and his guard of fifty Gentlemen Pensioners bearing gilt battle axes, to the throne room, where he proceeded to transact business of state. His "uncle," Lord Hertford, took his stand by the throne to assist the royal mind with wise counsel.

The body of illustrious men named by the late king as his executors appeared to ask Tom's approval of certain acts of theirs—rather a form, and yet not wholly a form, since there was no Protector as yet. The Archbishop of Canterbury made report of the decree of the Council of Executors concerning the obsequies of his late most illustrious Majesty and finished by reading the signatures of the executors, to wit: the Archbishop of Canterbury, the Lord Chancellor of England, William Lord St. John, John Lord Russell, Edward Earl of Hertford, John Viscount Lisle, Cuthbert Bishop of Durham—

Tom was not listening; an earlier clause of the document was puzzling him. At this point he turned and whispered to Lord Hertford, "What day did he say the burial hath been appointed for?"

"The sixteenth of the coming month, my liege."

" 'Tis a strange folly. Will he keep?"

Poor chap, he was still new to the customs of royalty; he was used to seeing the forlorn dead of Offal Court hustled out of the way with a very different sort of expedition. However, the lord Hertford set his mind at rest with a word or two.

A secretary of state presented an order of the council appointing the morrow at eleven for the reception of the foreign ambassadors, and desired the king's assent.

Tom turned an inquiring look toward Hertford, who

whispered, "Your Majesty will signify consent. They come to testify their royal masters' sense of the heavy calamity which hath visited your Grace and the realm of England."

Tom did as he was bidden. Another secretary began to read a preamble concerning the expenses of the late king's household, which had amounted to £28,000 during the preceding six months—a sum so vast that it made Tom Canty gasp; he gasped again when the fact appeared that £20,000 of this money were still owing and unpaid, and once more when it appeared that the king's coffers were about empty and his twelve hundred servants much embarrassed for lack of the wages due them. Tom spoke out with lively apprehension, "We be going to the dogs, 'tis plain. 'Tis meet and necessary that we take a smaller house and set the servants at large, sith they be of no value but to make delay, and trouble one with offices that harass the spirit and shame the soul, they misbecoming any but a doll, that hath nor brains nor hands to help itself withal. I remember me of a small house that standeth over against the fish market, by Billingsgate——"

A sharp pressure upon Tom's arm stopped his foolish tongue and sent a blush to his face; but no countenance there betrayed any sign that this strange speech had been remarked or given concern.

A secretary made report that forasmuch as the late king had provided in his will for conferring the ducal degree upon the Earl of Hertford and raising his brother, Sir Thomas Seymour, to the peerage, and likewise Hertford's son to an earldom, together with similar aggrandizements to other great servants of the Crown, the council had resolved to hold a sitting on the sixteenth of February for the delivering and confirming of these honors; and that meantime, the late king not

having granted in writing estates suitable to the support
of these dignities, the council, knowing his private
wishes in that regard, had thought proper to grant to
Seymour "£500 lands," and to Hertford's son "800
pound lands and 300 pound of the next bishop's lands
which should fall vacant," his present Majesty being
willing.

Tom was about to blurt out something about the
propriety of paying the late king's debts first before
squandering all this money, but a timely touch upon his
arm from the thoughtful Hertford saved him this indis-
cretion, wherefore he gave the royal assent, without
spoken comment but with much inward discomfort.
While he sat reflecting a moment over the ease with
which he was doing strange and glittering miracles, a
happy thought shot into his mind: why not make his
mother Duchess of Offal Court and give her an estate?
But a sorrowful thought swept it instantly away: he was
only a king in name, these grave veterans and great
nobles were his masters; to them his mother was only the
creature of a diseased mind; they would simply listen to
his project with unbelieving ears, then send for the
doctor.

The dull work went tediously on. Petitions were
read, and proclamations, patents, and all manner of
wordy, repetitious, and wearisome papers relating to the
public business; and at last Tom sighed pathetically and
murmured to himself, "In what have I offended, that the
good God should take me away from the fields and the
free air and the sunshine to shut me up here and make
me a king and afflict me so?" Then his poor muddled
head nodded awhile and presently drooped to his shoulder, and the business of the empire came to a standstill
for want of that august factor the ratifying power.
Silence ensued around the slumbering child, and the

sages of the realm ceased from their deliberations.

During the forenoon Tom had an enjoyable hour, by permission of his keepers, Hertford and St. John, with the lady Elizabeth and the little lady Jane Grey, though the spirits of the princesses were rather subdued by the mighty stroke that had fallen upon the royal house; and at the end of the visit his "elder sister"—afterwards the "Bloody Mary" of history—chilled him with a solemn interview which had but one merit in his eyes, its brevity. He had a few moments to himself, and then a slim lad of about twelve years of age was admitted to his presence, whose clothing, except his snowy ruff and the laces about his wrists, was of black—doublet, hose and all. He bore no badge of mourning but a knot of purple ribbon on his shoulder. He advanced hesitatingly with head bowed and bare and dropped upon one knee in front of Tom. Tom sat still and contemplated him soberly a moment. Then he said, "Rise, lad. Who art thou? What wouldst have?"

The boy rose and stood at graceful ease, but with an aspect of concern in his face. He said "Of a surety thou must remember me, my lord. I am thy whipping boy."

"My *whipping* boy?"

"The same, your Grace. I am Humphrey—Humphrey Marlow."

Tom perceived that here was someone whom his keepers ought to have posted him about. The situation was delicate. What should he do? Pretend he knew this lad, and then betray by his every utterance that he had never heard of him before? No, that would not do. An idea came to his relief: accidents like this might be likely to happen with some frequency now that business urgencies would often call Hertford and St. John from his side, they being members of the council of executors;

therefore perhaps it would be well to strike out a plan himself to meet the requirements of such emergencies. Yes, that would be a wise course; he would practice on this boy, and see what sort of success he might achieve. So he stroked his brow perplexedly a moment or two and presently said, "Now I seem to remember thee somewhat, but my wit is clogged and dim with suffering—"

"Alack, my poor master!" ejaculated the whipping boy with feeling, adding to himself, "In truth 'tis as they said—his mind is gone; alas, poor soul! But misfortune catch me, how am I forgetting! They said one must not seem to observe that aught is wrong with him."

" 'Tis strange how my memory doth wanton with me these days," said Tom. "But mind it not—I mend apace—a little clue doth often serve to bring me back again the things and names which had escaped me. [And not they only, forsooth, but e'en such as I ne'er heard before—as this lad shall see.] Give thy business speech."

" 'Tis matter of small weight, my liege, yet will I touch upon it an' it please your Grace. Two days gone by, when your Majesty faulted thrice in your Greek in the morning lessons—dost remember it?"

"Y-e-s—methinks I do. [It is not much of a lie—an' I had meddled with the Greek at all, I had not faulted simply thrice, but forty times.] Yes, I do recall it now; go on."

"The master, being wroth with what he termed such slovenly and doltish work, did promise that he would soundly whip me for it, and—"

"Whip *thee!*" said Tom, astonished out of his presence of mind. "Why should he whip thee for faults of mine?"

"Ah, your Grace forgetteth again. He always scourgeth me when thou dost fail in thy lessons."

"True, true—I had forgot. Thou teachest me in private; then if I fail, he argueth that thy office was lamely done, and—"

"Oh, my liege, what words are these? I, the humblest of thy servants, presume to teach *thee?*"

"Then where is thy blame? What riddle is this? Am I in truth gone mad, or is it thou? Explain—speak out."

"But good your Majesty, there's nought that needeth simplifying. None may visit the sacred person of the Prince of Wales with blows, wherefore when he faulteth, 'tis I that take them; and meet it is and right, for that it is mine office and my livelihood."

Tom stared at the tranquil boy, observing to himself, "Lo, it is a wonderful thing—a most strange and curious trade; I marvel they have not hired a boy to take my combings and my dressings for me—would heaven they would!—an' they will do this thing, I will take my lashings in mine own person, giving God thanks for the change." Then he said aloud, "And hast thou been beaten, poor friend, according to the promise?"

"No, good your Majesty, my punishment was appointed for this day, and peradventure it may be annulled as unbefitting the season of mourning that is come upon us; I know not, and so have made bold to come hither and remind your Grace about your gracious promise to intercede in my behalf—"

"With the master? To save thee thy whipping?"

"Ah, thou dost remember!"

"My memory mendeth, thou seest. Set thy mind at ease; thy back shall go unscathed; I will see to it."

"Oh, thanks, my good lord!" cried the boy, dropping upon his knee again. "Mayhap I have ventured far enow; and yet—"

Seeing Master Humphrey hesitate, Tom encouraged

him to go on, saying he was "in the granting mood."

"Then will I speak it out, for it lieth near my heart. Sith thou art no more Prince of Wales, but king, thou canst order matters as thou wilt, with none to say thee nay; wherefore it is not in reason that thou wilt longer vex thyself with dreary studies, but wilt burn thy books and turn thy mind to things less irksome. Then am I ruined, and mine orphan sisters with me!"

"Ruined? Prithee how?"

"My back is my bread, O my gracious liege! If it go idle, I starve. An' thou cease from study, mine office is gone, thou'lt need no whipping boy. Do not turn me away!"

Tom was touched with this pathetic distress. He said, with a right royal burst of generosity, "Discomfort thyself no further, lad. Thine office shall be permanent in thee and thy line forever." Then he struck the boy a light blow on the shoulder with the flat of his sword, exclaiming, "Rise, Humphrey Marlow, Hereditary Grand Whipping Boy to the royal house of England! Banish sorrow; I will betake me to my books again and study so ill that they must in justice treble thy wage, so mightily shall the business of thine office be augmented."

The grateful Humphrey responded fervidly, "Thanks, O most noble master; this princely lavishness doth far surpass my most distempered dreams of fortune. Now shall I be happy all my days, and all the house of Marlow after me."

Tom had wit enough to perceive that here was a lad who could be useful to him. He encouraged Humphrey to talk, and he was nothing loath. He was delighted to believe that he was helping in Tom's "cure," for always, as soon as he had finished calling back to Tom's diseased mind the various particulars of his experiences and

adventures in the royal schoolroom and elsewhere about
the palace, he noticed that Tom was then able to
"recall" the circumstances quite clearly. At the end of
an hour Tom found himself well freighted with very
valuable information concerning personages and matters pertaining to the court, so he resolved to draw
instruction from this source daily, and to this end he
would give order to admit Humphrey to the royal closet
whenever he might come, provided the majesty of
England was not engaged with other people. Humphrey
had hardly been dismissed when my lord Hertford
arrived with more trouble for Tom.

He said that the lords of the council, fearing that some
overwrought report of the king's damaged health might
have leaked out and got abroad, they deemed it wise and
best that his Majesty should begin to dine in public after
a day or two—his wholesome complexion and vigorous
step, assisted by a carefully guarded repose of manner
and ease and grace of demeanor, would more surely
quiet the general pulse, in case any evil rumors *had* gone
about, than any other scheme that could be devised.

Then the earl proceeded very delicately to instruct
Tom as to the observances proper to the stately occasion,
under the rather thin disguise of "reminding" him
concerning things already known to him; but to his vast
gratification it turned out that Tom needed very little
help in this line: he had been making use of Humphrey
in that direction, for Humphrey had mentioned that
within a few days he was to begin to dine in public,
having gathered it from the swift-winged gossip of the
court. Tom kept these facts to himself, however.

Seeing the royal memory so improved, the earl ventured to apply a few tests to it, in an apparently casual
way, to find out how far its amendment had progressed.
The results were happy, here and there, in spots—spots

My lord Hertford arrived with more trouble for Tom

where Humphrey's tracks remained; and on the whole my lord was greatly pleased and encouraged. So encouraged was he, indeed, that he spoke up and said in a quite hopeful voice, "Now am I persuaded that if your Majesty will but tax your memory yet a little further, it will resolve the puzzle of the Great Seal—a loss which was of moment yesterday, although of none today, since its term of service ended with our late lord's life. May it please your Grace to make the trial?"

Tom was at sea—a Great Seal was a something which he was totally unacquainted with. After a moment's hesitation he looked up innocently and asked, "What was it like, my lord?"

The earl started, almost imperceptibly, muttering to himself, "Alack, his wits are flown again! It was ill wisdom to lead him on to strain them." Then he deftly turned the talk to other matters, with the purpose of sweeping the unlucky Seal out of Tom's thoughts—a purpose which easily succeeded.

15

Tom as King

The next day the foreign ambassadors came, with their gorgeous trains; and Tom, throned in awful state, received them. The splendors of the scene delighted his eye and fired his imagination at first, but the audience was long and dreary, and so were most of the addresses; wherefore, what began as a pleasure grew into weariness and homesickness by and by. Tom said the words which Hertford put into his mouth from time to time and tried hard to acquit himself satisfactorily, but he was too new to such things and too ill at ease to accomplish more than a tolerable success. He looked sufficiently like a king, but he was ill able to feel like one. He was cordially glad when the ceremony was ended.

The larger part of his day was "wasted"—as he termed it in his own mind—in labors pertaining to his royal office. Even the two hours devoted to certain princely pastimes and recreations were rather a burden to him than otherwise, they were so fettered by restrictions and ceremonious observances. However, he had a private hour with his whipping boy, which he counted clear gain, since he got both entertainment and needful information out of it.

The third day of Tom Canty's kingship came and went much as the others had done, but there was a lifting of his cloud in one way: he felt less uncomfortable than at first; he was getting a little used to his circumstances and surroundings; his chains still galled, but not all the time; he found that the presence and homage of the great afflicted and embarrassed him less and less sharply with every hour that drifted over his head.

But for one single dread, he could have seen the fourth day approach without serious distress—the dining in public; it was to begin that day. There were greater matters in the program, for on that day he would have to preside at a council which would take his views and commands concerning the policy to be pursued toward various foreign nations scattered far and near over the great globe; on that day too, Hertford would be formally chosen to the grand office of Lord Protector; other things of note were appointed for that fourth day also, but to Tom they were all insignificant compared with the ordeal of dining all by himself with a multitude of curious eyes fastened upon him and a multitude of mouths whispering comments upon his performance— and upon his mistakes, if he should be so unlucky as to make any.

Still, nothing could stop that fourth day, and so it came. It found poor Tom low-spirited and absent-minded, and this mood continued; he could not shake it off. The ordinary duties of the morning dragged upon his hands and wearied him. Once more he felt the sense of captivity heavy upon him.

Late in the forenoon he was in a large audience chamber, conversing with the Earl of Hertford and dully awaiting the striking of the hour appointed for a visit of ceremony from a considerable number of great officials and courtiers.

After a little while Tom, who had wandered to a window and become interested in the life and movement of the great highway beyond the palace gates—and not idly interested, but longing with all his heart to take part in person in its stir and freedom—saw the van of a hooting and shouting mob of disorderly men, women, and children of the lowest and poorest degree approaching from up the road.

"I would I knew what 'tis about!" he exclaimed with all a boy's curiosity in such happenings.

"Thou art the king!" solemnly responded the earl with a reverence. "Have I your Grace's leave to act?"

"Oh, blithely, yes! Oh, gladly, yes!" exclaimed Tom excitedly, adding to himself with a lively sense of satisfaction, "In truth, being a king is not all dreariness; it hath its compensations and conveniences."

The earl called a page and sent him to the captain of the guard with the order, "Let the mob be halted, and inquiry made concerning the occasion of its movement. By the king's command!"

A few seconds later a long rank of the royal guards, cased in flashing steel, filed out at the gates and formed across the highway in front of the multitude. A messenger returned to report that the crowd was following a man, a woman, and a young girl to execution for crimes committed against the dignity of the realm.

Death—and a violent death—for these poor unfortunates! The thought wrung Tom's heartstrings. The spirit of compassion took control of him, to the exclusion of all other considerations: he never thought of the offended laws or of the grief or loss which these three criminals had inflicted upon their victims, he could think of nothing but the scaffold and the grisly fate hanging over the heads of the condemned. His concern made him even forget for the moment that he was but the false shadow of a king, not the substance; and before he knew it he had blurted out the command, "Bring them here!"

Then he blushed scarlet, and a sort of apology sprung to his lips; but observing that his order had wrought no sort of surprise in the earl or the waiting page, he suppressed the words he was about to utter. The page, in the most matter-of-fact way, made a profound obeisance and retired backwards out of the room to deliver the command. Tom experienced a glow of pride and a renewed sense of the compensating advantages of the kingly office. He said to himself, "Truly it is like what I was used to feel when I read the old priest's tales and did imagine mine own self a prince, giving law and command to all, saying, 'Do this, do that,' whilst none durst offer let or hindrance to my will."

Now the doors swung open; one high-sounding title after another was announced, the personages owning them followed, and the place was quickly half filled with noble folk and finery. But Tom was hardly conscious of the presence of these people, so wrought up was he and so intensely absorbed in that other and more interesting matter. He seated himself absently in his chair of state and turned his eyes upon the door with manifestations of impatient expectancy, seeing which, the company forebore to trouble him and fell to chatting a mixture of public business and court gossip one with another.

In a little while the measured tread of military men was heard approaching, and the culprits entered the presence in charge of an undersheriff and escorted by a detail of the king's guard. The civil officer knelt before Tom, then stood aside; the three doomed persons knelt also and remained so; the guard took position behind Tom's chair. Tom scanned the prisoners curiously. Something about the dress or appearance of the man had stirred a vague memory in him. "Methinks I have seen this man ere now, but the when or the where fail me—" Such was Tom's thought. Just then the man glanced

Tom scanned the prisoners curiously

quickly up, and quickly dropped his face again, not being able to endure the awful port of sovereignty; but the one full glimpse of the face which Tom got was sufficient. He said to himself, "Now is the matter clear; this is the stranger that plucked Giles Witt out of the Thames and saved his life that windy, bitter, first day of the new year—a brave good deed; pity he hath been doing baser ones and got himself in this sad case. I have not forgot the day, neither the hour; by reason that an hour after, upon the stroke of eleven, I did get a hiding by the hand of Gammer Canty which was of so goodly and admired severity that all that went before or followed after it were but fondlings and caresses by comparison."

Tom now ordered that the woman and the girl be removed from the presence for a little time, then addressed himself to the undersheriff, saying, "Good sir, what is this man's offense?"

The officer knelt and answered, "So please your Majesty, he hath taken the life of a subject by poison."

Tom's compassion for the prisoner and admiration of him as the daring rescuer of a drowning boy experienced a most damaging shock.

"The thing was proven upon him?" he asked.

"Most clearly, sire."

Tom sighed and said, "Take him away—he hath earned his death. 'Tis a pity, for he was a brave heart—na—na, I mean he hath the *look* of it!"

The prisoner clasped his hands together with sudden energy and wrung them despairingly, at the same time appealing imploringly to the "king" in broken and terrified phrases, "O my lord the king, an' thou canst pity the lost, have pity upon me! I am innocent—neither hath that wherewith I am charged been more than but lamely proved—yet I speak not of that; the judgment is gone forth against me and may not suffer alteration; yet in mine extremity I beg a boon, for my doom is more than I can bear. A grace, a grace, my lord the King! In thy royal compassion grant my prayer; give commandment that I be hanged!"

Tom was amazed. This was not the outcome he had looked for.

"Odds my life, a strange *boon*! Was it not the fate intended thee?"

"O good my liege, not so! It is ordered that I be *boiled alive!*"

The hideous surprise of these words almost made Tom spring from his chair. As soon as he could recover his wits he cried out, "Have thy wish, poor soul! An' thou had poisoned a hundred men thou shouldst not suffer so miserable a death."

The prisoner bowed his face to the ground and burst into passionate expressions of gratitude, ending with, "If ever thou shouldst know misfortune—which God forefend!—may thy goodness to me this day be remembered and requited!"

Tom turned to the Earl of Hertford and said, "My lord, is it believable that there was warrant for this man's ferocious doom?"

"It is the law, your Grace—for poisoners. In Germany coiners be boiled to death in *oil*—not cast in of a sudden, but by a rope let down into the oil by degrees, and slowly; first the feet, then the legs, then—"

"Oh, prithee no more, my lord; I cannot bear it!" cried Tom, covering his eyes with his hands to shut out the picture. "I beseech your good lordship that order be taken to change this law. Oh, let no more poor creatures be visited with its tortures."

The earl's face showed profound gratification, for he was a man of merciful and generous impulses—a thing not very common with his class in that fierce age. He said, "These your Grace's noble words have sealed its doom. History will remember it to the honor of your royal house."

The undersheriff was about to remove his prisoner; Tom gave him a sign to wait; then he said, "Good sir, I would look into this matter further. The man has said his deed was but lamely proved. Tell me what thou knowest."

"If the king's grace please, it did appear upon the trial that this man entered into a house in the hamlet of Islington where one lay sick—three witnesses say it was at ten of the clock in the morning and two say it was some minutes later—the sick man being alone at the time, and sleeping; and presently the man came forth again and went his way. The sick man died within the hour, being torn with spasms and retchings."

"Did any see the poison given? Was poison found?"

"Marry, no, my liege."

"Then how doth one know there was poison given at all?"

"Please your Majesty, the doctors testified that none die with such symptoms but by poison."

Weighty evidence, this—in that simple age. Tom recognized its formidable nature and said, "The doctor knoweth his trade; belike they were right. The matter hath an ill look for this poor man."

"Yet was not this all, your Majesty; there is more and worse. Many testified that a witch, since gone from the village, none know whither, did foretell, and speak it privately in their ears, that the sick man *would die by poison,* and more, that a stranger would give it—a stranger with brown hair and clothed in a worn and common garb; and surely this prisoner doth answer woundily to the bill. Please your Majesty to give the circumstance that solemn weight which is its due, seeing it was *foretold*."

This was an argument of tremendous force in that superstitious day. Tom felt that the thing was settled; if evidence was worth anything, this poor fellow's guilt was proved. Still he offered the prisoner a chance, saying, "If thou canst say aught in thy behalf, speak."

"Nought that will avail, my king. I am innocent, yet cannot I make it appear. I have no friends, else might I show that I was not in Islington that day; so also might I show that at that hour they name I was above a league away, seeing I was at Wapping Old Stairs; yea more, my king, for I could show that whilst they say I was *taking* life, I was *saving* it. A drowning boy—"

"Peace! Sheriff, name the day the deed was done!"

"At ten in the morning, or some minutes later, the first day of the new year, most illustrious—"

"Let the prisoner go free; it is the king's will!"

Another blush followed this unregal outburst, and he covered his indecorum as well as he could by adding, "It enrageth me that a man should be hanged upon such idle, harebrained evidence!"

A low buzz of admiration swept through the assemblage. It was not admiration of the decree that had been delivered by Tom, for the propriety or expediency of pardoning a convicted poisoner was a thing which few there would have felt justified in either admitting or admiring—no, the admiration was for the intelligence and spirit which Tom had displayed. Some of the low-voiced remarks were to this effect: "This is no mad king; he hath his wits sound." "How sanely he put his questions; how like his former natural self was this abrupt, imperious disposal of the matter!" "God be thanked his infirmity is spent! This is no weakling, but a king. He hath borne himself like to his own father."

The air being filled with applause, Tom's ear necessarily caught a little of it. The effect which this had upon him was to put him greatly at his ease and also to charge his system with very gratifying sensations.

However, his juvenile curiosity soon rose superior to these pleasant thoughts and feelings; he was eager to know what sort of deadly mischief the woman and the little girl could have been about; so, by his command the two terrified and sobbing creatures were brought before him.

"What is it that these have done?" he inquired of the sheriff.

"Please your Majesty, a black crime is charged upon them, and clearly proven; wherefore the judges have decreed, according to the law, that they be hanged. They sold themselves to the devil; such is their crime."

Tom shuddered. He had been taught to abhor people who did this wicked thing. Still, he was not going to deny himself the pleasure of feeding his curiosity, for all that; so he asked, "Where was this done? And when?"

"On a midnight, in December, in a ruined church, your Majesty."

Tom shuddered again. "Who was there present?"

"Only these two, your Grace—and *that other.*"

"Have these confessed?"

"Nay, not so, sire; they do deny it."

"Then prithee, how was it known?"

"Certain witnesses did see them wending thither, good your Majesty; this bred the suspicion, and dire effects have since confirmed and justified it. In particular, it is in evidence that through the wicked power so obtained, they did invoke and bring about a storm that wasted all the region round about. Above forty witnesses have proved the storm; and sooth one might have had a thousand, for all had reason to remember it, sith all had suffered by it."

"Certes this is a serious matter." Tom turned this dark piece of scoundrelism over in his mind awhile, then asked, "Suffered the woman also by the storm?"

Several old heads among the assemblage nodded their recognition of the wisdom of this question. The sheriff, however, saw nothing consequential in the inquiry; he answered with simple directness, "Indeed did she, your Majesty, and most righteously, as all aver. Her habitation was swept away, and herself and child left shelterless."

"Methinks the power to do herself so ill a turn was dearly bought. She had been cheated had she paid but a farthing for it; that she paid her soul, and her child's, argueth that she is mad; if she is mad she knoweth not what she doth, therefore sinneth not."

The elderly heads nodded recognition of Tom's wisdom once more, and one individual murmured, "An' the king be mad himself, according to report, then is it a madness of a sort that would improve the sanity of some I wot of, if by the gentle providence of God they could but catch it."

"What age hath the child?" asked Tom.

"Nine years, please your Majesty."

"By the law of England may a child enter into covenant and sell itself, my lord?" asked Tom, turning to a learned judge.

"The law doth not permit a child to make or meddle in any weighty matter, good my liege, holding that its callow wit unfitteth it to cope with the riper wit and evil schemings of them that are its elders. The *devil* may buy a child if he so choose, and the child agree thereto, but not an Englishman; in this latter case the contract would be null and void."

"It seemeth a rude, unchristian thing, and ill-contrived, that English law denieth privileges to Englishmen, to waste them on the devil!" cried Tom with honest heat.

This novel view of the matter excited many smiles, and was stored away in many heads to be repeated about the court as evidence of Tom's originality as well as progress toward mental health.

The elder culprit had ceased from sobbing and was hanging upon Tom's words with an excited interest and a growing hope. Tom noticed this, and it strongly inclined his sympathies toward her in her perilous and unfriended situation. Presently he asked, "How wrought they to bring the storm?"

"By pulling off their stockings, sire."

This astonished Tom and also fired his curiosity to fever heat. He said eagerly, "It is wonderful! Hath it always this dread effect?"

"Always, my liege, at least if the woman desire it and utter the needful words, either in her mind or with her tongue."

Tom turned to the woman and said with impetuous zeal, "Exert thy power; I would see a storm!"

There was a sudden paling of cheeks in the superstitious assemblage, and a general though unexpressed desire to get out of the place, all of which was lost upon Tom, who was dead to everything but the proposed cataclysm. Seeing a puzzled and astonished look in the woman's face, he added excitedly, "Never fear; thou shalt be blameless. More, thou shalt go free; none shall touch thee. Exert thy power."

"Oh, my lord the king, I have it not; I have been falsely accused."

"Thy fears stay thee. Be of good heart; thou shalt suffer no harm. Make a storm; it mattereth not how small a one—I require nought great or harmful, but indeed prefer the opposite; do this and thy life is spared; thou shalt go out free, with thy child, bearing the king's pardon, and safe from hurt or malice from any in the realm."

The woman prostrated herself and protested with tears that she had no power to do the miracle, else she would gladly win her child's life alone and be content to lose her own, if by obedience to the king's command so precious a grace might be acquired.

Tom urged; the woman still adhered to her declarations. Finally he said, "I think the woman hath said true. An' *my* mother were in her place and gifted with the devil's functions, she had not stayed a moment to call her storms and lay the whole land in ruins if the saving of my forfeit life were the price she got! It is argument that other mothers are made in like mold. Thou art free, goodwife—thou and thy child—for I do think thee innocent. *Now* thou'st nought to fear, being pardoned, pull off thy stockings! An' thou canst make me a storm, thou shalt be rich!"

The redeemed creature was loud in her gratitude and proceeded to obey, whilst Tom looked on with eager expectancy, a little marred by apprehension, the courtiers at the same time manifesting decided discomfort and uneasiness. The woman stripped her own feet and her little girl's also, and plainly did her best to reward the king's generosity with an earthquake, but it was all a failure and a disappointment.

Tom sighed and said, "There, good soul, trouble thyself no further; thy power is departed out of thee. Go thy way in peace; and if it return to thee at any time, forget me not, but fetch me a storm."

16

The State Dinner

The dinner hour drew near, yet strangely enough the thought brought but slight discomfort to Tom, and hardly any terror. The morning's experiences had wonderfully built up his confidence; the poor little ash-cat was already more wonted to his strange garret after four days' habit than a mature person could have become in a full month. A child's facility in accommodating itself to circumstances was never more strikingly illustrated.

Let us privileged ones hurry to the great banqueting room and have a glance at matters there whilst Tom is being made ready for the imposing occasion. It is a spacious apartment, with gilded pillars and pilasters, and pictured walls and ceilings. At the door stand tall guards, as rigid as statues, dressed in rich and picturesque costumes, and bearing halberds. In a high gallery which runs all around the place is a band of musicians and a packed company of citizens of both sexes in brilliant attire. In the center of the room, upon a raised platform, is Tom's table. Now let the ancient chronicler speak:

"A gentleman enters the room bearing a rod, and along with him another bearing a tablecloth, which, after they have both kneeled three times with the utmost veneration, he spreads upon the table, and after kneeling again they both retire; then come two others, one with the rod again, the other with a salt cellar, a plate, and bread; when they have kneeled as the others had done and placed what was brought upon the table, they too retire with the same ceremonies performed by the first; at last come two nobles, richly clothed, one bearing a tasting knife, who, after prostrating themselves three times in the most graceful manner, approach and rub the table with bread and salt with as much awe as if the king had been present."

So end the solemn preliminaries. Now, far down the echoing corridors we hear a bugle blast and the indistinct cry, "Place for the king! Way for the king's most excellent majesty!" These sounds are momently repeated—they grow nearer and nearer—and presently, almost in our faces, the martial note peals and the cry rings out, "Way for the king!" At this instant the shining pageant appears and files in at the door with a measured march. Let the chronicler speak again:

"First come gentlemen, barons, earls, knights of the Garter, all richly dressed and bareheaded; next comes the Chancellor, between two, one of which carries the royal scepter, the other the Sword of State in a red scabbard studded with golden fleurs-de-lis, the point upwards; next comes the king himself, whom, upon his appearing, twelve trumpets and many drums salute with a great burst of welcome, whilst all in the galleries rise in their places, crying, 'God save the king!' After him come nobles attached to his person, and on his right and left march his guard of honor, his fifty gentlemen pensioners, with gilt battle-axes."

This was all fine and pleasant. Tom's pulse beat high, and a glad light was in his eyes. He bore himself right gracefully, and all the more so because he was not thinking of how he was doing it, his mind being charmed and occupied with the blithe sights and sounds about him; and besides, nobody can be very ungraceful in nicely fitting beautiful clothes after he has grown a little used to them, especially if he is for the moment unconscious of them. Tom remembered his instructions and acknowledged his greeting with a slight inclination of his plumed head and a courteous, "I thank ye, my good people."

He seated himself at table without removing his cap, and did it without the least embarrassment, for to eat with one's cap on was the one solitary royal custom upon which the kings and the Cantys met upon common ground, neither party having any advantage over the other in the matter of old familiarity with it. The pageant broke up and grouped itself picturesquely, and remained bareheaded.

Now, to the sound of gay music, the yeomen of the guard entered, "the tallest and mightiest men in England, they being carefully selected in this regard." But we will let the chronicler tell about it:

"The yeomen of the guard entered, bareheaded, clothed in scarlet, with golden roses upon their backs; and these went and came, bringing in each turn a course of dishes, served in plate. These dishes were received by a gentleman in the same order they were brought, and placed upon the table, while the taster gave to each guard a mouthful to eat of the particular dish he had brought, for fear of any poison."

Tom made a good dinner, notwithstanding he was conscious that hundreds of eyes followed each morsel to his mouth and watched him eat it with an interest which could not have been more intense if it had been a deadly explosive and was expected to blow him up and scatter him all about the place. He was careful not to hurry, and equally careful not to do anything whatever for himself, but wait till the proper official knelt down and did it for him. He got through without a mistake— flawless and precious triumph.

When the meal was over at last and he marched away in the midst of his bright pageant, with the happy noises in his ears of blaring bugles, rolling drums, and thundering acclamations, he felt that if he had seen the worst of dining in public, it was an ordeal which he would be glad to endure several times a day if by that means he could but buy himself free from some of the more formidable requirements of his royal office.

17

Foo-foo the First

Miles Hendon hurried along toward the Southwark end of the bridge, keeping a sharp lookout for the persons he sought and hoping and expecting to overtake them presently. He was disappointed in this, however. By asking questions, he was enabled to track them part of the way through Southwark; then all traces ceased, and he was perplexed as to how to proceed. Still, he continued his efforts as best he could during the rest of the day. Nightfall found him leg-weary, half famished, and his desire as far from accomplishment as ever; so he supped at the Tabard Inn and went to bed, resolved to make an early start in the morning and give the town an exhaustive search. As he lay thinking and planning, he presently began to reason thus: The boy would escape from the ruffian, his reputed father, if possible; would he go back to London and seek his former haunts? No, he would not do that; he would avoid recapture. What, then, would he do? Never having had a friend in the world or a protector until he met Miles Hendon, he would naturally try to find that friend again, provided the effort did not require him to go toward London and danger. He would strike for

Hendon Hall, that is what he would do, for he knew Hendon was homeward bound and there he might expect to find him. Yes, the case was plain to Hendon—he must lose no more time in Southwark, but move at once through Kent, toward Monk's Holm, searching the wood and inquiring as he went. Let us return to the vanished little king now.

The ruffian whom the waiter at the inn on the bridge saw "about to join" the youth and the king did not exactly join them, but fell in close behind them and followed their steps. He said nothing. His left arm was in a sling, and he wore a large green patch over his left eye; he limped slightly and used an oaken staff as a support. The youth led the king a crooked course through Southwark, and by and by struck into the high road beyond. The king was irritated now and said he would stop here—it was Hendon's place to come to him, not his to go to Hendon. He would not endure such insolence; he would stop where he was. The youth said, "Thou'lt tarry here, and thy friend lying wounded in the wood yonder? So be it then."

The king's manner changed at once. He cried out, "Wounded? And who hath dared to do it? But that is apart; lead on, lead on! Faster, sirrah! Art shod with lead? Wounded, is he? Now though the doer of it be a duke's son, he shall rue it!"

It was some distance to the wood, but the space was speedily traversed. The youth looked about him, discovered a bough sticking in the ground, with a small bit of rag tied to it, then led the way into the forest, watching for similar boughs and finding them at intervals: they were evidently guides to the point he was aiming at. By and by an open place was reached, where were the charred remains of a farmhouse, and near them a barn which was falling to ruin and decay. There was no sign of life anywhere, and utter silence prevailed. The youth entered the barn, the king following eagerly upon his heels. No one there! The king shot a surprised and suspicious glance at the youth and asked, "Where is he?"

A mocking laugh was his answer. The king was in a rage in a moment; he seized a billet of wood and was in the act of charging upon the youth when another mocking laugh fell upon his ear. It was from the lame ruffian who had been following at a distance. The king turned and said angrily, "Who art thou? What is thy business here?"

"Leave thy foolery," said the man, "and quiet thyself. My disguise is none so good that thou canst pretend thou knowest not thy father through it."

"Thou art not my father. I know thee not. I am the king. If thou hast hid my servant, find him for me, or thou shalt sup sorrow for what thou hast done."

John Canty replied in a stern and measured voice, "It is plain thou art mad, and I am loath to punish thee; but if thou provoke me, I must. Thy prating doth no harm here, where there are no ears that need to mind thy follies, yet is it well to practice thy tongue to wary speech, that it may do no hurt when our quarters change. I have done a murder and may not tarry at home; neither shalt thou, seeing I need thy service. My name is changed, for wise reasons; it is Hobbs—John Hobbs; thine is Jack; charge thy memory accordingly. Now then, speak. Where is thy mother? Where are thy sisters? They came not to the place appointed; knowest thou whither they went?"

The king answered sullenly, "Trouble me not with these riddles. My mother is dead; my sisters are in the palace."

The youth nearby burst into a derisive laugh, and the

king would have assaulted him, but Canty—or Hobbs, as he now called himself—prevented him, and said, "Peace, Hugo, vex him not; his mind is astray, and thy ways fret him. Sit thee down, Jack, and quiet thyself; thou shalt have a morsel to eat, anon."

Hobbs and Hugo fell to talking together in low voices, and the king removed himself as far as he could from their disagreeable company. He withdrew into the twilight of the farther end of the barn, where he found the earthen floor bedded a foot deep with straw. He lay down here, drew straw over himself in lieu of blankets, and was soon absorbed in thinking. He had many griefs, but the minor ones were swept almost into forgetfulness by the supreme one, the loss of his father. To the rest of the world the name of Henry VIII brought a shiver and suggested an ogre whose nostrils breathed destruction and whose hand dealt scourgings and death; but to this boy the name brought only sensations of pleasure, the figure it invoked wore a countenance that was all gentleness and affection. He called to mind a long succession of loving passages between his father and himself and dwelt fondly upon them, his unstinted tears attesting how deep and real was the grief that possessed his heart. As the afternoon wasted away, the lad, wearied with his troubles, sunk gradually into a tranquil and healing slumber.

After a considerable time—he could not tell how long—his senses struggled to a half consciousness, and as he lay with closed eyes vaguely wondering where he was and what had been happening, he noted a murmurous sound, the sullen beating of rain upon the roof. A snug sense of comfort stole over him, which was rudely broken the next moment by a chorus of piping cackles and coarse laughter. It startled him disagreeably, and he unmuffled his head to see whence this interruption proceeded. A grim and unsightly picture met his eye. A bright fire was burning in the middle of the floor at the other end of the barn; and around it, and lit weirdly up by the red glare, lolled and sprawled the motliest company of tattered gutter scum and ruffians, of both sexes, he had ever read or dreamed of. There were huge, stalwart men, brown with exposure, long-haired, and clothed in fantastic rags; there were middle-sized youths of truculent countenance, and similarly clad; there were blind mendicants with patched or bandaged eyes, crippled ones with wooden legs and crutches; there was a villain-looking peddler with his pack, a knife-grinder, a tinker, and a barber-surgeon with the implements of their trades; some of the females were hardly grown girls, some were at prime, some were old and wrinkled hags, and all were loud, brazen, foul-mouthed; and all soiled and slatternly; there were three sore-faced babies; there were a couple of starveling curs, with strings about their necks, whose office was to lead the blind.

The night was come, the gang had just finished feasting, an orgy was beginning, the can of liquor was passing from mouth to mouth. A general cry broke forth, "A song! A song from the Bat and Dick Dot-and-Go-One!"

One of the blind men got up and made ready by casting aside the patches that sheltered his excellent eyes and the pathetic placard which recited the cause of his calamity. Dot-and-Go-One disencumbered himself of his timber leg and took his place, upon sound and healthy limbs, beside his fellow rascal; then they roared out a rollicking ditty, and were reenforced by the whole crew at the end of each stanza in a rousing chorus. By the time the last stanza was reached, the half-drunken enthusiasm had risen to such a pitch that everybody joined in and sang it clear through from the beginning, producing a volume of villainous sound that made the rafters quake. These were the inspiring words:

> *Bien Darkmans then, Bouse Mort and Ken,*
> *The bien Coves bings awast,*
> *On Chates to trine by Rome Coves dine*
> *For his long lib at last.*
> *Bing'd out bien Morts and toure, and toure,*
> *Bing out of the Rome vile bine,*
> *And toure the Cove that cloy'd your duds,*
> *Upon the Chates to trine.*

Conversation followed; not in the thieves' dialect of the song, for that was only used in talk when unfriendly ears might be listening. In the course of it, it appeared that "John Hobbs" was not altogether a new recruit, but had trained in the gang at some former time. His later history was called for, and when he said he had "accidentally" killed a man, considerable satisfaction was expressed; when he added that the man was a priest, he was roundly applauded and had to take a drink with everybody. Old acquaintances welcomed him joyously, and new ones were proud to shake him by the hand. He was asked why he had "tarried away so many months." He answered, "London is better than the country, and safer these late years, the laws be so bitter and so diligently enforced. An' I had not had that accident, I had stayed there. I had resolved to stay and never more venture countrywards, but the accident has ended that."

He inquired how many persons the gang numbered now. The "Ruffler," or chief, answered, "Five and twenty sturdy budges, bulks, files, clapperdogeons and maunders, counting the dells and doxies and other morts. Most are here; the rest are wandering eastward along the winter lay. We follow at dawn."

"I do not see the Wen among the honest folk about me. Where may he be?"

"Poor lad, his diet is brimstone now, and over hot for a delicate taste. He was killed in a brawl, somewhere about midsummer."

"I sorrow to hear that; the Wen was a capable man, and brave."

"That was he, truly. Black Bess, his dell, is of us yet, but absent on the eastward tramp; a fine lass, of nice ways and orderly conduct, none ever seeing her drunk above four days in the seven."

"She was ever strict—I remember it well—a goodly wench and worthy all commendation. Her mother was more free and less particular, a troublesome and ugly tempered beldame, but furnished with a wit above the common."

"We lost her through it. Her gift of palmistry and other sorts of fortune-telling begot for her at last a witch's name and fame. The law roasted her to death at a slow fire. It did touch me to a sort of tenderness to see the gallant way she met her lot—cursing and reviling all the crowd that gaped and gazed around her, whilst the flames licked upward toward her face and catched her thin locks and crackled about her old gray head. Cursing them, said I? Cursing them! Why, an' thou shouldst live a thousand years thou'dst never hear so masterful a cursing. Alack, her art died with her. There be base and weakling imitations left, but no true blasphemy."

The Ruffler sighed; the listeners sighed in sympathy; a general depression fell upon the company for a moment, for even hardened outcasts like these are not wholly dead to sentiment, but are able to feel a fleeting sense of loss and affliction at wide intervals and under peculiarly favoring circumstances—as in cases like to this, for instance, when genius and culture depart and leave no heir. However, a deep drink all round soon restored the spirits of the mourners.

"Have any others of our friends fared hardly?" asked Hobbs.

"Some—yes. Particularly newcomers, such as small husbandmen turned shiftless and hungry upon the world because their farms were taken from them to be changed to sheep ranges. They begged, and were whipped at the cart's tail, naked from the girdle up, till the blood ran, then set in the stocks to be pelted; they begged again, were whipped again, and deprived of an ear; they begged a third time—poor devils, what else could they do?—and were branded on the cheek with a red-hot iron, then sold for slaves; they ran away, were hunted down, and hanged. 'Tis a brief tale, and quickly told. Others of us have fared less hardly. Stand forth, Yokel, Burns, and Hodge—show your adornments!"

These stood up and stripped away some of their rags, exposing their backs, crisscrossed with ropy old welts left by the lash; one turned up his hair and showed the place where a left ear had once been; another showed a brand upon his shoulder—the letter V—and a mutilated ear; the third said, "I am Yokel, once a farmer and prosperous, with loving wife and kids, now am I somewhat different in estate and calling, and the wife and kids are gone; mayhap they are in heaven, mayhap in—in the other place; but the kindly God be thanked, they bide no more in *England!* My good old blameless mother strove to earn bread by nursing the sick; one of these died, the doctors knew not how, so my mother was burnt for a witch, whilst my babes looked on and wailed. English law! Up, all, with your cups! Now altogether and with a cheer! Drink to the merciful English law that delivered *her* from the English hell! Thank you, mates, one and all. I begged, from house to house—I and the wife—bearing with us the hungry kids; but it was crime to be hungry in England, so they stripped us and lashed us through three towns. Drink ye all again to the merciful English law! For its lash drank deep of my Mary's blood and its blessed deliverance came quick. She lies there, in the potter's field, safe from all harms. And the kids—well, whilst the law lashed me from town to town, they starved. Drink lads—only a drop—a drop to the poor kids, that never did any creature harm. I begged again—begged for a crust, and got the stocks and lost an ear—see, here bides the stump; I begged again, and here is the stump of the other to keep me minded of it. And still I begged again, and was sold for a slave—here on my cheek under this stain, if I washed it off, ye might see the red S the branding iron left there! A *slave!* Do ye understand that word! An English *slave!* That is he that stands before ye. I have run from my master, and when I am found—the heavy curse of heaven fall on the law of the land that hath commanded it!—I shall hang!"

A ringing voice came through the murky air, "Thou shalt *not!* And this day the end of that law is come!"

All turned and saw the fantastic figure of the little king approaching hurriedly; as it emerged into the light and was clearly revealed, a general explosion of inquiries broke out: "Who is it? *What* is it? Who art thou, manikin?"

The boy stood unconfused in the midst of all those surprised and questioning eyes and answered with princely dignity, "I am Edward, king of England."

A wild burst of laughter followed, partly of derision and partly of delight in the excellence of the joke. The king was stung. He said sharply, "Ye mannerless vagrants, is this your recognition of the royal boon I have promised?"

He said more, with angry voice and excited gesture, but it was lost in a whirlwind of laughter and mocking exclamations. "John Hobbs" made several attempts to make himself heard above the din, and at last succeeded, saying, "Mates, he is my son, a dreamer, a fool, and stark mad; mind him not—he thinketh he *is* the king."

"I *am* the king," said Edward, turning toward him, "as thou shalt know to thy cost, in good time. Thou hast confessed a murder—thou shalt swing for it."

"*Thou'lt* betray me? *Thou?* An' I get my hands upon thee—"

"Tut-tut!" said the burly Ruffler, interposing in time to save the king, and emphasizing this service by knocking Hobbs down with his fist. "Hast respect for neither king *nor* Rufflers? An' thou insult my presence so again, I'll hang thee up myself." Then he said to his Majesty, "Thou must make no threats against thy mates, lad; and thou must guard thy tongue from saying evil of them elsewhere. *Be* king, if it please thy mad humor, but be not harmful in it. Sink the title thou hast uttered—'tis treason; we be bad men in some few trifling ways, but none among us is so base as to be traitor to his king; we be loving and loyal hearts in that regard. Note if I speak truth. Now, all together: 'Long live Edward, king of England!' "

"*Long live Edward, king of England!*"

The response came with such a thundergust from the motley crew that the crazy building vibrated to the sound. The little king's face lighted with pleasure for an instant, and he slightly inclined his head and said with grave simplicity, "I thank you, my good people."

This unexpected result threw the company into convulsions of merriment. When something like quiet was presently come again, the Ruffler said firmly but with an accent of good nature, "Drop it, boy; 'tis not wise nor well. Humor thy fancy if thou must, but choose some other title."

A tinker shrieked out a suggestion, "Foo-foo the First, king of the Mooncalves!"

The title "took" at once, every throat responded, and a roaring shout went up of "Long live Foo-foo the First, king of the Mooncalves!" followed by hootings, catcalls, and peals of laughter.

"Hale him forth and crown him!"

"Robe him!"

"Scepter him!"

"Throne him!"

These and twenty other cries broke out at once; and almost before the poor little victim could draw a breath he was crowned with a tin basin, robed in a tattered blanket, throned upon a barrel, and sceptered with the tinker's soldering iron. Then all flung themselves upon their knees about him and sent up a chorus of ironical wailings and mocking supplications, whilst they swabbed their eyes with their soiled and ragged sleeves and aprons: "Be gracious to us, O sweet king!" "Trample not upon thy beseeching worms, O noble Majesty!" "Pity thy slaves, and comfort them with a royal kick!" "Cheer us and warm us with thy gracious rays, O flaming sun of sovereignty!" "Sanctify the ground with the touch of thy foot, that we may eat the dirt and be ennobled!" "Deign to spit upon us, O sire, that our children's children may tell of thy princely condescension, and be proud and happy forever!"

But the humorous tinker made the "hit" of the evening and carried off the honors. Kneeling, he pretended to kiss the king's foot, and was indignantly spurned; whereupon he went about begging for a rag to paste over the place upon his face which had been touched by the foot, saying it must be preserved from contact with the vulgar air and that he should make his fortune by going to the highway and exposing it to view at the rate of a hundred shillings a sight. He made himself so killingly funny that he was the envy and admiration of the whole mangy rabble.

Tears of shame and indignation stood in the little monarch's eyes; and the thought in his heart was, "Had I offered them a deep wrong they could not be more cruel; yet have I proffered nought but to do them a kindness, and it is thus they use me for it!"

18

The Prince with the Tramps

The troop of vagabonds turned out at early dawn and set forward on their march. There was a lowering sky overhead, sloppy ground underfoot, and a winter chill in the air. All gaiety was gone from the company; some were sullen and silent, some were irritable and petulant, none were gentle-humored, all were thirsty.

The Ruffler put "Jack" in Hugo's charge, with some brief instructions, and commanded John Canty to keep away from him and let him alone; he also warned Hugo not to be too rough with the lad.

After a while the weather grew milder and the clouds lifted somewhat. The troop ceased to shiver, and their spirits began to improve. They grew more and more cheerful and finally began to chaff each other and insult passengers along the highway. This showed that they were awaking to an appreciation of life and its joys once more. The dread in which their sort was held was apparent in the fact that everybody gave them the road and took their ribald insolences meekly, without venturing to talk back. They snatched linen from the hedges occasionally, in full view of the owners, who made no protest but only seemed grateful that they did not take the hedges too.

By and by they invaded a small farmhouse and made themselves at home while the trembling farmer and his people swept the larder clean to furnish a breakfast for them. They chucked the housewife and her daughters under the chin whilst receiving the food from their hands, and made coarse jests about them, accompanied with insulting epithets and bursts of horselaughter. They threw bones and vegetables at the farmer and his sons, kept them dodging all the time, and applauded uproariously when a good hit was made. They ended by buttering the head of one of the daughters who resented some of their familiarities. When they took their leave they threatened to come back and burn the house over the heads of the family if any report of their doings got to the ears of the authorities.

About noon, after a long and heavy tramp, the gang came to a halt behind a hedge on the outskirts of a considerable village. An hour was allowed for rest, then the crew scattered themselves abroad to enter the village at different points to ply their various trades.

"Jack" was sent with Hugo. They wandered hither and thither for some time, Hugo watching for opportunities to do a stroke of business but finding none; so he finally said, "I see nought to steal; it is a paltry place. Wherefore we will beg."

"*We*, forsooth! Follow thy trade—it befits thee. But *I* will not beg."

"Thou'lt not beg!" exclaimed Hugo, eyeing the king with surprise. "Prithee, since when hast thou reformed?"

"What dost thou mean?"

"Mean? Hast thou not begged the streets of London all thy life?"

"I? Thou idiot!"

"Spare thy compliments—thy stock will last longer. Thy father says thou hast begged all thy days. Mayhap he lied. Peradventure you will even make so bold as to *say* he lied," scoffed Hugo.

"Him *you* call my father? Yes, he lied."

"Come, play not thy merry game of madman so far, mate; use it for thy amusement, not thy hurt. An' I tell him this, he will scorch thee finely for it."

"Save thyself the trouble. I will tell him."

"I like thy spirit, I do in truth; but I do not admire thy judgment. Bone-rackings and bastings be plenty enow in this life without going out of one's way to invite them. But a truce to these matters; *I* believe your father. I doubt not he can lie; I doubt not he *doth* lie upon occasion, for the best of us do that; but there is no occasion here. A wise man does not waste so good a commodity as lying for nought. But come; sith it is thy humor to give over begging, wherewithal shall we busy ourselves? With robbing kitchens?"

The king said impatiently, "Have done with this folly; you weary me!"

Hugo replied with temper, "Now harkee, mate; you will not beg, you will not rob; so be it. But I will tell you what you *will* do. You will play decoy whilst *I* beg. Refuse, an' you think you may venture!"

The king was about to reply contemptuously when Hugo said, interrupting, "Peace! Here comes one with a kindly face. Now will I fall down in a fit. When the stranger runs to me, set you up a wail and fall upon your knees, seeming to weep; then cry out as all the devils of misery were in your belly and say, 'Oh, sir, it is my poor afflicted brother, and we be friendless; o' God's name cast through your merciful eyes one pitiful look upon a sick, forsaken, and most miserable wretch; bestow one little penny out of thy riches upon one smitten of God and ready to perish!' And mind you, keep you *on* wailing, and abate not till we bilk him of his penny, else shall you rue it."

Then immediately Hugo began to moan, and groan, and roll his eyes, and reel and totter about; and when the stranger was close at hand, down he sprawled before him, with a shriek, and began to writhe and wallow in the dirt, in seeming agony.

"Oh dear, oh dear!" cried the benevolent stranger, "Oh, poor soul, poor soul, how he doth suffer! There, let me help thee up."

"Oh, noble sir, forbear, and God love you for a princely gentleman—but it giveth me cruel pain to touch me when I am taken so. My brother there will tell your worship how I am racked with anguish when these fits be upon me. A penny, dear sir, a penny to buy a little food; then leave me to my sorrows."

"A penny! Thou shalt have three, thou hapless creature"—and he fumbled in his pocket with nervous haste and got them out. "There, poor lad, take them, and most welcome. Now come hither, my boy, and help me carry thy stricken brother to yon house, where—"

"I am not his brother," said the king, interrupting.

"What! Not his brother?"

"Oh, hear him!" groaned Hugo, then privately ground his teeth. "He denies his own brother—and he with one foot in the grave!"

"Boy, thou art indeed hard of heart if this is thy brother. For shame! And he scarce able to move hand or foot. If he is not thy brother, who is he then?"

"A beggar and a thief! He has got your money and has picked your pocket likewise. An' thou wouldst do a healing miracle, lay thy staff over his shoulders, and trust Providence for the rest."

But Hugo did not tarry for the miracle. In a moment he was up and off like the wind, the gentleman following after and raising the hue and cry lustily as he went. The king, breathing deep gratitude to heaven for his own release, fled in the opposite direction and did not slacken his pace until he was out of harm's reach. He took the first road that offered and soon put the village behind him. He hurried along as briskly as he could during several hours, keeping a nervous watch over his shoulder for pursuit; but his fears left him at last, and a grateful sense of security took their place. He recognized now that he was hungry, and also very tired. So he halted at a farmhouse, but when he was about to speak he was cut short and driven rudely away. His clothes were against him.

He wandered on, wounded and indignant, and was resolved to put himself in the way of like treatment no more. But hunger is pride's master; so as the evening drew near, he made an attempt at another farmhouse, but here he fared worse than before, for he was called hard names and was promised arrest as a vagrant except he moved on promptly.

The night came on, chilly and overcast; and still the footsore monarch labored slowly on. He was obliged to keep moving, for every time he sat down to rest he was soon penetrated to the bone with the cold. All his sensations and experiences as he moved through the solemn gloom and the empty vastness of the night were new and strange to him. At intervals he heard voices approach, pass by, and fade into silence; and as he saw nothing more of the bodies they belonged to than a sort of formless drifting blur, there was something spectral and uncanny about it all that made him shudder. Occasionally he caught the twinkle of a light—always far away apparently, almost in another world; if he heard the tinkle of a sheep's bell, it was vague, distant, indistinct; the muffled lowing of the herds floated to him on the night wind in vanishing cadences, a mournful sound; now and then came the complaining howl of a dog over viewless expanses of field and forest; all sounds were remote; they made the little king feel that all life and activity were far removed from him and that he stood solitary, companionless, in the center of a measureless solitude.

He stumbled along through the gruesome fascinations of this new experience, startled occasionally by the soft rustling of the dry leaves overhead, so like human whispers they seemed to sound; and by and by he came suddenly upon the freckled light of a tin lantern near at hand. He stepped back into the shadows and waited. The lantern stood by the open door of a barn. The king waited some time; there was no sound, and nobody stirring. He got so cold, standing still, and the hospitable barn looked so enticing that at last he resolved to risk everything and enter. He started swiftly and stealthily, and just as he was crossing the threshold he heard voices behind him. He darted behind a cask within the barn and stooped down. Two farm laborers came in, bringing the lantern with them, and fell to work, talking meanwhile. Whilst they moved about with the light, the king made good use of his eyes and took the bearings of what seemed to be a good-sized stall at the further end of the place, purposing to grope his way to it when he should be left to himself. He also noted the position of a pile of horse blankets, midway of the route, with the intent to levy upon them for the service of the Crown of England for one night.

By and by the men finished and went away, fastening the door behind them and taking the lantern with them. The shivering king made for the blankets with as good speed as the darkness would allow, gathered them up, and then groped his way safely to the stall. Of two of the blankets he made a bed, then covered himself with the remaining two. He was a glad monarch now, though the blankets were old and thin and not quite warm enough, and besides, gave out a pungent horsey odor that was almost suffocatingly powerful.

Although the king was hungry and chilly, he was also so tired and so drowsy that these latter influences soon began to get the advantage of the former, and he presently dozed off into a state of semiconsciousness. Then, just as he was on the point of losing himself wholly, he distinctly felt something touching him! He was broad awake in a moment, and gasping for breath. The cold horror of that mysterious touch in the dark almost made his heart stand still. He lay motionless and listened, scarcely breathing. But nothing stirred, and there was no sound. He continued to listen and wait during what seemed a long time, but still nothing stirred, and there was no sound. So he began to drop into a drowse once more at last; and all at once he felt that mysterious touch again! It was a grisly thing, this light touch from this noiseless and invisible presence; it made the boy sick with ghostly fears. What should he do? That was the question, but he did not know how to answer it. Should he leave these reasonably comfortable quarters and fly from this inscrutable horror? But fly whither? He could not get out of the barn, and the idea of scurrying blindly hither and thither in the dark within the captivity of the four walls, with this phantom gliding after him and visiting him with that soft, hideous touch upon cheek or shoulder at every turn, was intolerable. But to stay where he was and endure this living death all night? Was that better? No. What, then, was there left to do? Ah, there was but one course; he knew it well—he must put out his hand and find that thing!

It was easy to think this, but it was hard to brace himself up to try it. Three times he stretched his hand a little way out into the dark, gingerly, and snatched it suddenly back, with a gasp—not because it had encountered anything, but because he had felt so sure it was just *going* to. But the fourth time, he groped a little further, and his hand lightly swept against something soft and warm. This petrified him, nearly, with fright: his mind was in such a state that he could imagine the thing to be nothing else than a corpse newly dead and still warm. He thought he would rather die than touch it again. But he thought this false thought because he did not know the immortal strength of human curiosity. In no long time his hand was tremblingly groping again—against his judgment, and without his consent, but groping persistently on just the same. It encountered a bunch of long hair; he shuddered, but followed up the hair and found what seemed to be a warm rope; followed up the rope and found an innocent calf! For the rope was not a rope at all, but a calf's tail.

The king was cordially ashamed of himself for having gotten all that fright and misery out of so paltry a matter as a slumbering calf; but he need not have felt so about it, for it was not the calf that frightened him but a dreadful nonexistent something which the calf stood for; and any other boy in those old superstitious times would have acted and suffered just as he had done.

The king was not only delighted to find that the creature was only a calf, but delighted to have the calf's company, for he had been feeling so lonesome and friendless that the company and comradeship of even this humble animal was welcome. And he had been so buffeted, so rudely entreated by his own kind, that it was a real comfort to him to feel that he was at last in the society of a fellow creature that had at least a soft heart and a gentle spirit, whatever loftier attributes might be lacking. So he resolved to waive rank and make friends with the calf.

While stroking its sleek warm back—for it lay near him and within easy reach—it occurred to him that this calf might be utilized in more ways than one. Whereupon he rearranged his bed, spreading it down close to the calf; then he cuddled himself up to the calf's back, drew the covers up over himself and his friend, and in a minute or two was as warm and comfortable as he had ever been in the downy couches of the regal palace of Westminster.

Pleasant thoughts came at once; life took on a cheerfuller seeming. He was free of the bonds of servitude and crime, free of the companionship of base and brutal outlaws; he was warm, he was sheltered; in a word, he was happy. The night wind was rising; it swept by in fitful gusts that made the old barn quake and rattle; then its forces died down at intervals and went moaning and wailing around corners and projections; but it was all music to the king, now that he was snug and comfortable: let it blow and rage, let it batter and bang, let it moan and wail, he minded it not, he only enjoyed it. He merely snuggled the closer to his friend, in a luxury of warm contentment, and drifted blissfully out of consciousness into a deep and dreamless sleep that was full of serenity and peace. The distant dogs howled, the melancholy kine complained, and the winds went on raging, whilst furious sheets of rain drove along the roof; but the Majesty of England slept on, undisturbed, and the calf did the same, it being a simple creature and not easily troubled by storms or embarrassed by sleeping with a king.

19

The Prince
with the Peasants

When the king awoke in the early morning, he found that a wet but thoughtful rat had crept into the place during the night and made a cozy bed for itself in his bosom. Being disturbed now, it scampered away. The boy smiled and said, "Poor fool, why so fearful? I am as forlorn as thou. 'Twould be a shame in me to hurt the helpless, who am myself so helpless. Moreover, I owe you thanks for a good omen; for when a king has fallen so low that the very rats do make a bed of him, it surely meaneth that his fortunes be upon the turn, since it is plain he can no lower go."

He got up and stepped out of the stall, and just then he heard the sound of children's voices. The barn door opened and a couple of little girls came in. As soon as they saw him their talking and laughing ceased, and they stopped and stood still, gazing at him with strong curiosity; they presently began to whisper together, then they approached nearer, and stooped again to gaze and whisper. By and by they gathered courage and began to discuss him aloud. One said, "He hath a comely face."

The other added, "And pretty hair."

"But is ill-clothed enow."

"And how starved he looketh."

They came still nearer, sidling shyly around and about him, examining him minutely from all points as if he were some strange new kind of animal, but warily and watchfully the while, as if they half feared he might be a sort of animal that would bite upon occasion. Finally they halted before him, holding each other's hands for protection, and took a good satisfying stare with their innocent eyes; then one of them plucked up all her courage and inquired with honest directness, "Who are thou, boy?"

"I am the king," was the grave answer.

The children gave a little start, and their eyes spread themselves wide open and remained so during a speechless half minute. Then curiosity broke the silence, "The *king*? What king?"

"The king of England."

The children looked at each other, then at him, then at each other again—wonderingly, perplexedly; then one said, "Didst hear him, Margery? He saith he is the king. Can that be true?"

"How can it be else but true, Prissy? Would he say a lie? For look you, Prissy, an' it were not true, it *would* be a lie. It surely would be. Now think on't. For all things that be not true be lies; thou canst make nought else out of it."

It was a good tight argument, without a leak in it anywhere; and it left Prissy's half doubts not a leg to stand on. She considered a moment, then put the king upon his honor with the simple remark, "If thou art truly the king, then I believe thee."

"I am truly the king."

This settled the matter. His Majesty's royalty was

accepted without further question or discussion, and the two little girls began at once to inquire into how he came to be where he was, and how he came to be so unroyally clad, and whither he was bound, and all about his affairs. It was a mighty relief to him to pour out his troubles where they would not be scoffed at or doubted, so he told his tale with feeling, forgetting even his hunger for the time; and it was received with the deepest and tenderest sympathy by the gentle little maids. But when he got down to his latest experiences and they learned how long he had been without food, they cut him short and hurried him away to the farmhouse to find a breakfast for him.

The king was cheerful and happy now and said to himself, "When I am come to mine own again, I will always honor little children, remembering how that these trusted me and believed in me in my time of trouble, whilst they that were older and thought themselves wiser mocked at me and held me for a liar."

The children's mother received the king kindly and was full of pity, for his forlorn condition and apparently crazed intellect touched her womanly heart. She was a widow and rather poor; consequently she had seen trouble enough to enable her to feel for the unfortunate. She imagined that the demented boy had wandered away from his friends or keepers, so she tried to find out whence he had come in order that she might take measures to return him; but all her references to neighboring towns and villages, and all her inquiries in the same line, went for nothing: the boy's face, and his answers too, showed that the things she was talking of were not familiar to him. He spoke earnestly and simply about court matters and broke down more than once when speaking of the late king "his father"; but whenever the conversation changed to baser topics, he lost interest and became silent.

The woman was mightily puzzled, but she did not give up. As she proceeded with her cooking, she set herself to contriving devices to surprise the boy into betraying his real secret. She talked about cattle—he showed no concern; then about sheep—the same result, so her guess that he had been a shepherd boy was an error; she talked about mills; and about weavers, tinkers, smiths, trades, and tradesmen of all sorts; and about Bedlam, and jails, and charitable retreats; but no matter, she was baffled at all points. Not altogether, either, for she argued that she had narrowed the thing down to domestic service. Yes, she was sure she was on the right track now; he must have been a house servant. So she led up to that. But the result was discouraging. The subject of sweeping appeared to weary him; firebuilding failed to stir him; scrubbing and scouring awoke no enthusiasm. Then the goodwife touched, with a perishing hope, and rather as a matter of form, upon the subject of cooking. To her surprise and her vast delight, the king's face lighted at once! Ah, she had hunted him down at last, she thought; and she was right proud too of the devious shrewdness and tact which had accomplished it.

Her tired tongue got a chance to rest now, for the king's, inspired by gnawing hunger and the fragrant smells that came from the sputtering pots and pans, turned itself loose and delivered itself up to such an eloquent dissertation upon certain toothsome dishes that within three minutes the woman said to herself, "Of a truth I was right—he hath holpen in a kitchen!" Then he broadened his bill of fare, and discussed it with such appreciation and animation that the goodwife said to herself, "Good lack! How can he know so many dishes, and so fine ones withal? For these belong only upon the tables of the rich and great. Ah, now I see! Ragged outcast as he is, he must have served in the palace before his reason went astray; yes, he must have helped in the very kitchen of the king himself! I will test him."

Full of eagerness to prove her sagacity, she told the king to mind the cooking a moment, hinting that he might manufacture and add a dish or two if he chose; then she went out of the room and gave her children a sign to follow after. The king muttered, "Another English king had a commission like to this in a bygone time; it is nothing against my dignity to undertake an office which the great Alfred stooped to assume. But I will try to better serve my trust than he, for he let the cakes burn."

The intent was good, but the performance was not answerable to it; for this king, like the other one, soon fell into deep thinkings concerning his vast affairs, and the same calamity resulted—the cookery got burned. The woman returned in time to save the breakfast from entire destruction, and she promptly brought the king out of his dreams with a brisk and cordial tongue-lashing. Then, seeing how troubled he was over his violated trust, she softened at once and was all goodness and gentleness toward him.

The boy made a hearty and satisfying meal, and was greatly refreshed and gladdened by it. It was a meal which was distinguished by this curious feature, that rank was waived on both sides; yet neither recipient of the favor was aware that it had been extended. The goodwife had intended to feed this young tramp with broken victuals in a corner like any other tramp or like a dog, but she was so remorseful for the scolding she had given him that she did what she could to atone for it by

allowing him to sit at the family table and eat with his
betters, on ostensible terms of equality with them; and
the king, on his side, was so remorseful for having
broken his trust after the family had been so kind to him
that he forced himself to atone for it by humbling
himself to the family level, instead of requiring the
woman and her children to stand and wait upon him
while he occupied their table in the solitary state due his
birth and dignity.   It does us all good to unbend
sometimes.   This good woman was made happy all the
day long by the applauses which she got out of herself for
her magnanimous condescension to a tramp, and the
king was just as self-complacent over his gracious humil-
ity toward a humble peasant woman.

When breakfast was over, the housewife told the king
to wash up the dishes.   This command was a staggerer
for a moment, and the king came near rebelling; but
then he said to himself, "Alfred the Great watched the
cakes; doubtless he would have washed the dishes too;
therefore will I essay it."

He made a sufficiently poor job of it; and to his
surprise too, for the cleaning of wooden spoons and
trenchers had seemed an easy thing to do.   It was a
tedious and troublesome piece of work, but he finished
it at last.   He was becoming impatient to get away on his
journey now; however, he was not to lose this thrifty
dame's society so easily.   She furnished him some little
odds and ends of employment, which he got through
with after a fair fashion and with some credit.   Then she
set him and the little girl to paring some winter apples,
but he was so awkward at this service that she retired
him from it and gave him a butcher knife to grind.
Afterward she kept him carding wool until he began to
think he had laid the good king Alfred about far enough
in the shade for the present in the matter of showy

menial heroisms that would read picturesquely in story-books and histories, and so he was half minded to resign. And when, just after the noonday dinner, the goodwife gave him a basket of kittens to drown, he did resign. At least he was just going to resign—for he felt that he must draw the line somewhere, and it seemed to him that to draw it at kitten drowning was about the right thing—when there was an interruption. The interruption was John Canty, with a peddler's pack on his back, and Hugo!

The king discovered these rascals approaching the front gate before they had had a chance to see him; so he said nothing about drawing the line, but took up his basket of kittens and stepped quietly out the back way, without a word. He left the creatures in an outhouse and hurried on into a narrow lane at the rear.

20

The Prince
and the Hermit

The high hedge hid him from the house now, and so under the impulse of a deadly fright he let out all his forces and sped toward a wood in the distance. He never looked back until he had almost gained the shelter of the forest; then he turned and descried two figures in the distance. That was sufficient; he did not wait to scan them critically, but hurried on, and never abated his pace till he was far within the twilight depths of the wood. Then he stopped, being persuaded that he was now tolerably safe. He listened intently, but the stillness was profound and solemn—awful, even, and depressing to the spirits. At wide intervals his straining ear did detect sounds, but they were so remote, and hollow, and mysterious that they seemed not to be real sounds, but only the moaning and complaining ghosts of departed ones. So the sounds were yet more dreary than the silence which they interrupted.

It was his purpose, in the beginning, to stay where he was the rest of the day; but a chill soon invaded his perspiring body, and he was at last obliged to resume movement in order to get warm. He struck straight through the forest, hoping to pierce to a road presently, but he was disappointed in this. He traveled on and on, but the farther he went, the denser the wood became apparently. The gloom began to thicken by and by, and the king realized that the night was coming on. It made him shudder to think of spending it in such an uncanny place; so he tried to hurry faster, but he only made the less speed, for he could not now see well enough to choose his steps judiciously; consequently he kept tripping over roots and tangling himself in vines and briers.

And how glad he was when at last he caught the glimmer of a light! He approached it warily, stopping often to look about him and listen. It came from an unglazed window opening in a shabby little hut. He heard a voice now and felt a disposition to run and hide; but he changed his mind at once, for this voice was praying evidently. He glided to the one window of the hut, raised himself on tiptoes, and stole a glance within. The room was small; its floor was the natural earth, beaten hard by use; in a corner was a bed of rushes and a ragged blanket or two; near it was a pail, a cup, a basin, and two or three pots and pans; there was a short bench and a three-legged stool; on the hearth the remains of a fagot fire were smoldering; before a shrine, which was lighted by a single candle, knelt an aged man; and on an old wooden box at his side lay an open book and a human skull. The man was of large, bony frame; his hair and whiskers were very long and snowy white; he was clothed in a robe of sheepskins which reached from his neck to his heels.

"A holy hermit!" said the king to himself. "Now am I indeed fortunate."

The hermit rose from his knees; the king knocked. A deep voice responded, "Enter! But leave sin behind, for the ground whereon thou shalt stand is holy!"

The king entered and paused. The hermit turned a pair of gleaming, unrestful eyes upon him and said, "Who art thou?"

"I am the king," came the answer, with placid simplicity.

"Welcome, king!" cried the hermit with enthusiasm. Then, bustling about with feverish activity and constantly saying "Welcome, welcome," he arranged his bench, seated the king on it, by the hearth, threw some fagots on the fire, and finally fell to pacing the floor with a nervous stride.

"Welcome! Many have sought sanctuary here, but they were not worthy, and were turned away. But a king who casts his crown away, and despises the vain splendors of his office, and clothes his body in rags to devote his life to holiness and the mortification of the flesh—he is worthy, he is welcome! Here shall he abide all his days till death come." The king hastened to interrupt and explain, but the hermit paid no attention to him, did not even hear him apparently, but went right on with his talk with a raised voice and a growing energy. "And thou shalt be at peace here. None shall find out thy refuge to disquiet thee with supplications to return to that empty and foolish life which God hath moved thee to abandon. Thou shalt pray here; thou shalt study the Book; thou shalt meditate upon the follies and delusions of this world, and upon the sublimities of the world to come; thou shalt feed upon crusts and herbs, and scourge thy body with whips daily to the purifying of thy soul. Thou shalt wear a hair shirt next thy skin; thou shalt drink water only; and thou shalt be at peace, yes, wholly at peace, for whoso comes to seek thee shall go his way again, baffled; he shall not find thee, he shall not molest thee."

The old man, still pacing back and forth, ceased to speak aloud and began to mutter. The king seized this opportunity to state his case, and he did it with an eloquence inspired by uneasiness and apprehension. But the hermit went on muttering and gave no heed. And still muttering, he approached the king and said impressively, "Sh! I will tell you a secret!" He bent down to impart it, but checked himself and assumed a listening attitude. After a moment or two he went on tiptoe to the window opening, put his head out and peered around in the gloaming, then came tiptoeing back again, put his face close down to the king's, and whispered, "I am an archangel!"

The king started violently and said to himself, "Would God I were with the outlaws again; for lo, now am I the prisoner of a madman!" His apprehensions were heightened, and they showed plainly in his face.

In a low, excited voice the hermit continued, "I see you feel my atmosphere! There's awe in your face! None may be in this atmosphere and not be thus affected, for it is the very atmosphere of heaven. I go thither and return in the twinkling of an eye. I was made an archangel on this very spot, it is five years ago, by angels sent from heaven to confer that awful dignity. Their presence filled this place with an intolerable brightness. And they knelt to me, king! Yes, they knelt to me! For I was greater than they. I have walked in the courts of heaven and held speech with the patriarchs. Touch my hand—be not afraid—touch it. There, now thou hast touched a hand which has been clasped by Abraham and Isaac and Jacob! For I have walked in the golden courts, I have seen the Deity face to face!" He paused to give this speech effect; then his face suddenly changed, and he started to his feet again, saying with angry energy, "Yes, I am an archangel, *a mere archangel!* I that might have been pope! It is verily true. I was told it from heaven in a dream twenty years ago; ah, yes, I was to be pope! And I *should* have been pope, for heaven had said it, but the king dissolved my religious house, and I, poor, obscure, unfriended monk, was cast homeless upon the world, robbed of my mighty destiny!" Here he began to mumble again and beat his forehead in futile rage with his fist, now and then articulating a venomous curse, and now and then a pathetic, "Wherefore I am nought but an archangel—I that should have been pope!"

So he went on for an hour, whilst the poor little king sat and suffered. Then all at once the old man's frenzy departed and he became all gentleness. His voice softened, he came down out of his clouds and fell to prattling along so simply and so humanly that he soon won the king's heart completely. The old devotee moved the boy nearer to the fire and made him comfortable, doctored his small bruises and abrasions with a deft and tender hand, and then set about preparing and cooking a supper, chatting pleasantly all the time and occasionally stroking the lad's cheek or patting his head in such a gently caressing way that in a little while all the fear and repulsion inspired by the archangel were changed to reverence and affection for the man.

This happy state of things continued while the two ate the supper; then, after a prayer before the shrine, the hermit put the boy to bed in a small adjoining room, tucking him in as snugly and lovingly as a mother might; and so, with a parting caress, left him and sat down by the fire and began to poke the brands about in an absent and aimless way. Presently he paused, then tapped his forehead several times with his fingers as if trying to recall some thought which had escaped from his mind. Apparently he was unsuccessful. Now he started quickly up and entered his guest's room and said, "Thou art king?"

"Yes," was the response drowsily uttered.

"What king?"

"Of England."

"Of England! Then Henry is gone!"

"Alack, it is so. I am his son."

A black frown settled down upon the hermit's face, and he clenched his bony hands with a vindictive energy. He stood a few moments, breathing fast and swallowing repeatedly, then said in a husky voice, "Dost know it was he that turned us out into the world houseless and homeless?"

There was no response. The old man bent down and scanned the boy's reposeful face and listened to his placid breathing. "He sleeps—sleeps soundly"; and the frown vanished away and gave place to an expression of evil satisfaction. A smile flitted across the dreaming boy's features. The hermit muttered, "So, his heart is happy," and he turned away. He went stealthily about the place, seeking here and there for something, now and then halting to listen, now and then jerking his head around and casting a quick glance toward the bed, and always muttering, always mumbling to himself. At last he found what he seemed to want—a rusty old butcher knife and a whetstone. Then he crept to his place by the fire, sat himself down, and began to whet the knife softly on the stone, still muttering, mumbling, ejaculating. The winds sighed around the lonely place, the mysterious voices of the night floated by out of the distances. The shining eyes of venturesome mice and rats peered out at the old man from cracks and coverts, but he went on with his work, rapt absorbed, and noted none of these things.

At long intervals he drew his thumb along the edge of his knife and nodded his head with satisfaction. "It grows sharper," he said; "yes, it grows sharper."

He took no note of the flight of time, but worked tranquilly on, entertaining himself with his thoughts, which broke out occasionally in articulate speech: "His father wrought us evil, he destroyed us—and is gone down into the eternal fires! Yes, down into the eternal fires! He escaped us, but it was God's will, yes, it was God's will, we must not repine. But he hath not escaped the fires! No, he hath not escaped the fires, the consuming, unpitying, remorseless fires—and *they* are everlasting!"

And so he wrought, and still wrought, mumbling—chuckling a low rasping chuckle at times, and at times breaking again into words: "It was his father that did it all. I am but an archangel; but for him, I should be pope!"

The king stirred. The hermit sprang noiselessly to the bedside and went down upon his knees, bending over the prostrate form with his knife uplifted. The boy stirred again; his eyes came open for an instant, but there was no speculation in them, they saw nothing; the next moment his tranquil breathing showed that his sleep was sound once more.

The hermit watched and listened for a time, keeping his position and scarcely breathing; then he slowly lowered his arm and presently crept away, saying, "It is long past midnight; it is not best that he should cry out, lest by accident someone be passing."

He glided about his hovel, gathering a rag here, a thong there, and another one yonder; then he returned, and by careful and gentle handling he managed to tie

The hermit sprang noiselessly to the bedside

the king's ankles together without waking him.   Next he essayed to tie the wrists; he made several attempts to cross them, but the boy always drew one hand or the other away just as the cord was ready to be applied; but at last, when the archangel was almost ready to despair, the boy crossed his hands himself, and the next moment they were bound.   Now a bandage was passed under the sleeper's chin and brought up over his head and tied fast; and so softly, so gradually, and so deftly were the knots drawn together and compacted that the boy slept peacefully through it all without stirring.

21

Hendon to the Rescue

The old man glided away, stooping, stealthy, catlike, and brought the low bench. He seated himself upon it, half his body in the dim and flickering light and the other half in shadow; and so, with his craving eyes bent upon the slumbering boy, he kept his patient vigil there, heedless of the drift of time, and softly whetted his knife and mumbled and chuckled; and in aspect and attitude he resembled nothing so much as a grisly, monstrous spider gloating over some hapless insect that lay bound and helpless in his web.

After a long while the old man, who was still gazing, yet not seeing, his mind having settled into a dreamy abstraction, observed on a sudden that the boy's eyes were open—wide open and staring, staring up in frozen horror at the knife! The smile of a gratified devil crept over the old man's face, and he said, without changing his attitude or his occupation, "Son of Henry the Eighth, hast thou prayed?"

The boy struggled helplessly in his bonds and at the same time forced a smothered sound through his closed jaws, which the hermit chose to interpret as an affirmative answer to his question.

"Then pray again. Pray the prayer for the dying!"

A shudder shook the boy's frame, and his face blenched. Then he struggled again to free himself, turning and twisting himself this way and that, tugging frantically, fiercely, desperately—but uselessly—to burst his fetters; and all the while, the old ogre smiled down upon him, and nodded his head, and placidly whetted his knife, mumbling from time to time. "The moments are precious; they are few and precious; pray the prayer for the dying!"

The boy uttered a despairing groan and ceased from his struggles, panting. The tears came then and trickled, one after the other, down his face; but this piteous sight wrought no softening effect upon the savage old man.

The dawn was coming now; the hermit observed it and spoke up sharply with a touch of nervous apprehension in his voice, "I may not indulge this ecstasy longer! The night is already gone. It seems but a moment, only a moment; would it had endured a year! Seed of the Church's spoiler, close thy perishing eyes, an' thou fearest to look upon—"

The rest was lost in inarticulate mutterings. The old man sunk upon his knees, his knife in his hand, and bent himself over the moaning boy.

Hark! There was a sound of voices near the cabin; the knife dropped from the hermit's hand; he cast a sheepskin over the boy and started up, trembling. The sounds increased, and presently the voices became rough and angry; then came blows, and cries for help; then a clatter of swift footsteps retreating. Immediately came a succession of thundering knocks upon the cabin door, followed by, "Hullo-o-o! Open! And dispatch, in the name of all the devils!"

Oh, this was the blessedest sound that had ever made music in the king's ears, for it was Miles Hendon's voice!

The hermit, grinding his teeth in impotent rage,

moved swiftly out of the bedchamber, closing the door behind him; and straightway the king heard a talk to this effect proceeding from the "chapel":

"Homage and greeting, reverend sir! Where is the boy—*my* boy?"

"What boy, friend?"

"What boy! Lie me no lies, sir priest, play me no deceptions! I am not in the humor for it. Near to this place I caught the scoundrels who I judged did steal him from me, and I made them confess; they said he was at large again, and they had tracked him to your door. They showed me his very footprints. Now palter no more; for look you, holy sir, an' thou produce him not— Where is the boy?"

"Oh, good sir, peradventure you mean the ragged regal vagrant that tarried here the night. If such as you take interest in such as he, know then that I have sent him of an errand. He will be back anon."

"How soon? How soon? Come, waste not the time; cannot I overtake him? How soon will he be back?"

"Thou needst not stir; he will return quickly."

"So be it then. I will try to wait. But stop! *You* sent him of an errand? You! Verily this is a lie—he would not go. He would pull thy old beard, an' thou didst offer him such an insolence. Thou hast lied, friend; thou hast surely lied! He would not go for any man."

"For any *man,* no; haply not. But I am not a man."

"*What!* Now o' God's name what art thou then?"

"It is a secret; mark thou reveal it not. I am an archangel!"

There was a tremendous ejaculation from Miles Hendon—not altogether unprofane—followed by, "This doth well and truly account for his complaisance! Right well I knew he would budge nor hand nor foot in the menial service of any mortal; but lord, even a king must obey when an archangel gives the word o' command! Let me—sh! What noise was that?"

All this while the little king had been yonder, alternately quaking with terror and trembling with hope; and all the while too he had thrown all the strength he could into his anguished moanings, constantly expecting them to reach Hendon's ear but always realizing, with bitterness, that they failed, or at least made no impression. So this last remark of his servant came as comes a reviving breath from fresh fields to the dying; and he exerted himself once more, and with all his energy, just as the hermit was saying, "Noise? I hear only the wind."

"Mayhap it was. Yes, doubtless that was it. I have been hearing it faintly all the—here it is again! It is not the wind! What an odd sound! Come, we will hunt it out!"

Now the king's joy was nearly insupportable. His tired lungs did their utmost—and hopefully, too—but the sealed jaws and the muffling sheepskin sadly crippled the effort. Then the poor fellow's heart sank to hear the hermit say, "Ah, it came from without—I think from the copse yonder. Come, I will lead the way."

The king heard the two pass out, talking; heard their footsteps die quickly away; then he was alone with a boding, brooding, awful silence.

It seemed an age till he heard the steps and voices approaching again, and this time he heard an added sound—the trampling of hoofs apparently. Then he heard Hendon say, "I will not wait longer. I *cannot* wait longer. He has lost his way in this thick wood. Which direction took he? Quick, point it out to me."

"He— But wait; I will go with thee."

"Good—good! Why, truly thou art better than thy

looks. Marry I do not think there's not another archangel with so right a heart as thine. Wilt ride? Wilt
take the wee donkey that's for my boy, or wilt thou fork
thy holy legs over this ill-conditioned slave of a mule
that I have provided for myself? And had been cheated
in too, had he cost but the indifferent sum of a month's
usury on a brass farthing let to a tinker out of work."

"No, ride thy mule and lead thine ass; I am surer on
mine own feet and will walk."

"Then prithee mind the little beast for me while I
take my life in my hands and make what success I may
toward mounting the big one."

Then followed a confusion of kicks, cuffs, tramplings,
and plungings, accompanied by a thunderous intermin-
gling of volleyed curses, and finally a bitter apostrophe
to the mule, which must have broken its spirit, for
hostilities seemed to cease from that moment.

With unutterable misery the fettered little king heard
the voices and footsteps fade away and die out. All hope
forsook him now for the moment, and a dull despair
settled down upon his heart. "My only friend is
deceived and got rid of," he said; "the hermit will return
and—" He finished with a gasp, and at once fell to
struggling so frantically with his bonds again that he
shook off the smothering sheepskin.

And now he heard the door open! The sound chilled
him to the marrow; already he seemed to feel the knife
at his throat. Horror made him close his eyes; horror
made him open them again—and before him stood John
Canty and Hugo!

He would have said, "Thank God!" if his jaws had
been free.

A moment or two later his limbs were at liberty, and
his captors, each gripping him by an arm, were hurrying
him with all speed through the forest.

22

A Victim of Treachery

Once more "King Foo-foo the First" was roving with the tramps and outlaws, a butt for their coarse jests and dull-witted railleries, and sometimes the victim of small spitefulnesses at the hands of Canty and Hugo when the Ruffler's back was turned. None but Canty and Hugo really disliked him. Some of the others liked him, and all admired his pluck and spirit. During two or three days, Hugo, in whose ward and charge the king was, did what he covertly could to make the boy uncomfortable; and at night, during the customary orgies, he amused the company by putting small indignities upon him—always as if by accident. Twice he stepped upon the king's toes—accidentally—and the king, as became his royalty, was contemptuously unconscious of it and indifferent to it; but the third time Hugo entertained himself in that way, the king felled him to the ground with a cudgel, to the prodigious delight of the tribe. Hugo, consumed with anger and shame, sprang up, seized a cudgel, and came at his small adversary in a fury. Instantly a ring was formed around the gladiators, and the betting and cheering began. But poor Hugo stood no chance whatever. His frantic and lubberly 'prentice-

*Once more "King Foo-foo the First" was roving
with the tramps and outlaws*

work found but a poor market for itself when pitted against an arm which had been trained by the first masters of Europe in single-stick, quarter-staff, and every art and trick of swordmanship. The little king stood, alert but at graceful ease, and caught and turned aside the thick rain of blows with a facility and precision which set the motley onlookers wild with admiration; and every now and then, when his practiced eye detected an opening, and a lightning-swift rap upon Hugo's head followed as a result, the storm of cheers and laughter that swept the place was something wonderful to hear. At the end of fifteen minutes, Hugo, all battered, bruised, and the target for a pitiless bombardment of ridicule, slunk from the field; and the unscathed hero of the fight was seized and borne aloft upon the shoulders of the joyous rabble to the place of honor beside the Ruffler, where with vast ceremony he was crowned king of the Gamecocks, his meaner title being at the same time solemnly canceled and annulled, and a decree of banishment from the gang pronounced against any who should thenceforth utter it.

All attempts to make the king serviceable to the troop had failed. He had stubbornly refused to act; moreover, he was always trying to escape. He had been thrust into an unwatched kitchen the first day of his return; he not only came forth empty-handed, but tried to rouse the housemates. He was sent out with a tinker to help him at his work; he would not work; moreover, he threatened the tinker with his own soldering iron; and finally both Hugo and the tinker found their hands full with the mere matter of keeping him from getting away. He delivered the thunders of his royalty upon the heads of all who hampered his liberties or tried to force him to service. He was sent out, in Hugo's charge, in company with a slatternly woman and a diseased baby to beg; but the result was not encouraging: he declined to plead for the mendicants or be a party to their cause in any way.

Thus several days went by; and the miseries of this tramping life, and the weariness and sordidness and meanness and vulgarity of it, became gradually and steadily so intolerable to the captive that he began at last to feel that his release from the hermit's knife must prove only a temporary respite from death at best.

But at night, in his dreams, these things were forgotten, and he was on his throne, and master again. This, of course, intensified the sufferings of the awakening, so the mortifications of each succeeding morning of the few that passed between his return to bondage and the combat with Hugo grew bitterer and bitterer, and harder and harder to bear.

The morning after that combat, Hugo got up with a heart filled with vengeful purposes against the king. He had two plans in particular. One was to inflict upon the lad what would be, to his proud spirit and "imagined" royalty, a peculiar humiliation; and if he failed to accomplish this, his other plan was to put a crime of some kind upon the king and then betray him into the implacable clutches of the law.

In pursuance of the first plan, he purposed to put a "clime" upon the king's leg, rightly judging that that would mortify him to the last and perfect degree; and as soon as the clime should operate, he meant to get Canty's help, and *force* the king to expose his leg in the highway and beg for alms. "Clime" was the cant term for a sore artificially created. To make a clime, the operator made a paste or poultice of unslaked lime, soap, and the rust of old iron, and spread it upon a piece of leather, which was then bound tightly upon the leg. This would presently fret off the skin and make the flesh raw and angry looking; blood was then rubbed upon the limb, which, being fully dried, took on a dark and repulsive color. Then a bandage of soiled rags was put on in a cleverly careless way which would allow the hideous ulcer to be seen and move the compassion of the passerby.*

Hugo got the help of the tinker whom the king had cowed with the soldering iron; they took the boy on a tinkering tramp, and as soon as they were out of sight of the camp they threw him down and the tinker held him while Hugo bound the poultice tight and fast upon his leg.

The king raged and stormed and promised to hang the two the moment the scepter was in his hand again, but they kept a firm grip upon him and enjoyed his impotent struggling and jeered at his threats. This continued until the poultice began to bite, and in no long time its work would have been perfected if there had been no interruption. But there was, for about this time the "slave" who had made the speech denouncing England's laws appeared on the scene and put an end to the enterprise and stripped off the poultice and bandage.

The king wanted to borrow his deliverer's cudgel and warm the jackets of the two rascals on the spot; but the man said no, it would bring trouble—leave the matter till night; the whole tribe being together then, the outside world would not venture to interfere or interrupt. He marched the party back to camp and reported the affair to the Ruffler, who listened, pondered, and then decided that the king should not be again detailed to beg, since it was plain he was worthy of something higher and better, wherefore, on the spot he promoted him from the mendicant rank and appointed him to steal!

* From *The English Rogue;* London, 1665.

Hugo was overjoyed. He had already tried to make the king steal and failed, but there would be no more trouble of that sort now, for of course the king would not dream of defying a distinct command delivered directly from headquarters. So he planned a raid for that very afternoon, purposing to get the king in the law's grip in the course of it; and to do it, too, with such ingenious strategy that it should seem to be accidental and unintentional, for the king of the Gamecocks was popular now, and the gang might not deal overgently with an unpopular member who played so serious a treachery upon him as the delivering him over to the common enemy, the law.

Very well. All in good time Hugo strolled off to a neighboring village with his prey; and the two drifted slowly up and down one street after another, the one watching sharply for a sure chance to achieve his evil purpose, and the other watching as sharply for a chance to dart away and get free of his infamous captivity forever.

Both threw away some tolerably fair-looking opportunities; for both, in their secret hearts, were resolved to make absolutely sure work this time, and neither meant to allow his fevered desires to seduce him into any venture that had much uncertainty about it.

Hugo's chance came first. For at last a woman approached who carried a fat package of some sort in a basket. Hugo's eyes sparkled with sinful pleasure as he said to himself, "Breath o' my life an' I can but put *that* upon him, 'tis good-den and God keep thee, king of the Gamecocks!" He waited and watched, outwardly patient but inwardly consuming with excitement, till the woman had passed by and the time was ripe; then said in a low voice, "Tarry here till I come again," and darted stealthily after the prey.

The king's heart was filled with joy: he could make his escape now if Hugo's quest only carried him far enough away.

But he was to have no such luck. Hugo crept behind the woman, snatched the package, and came running back, wrapping it in an old piece of blanket which he carried on his arm. The hue and cry was raised in a moment by the woman, who knew her loss by the lightening of her burden, although she had not seen the pilfering done. Hugo thrust the bundle into the king's hands without halting, saying, "Now speed ye after me with the rest, and cry 'Stop, thief!' but mind ye lead them astray!"

The next moment Hugo turned a corner and darted down a crooked alley, and in another moment or two he lounged into view again, looking innocent and indifferent, and took up a position behind a post to watch results.

The insulted king threw the bundle on the ground, and the blanket fell away from it just as the woman arrived with an augmenting crowd at her heels; she seized the king's wrist with one hand, snatched up her bundle with the other, and began to pour out a tirade of abuse upon the boy while he struggled, without success, to free himself from her grip.

Hugo had seen enough—his enemy was captured and the law would get him now—so he slipped away, jubilant and chuckling, and wended campwards, framing a judicious version of the matter to give to the Ruffler's crew as he strode along.

The king continued to struggle in the woman's strong grasp, and now and then cried out in vexation, "Unhand me, thou foolish creature; it was not I that bereaved thee of thy paltry goods."

The crowd closed around, threatening the king and

calling him names; a brawny blacksmith in leather apron and sleeves rolled to his elbows made a reach for him, saying he would trounce him well for a lesson; but just then a long sword flashed in the air and fell with convincing force upon the man's arm, flat side down, the fantastic owner of it remarking pleasantly at the same time, "Marry, good souls, let us proceed gently, not with ill blood and uncharitable words.   This is a matter for the law's consideration, not private and unofficial handling.   Loose thy hold from the boy, goodwife."

The blacksmith averaged the stalwart soldier with a glance, then went muttering away, rubbing his arm; the woman released the boy's wrist reluctantly; the crowd eyed the stranger unlovingly, but prudently closed their mouths.   The king sprang to his deliverer's side, with flushed cheeks and sparkling eyes, exclaiming, "Thou hast lagged sorely, but thou comest in good season now, Sir Miles; carve me this rabble to rags!"

23

The Prince a Prisoner

Hendon forced back a smile and bent down and whispered in the king's ear, "Softly, softly, my prince; wag thy tongue warily; nay, suffer it not to wag at all. Trust in me—all shall go well in the end." Then he added to himself: "*Sir* Miles! Bless me, I had totally forgot I was a knight! Lord how marvelous a thing it is, the grip his memory doth take upon his quaint and crazy fancies! An empty and foolish title is mine, and yet it is something to have deserved it, for I think it is more honor to be held worthy to be a specter-knight in his Kingdom of Dreams and Shadows, than to be held base enough to be an earl in some of the *real* kingdoms of this world."

The crowd fell apart to admit a constable, who approached and was about to lay his hand upon the king's shoulder when Hendon said, "Gently, good friend, withhold your hand; he shall go peaceably; I am responsible for that. Lead on, we will follow."

The officer led, with the woman and her bundle; Miles and the king followed after, with the crowd at their heels. The king was inclined to rebel, but Hendon said to him in a low voice, "Reflect, sire; your laws are the wholesome breath of your own royalty; shall their source resist them, yet require the branches to respect them?   Apparently one of these laws has been broken; when the king is on his throne again, can it ever grieve him to remember that when he was seemingly a private person he loyally sunk the king in the citizen and submitted to its authority?"

"Thou art right; say no more; thou shalt see that whatsoever the king of England requires a subject to suffer under the law, he will himself suffer while he holdeth the station of a subject."

When the woman was called upon to testify before the justice of the peace, she swore that the small prisoner at the bar was the person who had committed the theft; there was none able to show the contrary, so the king stood convicted.   The bundle was now unrolled, and when the contents proved to be a plump little dressed pig, the judge looked troubled, whilst Hendon turned pale, and his body was thrilled with an electric shiver of dismay; but the king remained unmoved, protected by his ignorance.   The judge meditated during an ominous pause, then turned to the woman with the question, "What dost thou hold this property to be worth?"

The woman courtesied and replied, "Three shillings and eightpence, your worship; I could not abate a penny and set forth the value honestly."

The justice glanced around uncomfortably upon the crowd, then nodded to the constable and said, "Clear the court and close the doors."

It was done.   None remained but the two officials, the accused, the accuser, and Miles Hendon.   This latter was rigid and colorless, and on his forehead big drops of cold sweat gathered, broke and blended together, and trickled down his face.   The judge turned to the woman again and said in a compassionate voice, " 'Tis a poor ignorant lad, and mayhap was driven hard by hunger, for these be grievous times for the unfortunate; mark you, he hath not an evil face, but when hunger driveth— Good woman! Dost know that when one steals a thing above the value of thirteen pence ha'penny the law saith he shall *hang* for it!"

The little king started, wide-eyed with consternation, but controlled himself and held his peace; but not so the woman. She sprang to her feet, shaking with fright, and cried out, "Oh, good lack, what have I done! God-a-mercy, I would not hang the poor thing for the whole world! Ah, save me from this, your worship; what shall I do, what *can* I do?"

The justice maintained his judicial composure and simply said, "Doubtless it is allowable to revise the value, since it is not yet writ upon the record."

"Then in God's name call the pig eighteenpence, and heaven bless the day that freed my conscience of this awesome thing!"

Miles Hendon forgot all decorum in his delight, and surprised the king and wounded his dignity by throwing his arms around him and hugging him. The woman made her grateful adieux and started away with her pig; and when the constable opened the door for her, he followed her out into the narrow hall. The justice proceeded to write in his record book. Hendon, always alert, thought he would like to know why the officer followed the woman out; so he slipped softly into the dusky hall and listened. He heard a conversation to this effect:

"It is a fat pig and promises good eating; I will buy it of thee; here is the eighteenpence."

"Eighteenpence, indeed! Thou'lt do no such thing. It cost me three shillings and eightpence, good honest coin of the last reign, that old Harry that's just dead ne'er touched nor tampered with.   A fig for thy eightpence!"

"Stands the wind in that quarter?   Thou wast under oath, and so swore falsely when thou saidst the value was but eightpence.   Come straightway back with me before his worship and answer for the crime!   And then the lad will hang."

"There, there, dear heart, say no more, I am content. Give me the eightpence, and hold thy peace about the matter."

The woman went off crying; Hendon slipped back into the courtroom, and the constable presently followed, after hiding his prize in some convenient place. The justice wrote a while longer, then read the king a wise and kindly lecture and sentenced him to a short imprisonment in the common jail, to be followed by a public flogging.   The astounded king opened his mouth and was probably going to order the good judge to be beheaded on the spot, but he caught a warning sign from Hendon and succeeded in closing his mouth again before he lost anything out of it.   Hendon took him by the hand now, made reverence to the justice, and the two departed in the wake of the constable toward the jail. The moment the street was reached, the inflamed monarch halted, snatched away his hand, and exclaimed, "Idiot, dost imagine I will enter a common jail *alive?*"

Hendon bent down and said somewhat sharply, "*Will* you trust in me?   Peace!   And forbear to worsen our chances with dangerous speech.   What God wills, will happen; thou canst not hurry it, thou canst not alter it; therefore wait, and be patient; 'twill be time enow to rail or rejoice when what is to happen has happened."

24

The Escape

The short winter day was nearly ended. The streets were deserted save for a few random stragglers, and these hurried straight along, with the intent look of people who were only anxious to accomplish their errands as quickly as possible and then snugly house themselves from the rising wind and the gathering twilight. They looked neither to the right nor to the left; they paid no attention to our party; they did not even seem to see them. Edward the Sixth wondered if the spectacle of a king on his way to jail had ever encountered such marvelous indifference before. By and by the constable arrived at a deserted market square and proceeded to cross it. When he had reached the middle of it, Hendon laid his hand upon his arm and said in a low voice, "Bide a moment, good sir; there is none in hearing, and I would say a word to thee."

"My duty forbids it, sir; prithee hinder me not; the night comes on."

"Stay, nevertheless, for the matter concerns thee nearly. Turn thy back a moment and seem not to see: *let this poor lad escape.*"

"This to me, sir! I arrest thee in—"

"Nay, be not too hasty. See thou be careful and

"Turn thy back a moment and let this poor lad escape."

commit no foolish error"—then he shut his voice down to a whisper and said in the man's ear—"the pig thou hast purchased for eightpence may cost thee thy neck, man!"

The poor constable, taken by surprise, was speechless at first, then found his tongue and fell to blustering and threatening; but Hendon was tranquil and waited with patience till his breath was spent; then said, "I have a liking to thee, friend, and would not willingly see thee come to harm. Observe, I heard it all—every word. I will prove it to thee." Then he repeated the conversation which the officer and the woman had had together in the hall, word for word, and ended with, "There, have I set it forth correctly? Should not I be able to set it forth correctly before the judge, if occasion required?"

The man was dumb with fear and distress for a moment; then he rallied and said with forced lightness, " 'Tis making a mighty matter indeed out of a jest; I but plagued the woman for mine amusement."

"Kept you the woman's pig for amusement?"

The man answered sharply, "Nought else, good sir. I tell thee 'twas but a jest."

"I do begin to believe thee," said Hendon with a perplexing mixture of mockery and half conviction in his tone; "but tarry thou here a moment whilst I run and ask his worship, for nathless, he being a man experienced in law, in jests, in—"

He was moving away, still talking; the constable hesitated, fidgeted, spat out an oath or two, then cried out, "Hold, hold, good sir; prithee wait a little—the judge! Why, man, he hath no more sympathy with a jest than hath a dead corpse! Come, and we will speak further. Ods body! I seem to be in evil case, and all for an innocent and thoughtless pleasantry. I am a man of family; and my wife and little ones— List to reason, good your worship; what wouldst thou of me?"

"Only that thou be blind and dumb and paralytic whilst one may count a hundred thousand, counting slowly," said Hendon with the expression of a man who asks but a reasonable favor, and that a very little one.

"It is my destruction!" said the constable despairingly. "Ah, be reasonable, good sir; only look at this matter on all its sides, and see how mere a jest it is—how manifestly and how plainly it is so. And even if one granted it were not a jest, it is a fault so small that e'en the grimmest penalty it could call forth would be but a rebuke and warning from the judge's lips."

Hendon replied with a solemnity which chilled the air about him, "This jest of thine hath a name in law; wot you what it is?"

"I knew it not! Peradventure I have been unwise. I never dreamed it had a name; as, sweet heaven, I thought it was original."

"Yes, it hath a name. In the law this crime is called *Non compos mentis lex talionis sic transit gloria mundi.*"

"Ah, my God!"

"And the penalty is death!"

"God be merciful to me, a sinner!"

"By advantage taken of one in fault, in dire peril, and at thy mercy, thou hast seized goods above thirteen pence ha'penny, paying but a trifle for the same; and this, in the eye of the law, is constructive barratry, misprision of treason, malfeasance in office, *ad hominem expurgatis in statu quo*—and the penalty is death by the halter, without ransom, commutation, or benefit of clergy."

"Bear me up, bear me up, sweet sir, my legs do fail me! Be thou merciful; spare me this doom, and I will turn my back and see nought that shall happen."

"Good! Now thou'rt wise and reasonable. And thou'lt restore the pig?"

"I will, I will indeed, nor ever touch another, though heaven send it and an archangel fetch it. Go—I am blind for thy sake—I see nothing. I will say thou didst break in and wrest the prisoner from my hands by force. It is but a crazy, ancient door; I will batter it down myself betwixt midnight and the morning."

"Do it, good soul; no harm will come of it; the judge hath a loving charity for this poor lad and will shed no tears and break no jailer's bones for his escape."

25

Hendon Hall

As soon as Hendon and the king were out of sight of the constable, his Majesty was instructed to hurry to a certain place outside the town and wait there whilst Hendon should go to the inn and settle his account. Half an hour later the two friends were blithely jogging eastward on Hendon's sorry steeds. The king was warm and comfortable now, for he had cast his rags and clothed himself in the secondhand suit which Hendon had bought on London Bridge.

Hendon wished to guard against overfatiguing the boy; he judged that hard journeys, irregular meals, and illiberal measures of sleep would be bad for his crazed mind, whilst rest, regularity, and moderate exercise would be pretty sure to hasten its cure; he longed to see the stricken intellect made well again and its diseased visions driven out of the tormented little head; therefore he resolved to move by easy stages toward the home whence he had so long been banished, instead of obeying the impulse of his impatience and hurrying along night and day.

When he and the king had journeyed about ten miles, they reached a considerable village and halted there for the night at a good inn. The former relations were resumed; Hendon stood behind the king's chair while he dined, and waited upon him; undressed him when he was ready for bed; then took the floor for his own quarters and slept athwart the door rolled up in a blanket.

The next day, and the day after, they jogged lazily along talking over the adventures they had met since their separation, and mightily enjoying each other's narratives. Hendon detailed all his wide wanderings in search of the king and described how the archangel had led him a fool's journey all over the forest and taken him back to the hut finally when he found he could not get rid of him. Then, he said, the old man went into the bedchamber and came staggering back looking broken-hearted and saying he had expected to find that the boy had returned and lain down in there to rest, but it was not so. Hendon had waited at the hut all day; hope of the king's return died out then, and he departed upon the quest again.

"And old Sanctum Sanctorum *was* truly sorry your Highness came not back," said Hendon; "I saw it in his face."

"Marry I will never doubt *that!*" said the king; and then told his own story, after which Hendon was sorry he had not destroyed the archangel.

During the last day of the trip Hendon's spirits were soaring. His tongue ran constantly. He talked about his old father and his brother Arthur, and told of many things which illustrated their high and generous characters; he went into loving frenzies over his Edith, and was so gladhearted that he was even able to say some gentle and brotherly things about Hugh. He dwelt a deal on the coming meeting at Hendon Hall; what a surprise it would be to everybody, and what an outburst of thanksgiving and delight there would be.

It was a fair region, dotted with cottages and orchards,

and the road led through broad pasturelands whose receding expanses, marked with gentle elevations and depressions, suggested the swelling and subsiding undulations of the sea. In the afternoon the returning prodigal made constant deflections from his course to see if by ascending some hillock he might not pierce the distance and catch a glimpse of his home. At last he was successful and cried out excitedly, "There is the village, my prince, and there is the Hall close by! You may see the towers from here; and that wood there—that is my father's park. Ah, *now* thou'lt know what state and grandeur be! A house with seventy rooms—think of that!—and seven and twenty servants! A brave lodging for such as we, is it not so? Come, let us speed; my impatience will not brook further delay."

All possible hurry was made; still, it was after three o'clock before the village was reached. The travelers scampered through it, Hendon's tongue going all the time. "Here is the church—covered with the same ivy, none gone, none added." "Yonder is the inn, the old Red Lion; and yonder is the marketplace." "Here is the Maypole, and here the pump; nothing is altered—nothing but the people, at any rate; ten years make a change in people; some of these I seem to know, but none know me." So his chat ran on. The end of the village was soon reached; then the travelers struck into a crooked, narrow road, walled in with tall hedges, and hurried briskly along it for a half mile, then passed into a vast flower garden through an imposing gateway whose huge stone pillars bore sculptured armorial devices. A noble mansion was before them.

"Welcome to Hendon Hall, my king!" exclaimed Miles. "Ah, 'tis a great day! My father and my brother, and the lady Edith will be so mad with joy that they will have eyes and tongue for none but me in the first transports of the meeting, and so thou'lt seem but coldly welcomed; but mind it not; 'twill soon seem otherwise, for when I say thou art my ward and tell them how costly is my love for thee, thou'lt see them take thee to their breasts for Miles Hendon's sake and make their house and hearts thy home forever after!"

The next moment Hendon sprang to the ground before the great door, helped the king down, then took him by the hand and rushed within. A few steps brought him to a spacious apartment; he entered, seated the king with more hurry than ceremony, then ran toward a young man who sat at a writing table in front of a generous fire of logs.

"Embrace me, Hugh," he cried, "and say thou'rt glad I am come again! And call our father, for home is not home till I shall touch his hand, and see his face, and hear his voice once more!"

But Hugh only drew back, after betraying a momentary surprise, and bent a grave stare upon the intruder—a stare which indicated somewhat of offended dignity at first, then changed, in response to some inward thought or purpose, to an expression of marveling curiosity mixed with a real or assumed compassion. Presently he said in a mild voice, "Thy wits seem touched, poor stranger; doubtless thou hast suffered rude buffetings at the world's hands; thy looks and dress betoken it. Whom dost thou take me to be?"

"Take thee? Prithee for whom else than whom thou art? I take thee to be Hugh Hendon," said Miles sharply.

The other continued in the same soft tone, "And whom dost thou imagine thyself to be?"

"Imagination hath nought to do with it! Dost thou pretend thou knowest me not for thy brother Miles Hendon?"

An expression of pleased surprise flitted across Hugh's face, and he exclaimed, "What! Thou art not jesting? Can the dead come to life? God be praised if it be so! Our poor lost boy restored to our arms after all these cruel years! Ah, it seems too good to be true, it *is* too good to be true; I charge thee, have pity, do not trifle with me! Quick, come to the light—let me scan thee well!"

He seized Miles by the arm, dragged him to the window, and began to devour him from head to foot with his eyes, turning him this way and that and stepping briskly around him and about him to prove him from all points of view, whilst the returned prodigal, all aglow with gladness, smiled, laughed, and kept nodding his head and saying, "Go on, brother, go on, and fear not; thou'lt find nor limb nor feature that cannot bide the test. Scour and scan me to thy content, my good old Hugh. I am indeed thy old Miles, thy same old Miles, thy lost brother, is't not so? Ah, 'tis a great day—I *said* 'twas a great day! Give me thy hand, give me thy cheek; lord, I am like to die of very joy!"

He was about to throw himself upon his brother, but Hugh put up his hand in dissent, then dropped his chin mournfully upon his breast, saying with emotion, "Ah, God of his mercy give me strength to bear this grievous disappointment!"

Miles, amazed, could not speak for a moment; then he found his tongue and cried out, *"What* disappointment? Am I not thy brother?"

Hugh shook his head sadly and said, "I pray heaven it may prove so, and that other eyes may find the resemblances that are hid from mine. Alack, I fear me the letter spoke but too truly."

"What letter?"

"One that came from over sea, some six or seven years ago. It said my brother died in battle."

"It was a lie! Call thy father; he will know me."

"One may not call the dead."

"Dead?" Miles's voice was subdued, and his lips trembled. "My father dead! Oh, this is heavy news. Half my new joy is withered now. Prithee let me see my brother Arthur; he will know me and console me."

"He also is dead."

"God be merciful to me, a stricken man! Gone, both gone—the worthy taken and the worthless spared, in me! Ah! I crave your mercy! Do not say the lady Edith—"

"Is dead? No, she lives."

"Then, God be praised, my joy is whole again! Speed thee, brother, let her come to me! An' *she* say I am not myself, but she will not; no, no, *she* will know me; I were a fool to doubt it. Bring her, bring the old servants; they too will know me."

"All are gone but five—Peter, Halsey, David, Bernard, and Margaret."

So saying, Hugh left the room. Miles stood musing a while, then began to walk the floor, muttering, "The five arch villains have survived the two and twenty leal and honest—'tis an odd thing."

He continued walking back and forth, muttering to himself; he had forgotten the king entirely. By and by his Majesty said gravely, and with a touch of genuine compassion, though the words themselves were capable of being interpreted ironically, "Mind not thy mischance, good man; there be others in the world whose identity is denied and whose claims are derided."

"Ah, my king," cried Hendon, coloring slightly, "do not thou condemn me; wait, and thou shalt see. I am no impostor; she will say it; you shall hear it from the sweetest lips in England. I an impostor? Why, I know this old hall, these pictures of my ancestors, and all things that are about us as a child knoweth its own nursery. Here was I born and bred, my lord; I speak the truth; I would not deceive thee; and should none else believe, I pray thee do not *thou* doubt me; I could not bear it."

"I do not doubt thee," said the king with a childlike simplicity and faith.

"I thank thee out of my heart!" exclaimed Hendon with a fervency which showed that he was touched. The king added, with the same gentle simplicity, "Dost thou doubt *me?*"

A guilty confusion seized upon Hendon, and he was grateful that the door opened to admit Hugh at that moment and saved him the necessity of replying.

A beautiful lady, richly clothed, followed Hugh, and after her came several liveried servants. The lady walked slowly, with her head bowed and her eyes fixed upon the floor. The face was unspeakably sad. Miles Hendon sprang forward, crying out, "Oh, my Edith, my darling"—

But Hugh waved him back gravely and said to the lady, "Look upon him. Do you know him?"

At the sound of Miles's voice the woman had started slightly and her cheeks had flushed; she was trembling now. She stood still during an impressive pause of several moments, then slowly lifted up her head and looked into Hendon's eyes with a stony and frightened gaze; the blood sank out of her face, drop by drop, till nothing remained but the gray pallor of death; then she said, in a voice as dead as the face, "I know him not!" and turned, with a moan and a stifled sob, and tottered out of the room.

Miles Hendon sank into a chair and covered his face

with his hands. After a pause, his brother said to the servants, "You have observed him. Do you know him?"

They shook their heads; then the master said, "The servants know you not, sir. I fear there is some mistake. You have seen that my wife knew you not."

"Thy *wife!*" In an instant Hugh was pinned to the wall with an iron grip about his throat. "Oh, thou fox-hearted slave, I see it all! Thou'st writ the lying letter thyself, and my stolen bride and goods are its fruit. There, now get thee gone, lest I shame mine honorable soldiership with the slaying of so pitiful a manikin!"

Hugh, red-faced and almost suffocated, reeled to the nearest chair and commanded the servants to seize and bind the murderous stranger. They hesitated, and one of them said, "He is armed, Sir Hugh, and we are weaponless."

"Armed? What of it, and ye so many? Upon him, I say!"

But Miles warned them to be careful what they did, and added, "Ye know me of old—I have not changed; come on, an' it like you."

This reminder did not hearten the servants much; they held back.

"Then go, ye paltry cowards, and arm yourselves and guard the doors, whilst I send one to fetch the watch," said Hugh. He turned at the threshold and said to Miles, "You'll find it to your advantage to offend not with useless endeavors at escape."

"Escape? Spare thyself discomfort, an' that is all that troubles thee. For Miles Hendon is master of Hendon Hall and all its belongings. He will remain; doubt it not."

26

Disowned

The king sat musing a few moments, then looked up and said, " 'Tis strange—most strange. I cannot account for it."

"No, it is not strange, my liege. I know him, and this conduct is but natural. He was a rascal from his birth."

"Oh, I spake not of *him*, Sir Miles."

"Not of him? Then of what? What is it that is strange?"

"That the king is not missed."

"How? Which? I doubt I do not understand."

"Indeed? Doth it not strike you as being passing strange that the land is not filled with couriers and proclamations describing my person and making search for me? Is it no matter for commotion and distress that the head of the state is gone, that I am vanished away and lost?"

"Most true, my king, I had forgot." Then Hendon sighed and muttered to himself, "Poor ruined mind— still busy with its pathetic dream."

"But I have a plan that shall right us both. I will write a paper in three tongues—Latin, Greek, and English—and thou shalt haste away with it to London in the morning. Give it to none but my uncle the lord

Hertford; when he shall see it, he will know and say I wrote it. Then he will send for me."

"Might it not be best, my prince, that we wait here until I prove myself and make my rights secure to my domains? I should be so much the better able then to—"

The king interrupted him imperiously, "Peace! What are thy paltry domains, thy trivial interests, contrasted with matters which concern the weal of a nation and the integrity of a throne!" Then he added in a gentle voice, as if he were sorry for his severity, "Obey, and have no fear; I will right thee, I will make thee whole—yes, more than whole. I shall remember, and requite."

So saying, he took the pen and set himself to work. Hendon contemplated him lovingly awhile, then said to himself, "An' it were dark, I should think it *was* a king that spoke; there's no denying it, when the humor's upon him he doth thunder and lighten like your true king; now where got he that trick? See him scribble and scratch away contentedly at his meaningless pothooks, fancying them to be Latin and Greek; and except my wit shall serve me with a lucky device for diverting him from his purpose, I shall be forced to pretend to post away tomorrow on this wild errand he hath invented for me."

The next moment Sir Miles's thoughts had gone back to the recent episode. So absorbed was he in his musings that when the king presently handed him the paper which he had been writing, he received it and pocketed it without being conscious of the act. "How marvelous strange she acted," he muttered. "I think she knew me, and I think she did *not* know me. These opinions do conflict, I perceive it plainly; I cannot reconcile them; neither can I by argument dismiss either of the two or even persuade one to outweigh the other. The matter standeth simply thus: she *must* have known my face, my figure, my voice, for how could it be otherwise? Yet she *said* she knew me not, and that is proof perfect, for she cannot lie. But stop—I think I begin to see. Peradventure he hath influenced her—commanded her—compelled her to lie. That is the solution! The riddle is unriddled. She seemed dead with fear; yes, she was under his compulsion. I will seek her; I will find her; now that he is away, she will speak her true mind. She will remember the old times when we were little playfellows together, and this will soften her heart, and she will no more betray me, but will confess me. There is no treacherous blood in her; no, she was always honest and true. She has loved me in those old days; this is my security, for whom one has loved one cannot betray."

He stepped eagerly toward the door; at that moment it opened, and the lady Edith entered. She was very pale, but she walked with a firm step, and her carriage was full of grace and gentle dignity. Her face was sad as before.

Miles sprang forward with a happy confidence to meet her, but she checked him with a hardy perceptible gesture, and he stopped where he was. She seated herself and asked him to do likewise. Thus simply did she take the sense of old comradeship out of him and transform him into stranger and a guest. The surprise of it, the bewildering unexpectedness of it, made him begin to question, for a moment, if he *was* the person he was pretending to be after all.

The lady Edith said, "Sir, I have come to warn you. The mad cannot be persuaded out of their delusions, perchance; but doubtless they may be persuaded to avoid perils. I think this dream of yours hath the seeming of honest truth to you, and therefore is not criminal; but do not tarry here with it, for here it is dangerous." She looked steadily into Miles's face a moment, then added impressively, "It is the more dangerous for that you *are* much like what our lost lad must have grown to be if he had lived."

"Heavens, madam, but I *am* he!"

"I truly think you think it, sir. I question not your honesty in that; I but warn you, that is all. My husband is master in this region; his power hath hardly any limit; the people prosper or starve as he wills. If you resembled not the man whom you profess to be, my husband might bid you pleasure yourself with your dream in peace; but trust me, I know him well, I know what he will do; he will say to all that you are but a mad impostor, and straightway all will echo him." She bent upon Miles that same steady look once more and added, "If you *were* Miles Hendon, and he knew it and all the region knew it—consider what I am saying, weigh it well—you would stand in the same peril, your punishment would be no less sure; he would deny you and denounce you, and none would be bold enough to give you countenance."

"Most truly I believe it," said Miles bitterly. "The power that can command one lifelong friend to betray and disown another be obeyed, may well look to be obeyed in quarters where bread and life are on the stake and no cobweb ties of loyalty and honor are concerned."

A faint tinge appeared for a moment in the lady's cheek, and she dropped her eyes to the floor; but her voice betrayed no emotion when she proceeded, "I have warned you, I must still warn you, to go hence. This man will destroy you, else. He is a tyrant who knows no pity. I, who am his fettered slave, know this. Poor Miles, and Arthur, and my dear guardian, Sir Richard, are free of him and at rest; better that you were with them than that you bide here in the clutches of this miscreant. Your pretensions are a menace to his title and possessions; you have assaulted him in his own house; you are ruined if you stay. Go—do not hesitate. If you lack money, take this purse, I beg of you, and bribe the servants to let you pass. Oh, be warned, poor soul, and escape while you may."

Miles declined the purse with a gesture and rose up and stood before her.

"Grant me one thing," he said. "Let your eyes rest upon mine so that I may see if they be steady. There, now answer me. Am I Miles Hendon?"

"No. I know you not."

"Swear it!"

The answer was low but distinct, "I swear."

"Oh, this passes belief!"

"Fly! Why will you waste the precious time? Fly, and save yourself."

At that moment the officers burst into the room, and a violent struggle began; but Hendon was soon over-powered and dragged away. The king was taken also, and both were bound and led to prison.

27

In Prison

The cells were all crowded, so the two friends were chained in a large room where persons charged with trifling offenses were commonly kept. They had company, for there were some twenty manacled and fettered prisoners here, of both sexes and of varying ages—an obscene and noisy gang. The king chafed bitterly over the stupendous indignity thus put upon his royalty, but Hendon was moody and taciturn. He was pretty thoroughly bewildered. He had come home a jubilant prodigal expecting to find everybody wild with joy over his return, and instead had got the cold shoulder and a jail. The promise and the fulfillment differed so widely that the effect was stunning; he could not decide whether it was most tragic or most grotesque. He felt much as a man might who had danced blithely out to enjoy a rainbow and got struck by lightning.

But gradually his confused and tormenting thoughts settled down into some sort of order, and then his mind centered itself upon Edith. He turned her conduct over and examined it in all lights, but he could not make anything satisfactory out of it. Did she know him? Or didn't she know him? It was a perplexing puzzle and occupied him a long time, but he ended finally with the conviction that she did know him and had repudiated him for interested reasons. He wanted to load her name with curses now, but this name had so long been sacred to him that he found he could not bring his tongue to profane it.

Wrapped in prison blankets of a soiled and tattered condition, Hendon and the king passed a troubled night. For a bribe the jailer had furnished liquor to some of the prisoners; singing of ribald songs, fighting, shouting, and carousing was the natural consequence. At last, a while after midnight, a man attacked a woman and nearly killed her by beating her over the head with his manacles before the jailer could come to the rescue. The jailer restored peace by giving the man a sound clubbing about the head and shoulders; then the carousing ceased, and after that all had an opportunity to sleep who did not mind the annoyance of the moanings and groanings of the two wounded people.

During the ensuing week, the days and nights were of a monotonous sameness as to events; men whose faces Hendon remembered more or less distinctly came by day to gaze at the "impostor" and repudiate and insult him; and by night the carousing and brawling went on with symmetrical regularity.

However, there was a change of incident at last. The jailer brought in an old man and said to him, "The villain is in this room; cast thy old eyes about and see if thou canst say which is he."

Hendon glanced up and experienced a pleasant sensation for the first time since he had been in the jail. He said to himself, "This is Blake Andrews, a servant all his life in my father's family—a good honest soul, with a right heart in his breast. That is, formerly. But none are true now; all are liars. This man will know me—and will deny me too, like the rest."

The old man gazed around the room, glanced at each

face in turn, and finally said, "I see none here but paltry knaves, scum o' the streets. Which is he?"

The jailer laughed.

"Here," he said; "scan this big animal, and grant me an opinion."

The old man approached and looked Hendon over long and earnestly, then shook his head and said, "Marry, *this* is no Hendon—nor ever was!"

"Right! Thy old eyes are sound yet. An' I were Sir Hugh, I would take the shabby carl and—"

The jailer finished by lifting himself atiptoe with an imaginary halter, at the same time making a gurgling noise in his throat suggestive of suffocation. The old man said vindictively, "Let him bless God an' he fare no worse. An' I had the handling o' the villain, he should roast, or I am no true man!"

The jailer laughed a pleasant hyena laugh and said, "Give him a piece of thy mind, old man; they all do it. Thou'lt find it good diversion."

Then he sauntered toward his anteroom and disappeared. The old man dropped upon his knees and whispered, "God be thanked, thou'rt come again, my master! I believed thou wert dead these seven years, and lo, here thou art alive! I knew thee the moment I saw thee; and main hard work it was to keep a stony countenance and seem to see none here but tuppenny knaves and rubbish o' the streets. I am old and poor, Sir Miles; but say the word and I will go forth and proclaim the truth, though I be strangled for it."

"No," said Hendon; "thou shalt not. It would ruin thee, and yet help but little in my cause. But I thank thee, for thou hast given me back somewhat of my lost faith in my kind."

The old servant became very valuable to Hendon and the king, for he dropped in several times a day to "abuse" the former and always smuggled in a few delicacies to help out the prison bill of fare; he also furnished the current news. Hendon reserved the dainties for the king; without them his Majesty might not have survived, for he was not able to eat the coarse and wretched food provided by the jailer. Andrews was obliged to confine himself to brief visits in order to avoid suspicion, but he managed to impart a fair degree of information each time—information delivered in a low voice for Hendon's benefit, and interlarded with insulting epithets delivered in a louder voice for the benefit of other hearers.

So little by little the story of the family came out. Arthur had been dead six years. This loss, with the absence of news from Hendon, impaired the father's health; he believed he was going to die, and he wished to see Hugh and Edith settled in life before he passed away; but Edith begged hard for delay, hoping for Miles's return; then the letter came which brought the news of Miles's death; the shock prostrated Sir Richard; he believed his end was very near, and he and Hugh insisted upon the marriage; Edith begged for and obtained a month's respite; then another and finally a third; the marriage then took place by the deathbed of Sir Richard. It had not proved a happy one. It was whispered about the country that shortly after the nuptials the bride found among her husband's papers several rough and incomplete drafts of the fatal letter and had accused him of precipitating the marriage, and Sir Richard's death too, by a wicked forgery. Tales of cruelty to the lady Edith and the servants were to be heard on all hands; and since the father's death Sir Hugh had thrown off all soft disguises and become a pitiless master toward all who in any way depended upon him and his domains for bread.

There was a bit of Andrews' gossip which the king listened to with a lively interest, "There is rumor that the king is mad. But in charity forbear to say *I* mentioned it, for 'tis death to speak of it, they say."

His Majesty glared at the old man and said, "The king is *not* mad, good man, and thou'lt find it to thy advantage to busy thyself with matters that nearer concern thee than this seditious prattle."

"What doth the lad mean?" said Andrews, surprised at this brisk assault from an unexpected quarter. Hendon gave a sign, and he did not pursue his question, but went on with his budget, "The late king is to be buried **at** Windsor in a day or two—the sixteenth of the month— and the new king will be crowned at Westminster the twentieth."

"Methinks they must needs find him first," muttered his Majesty; then added confidently, "but they will look to that—and also shall I."

"In the name of—"

But the old man got no further: a warning sign **from** Hendon checked his remark. He resumed the thread of his gossip, "Sir Hugh goeth to the coronation, and with grand hopes. He confidently looketh to come back a peer, for he is high in favor with the Lord Protector."

"What Lord Protector?" asked his Majesty.

"His grace the Duke of Somerset."

"What Duke of Somerset?"

"Marry, there is but one—Seymour, Earl of Hert- ford."

The king asked sharply, "Since when is *he* a duke, and Lord Protector?"

"Since the last day of January."

"And prithee who made him so?"

"Himself and the Great Council, with help of the king."

His Majesty started violently. "The *king!*" he cried. "*What* king, good sir?"

"What king, indeed! (God-a-mercy, what aileth the boy?) Sith we have but one, 'tis not difficult to answer—his most sacred Majesty King Edward the Sixth, whom God preserve! Yea, and a dear and gracious little urchin is he too; and whether he be mad or no—and they say he mendeth daily—his praises are on all men's lips; and all bless him, likewise, and offer prayers that he may be spared to reign long in England, for he began humanely, with saving the old Duke of Norfolk's life, and now is he bent on destroying the cruelest of the laws that harry and oppress the people."

This news struck his Majesty dumb with amazement and plunged him into so deep dismal a reverie that he heard no more of the old man's gossip. He wondered if the "little urchin" was the beggar boy whom he left dressed in his own garments in the palace. It did not seem possible that this could be, for surely his manners and speech would betray him if he pretended to be the Prince of Wales; then he would be driven out, and search made for the true prince. Could it be that the court had set up some sprig of the nobility in his place? No, for his uncle would not allow that; he was all-powerful and could and would crush such a movement, of course. The boy's musings profited him nothing; the more he tried to unriddle the mystery, the more perplexed he became, the more his head ached, and the worse he slept. His impatience to get to London grew hourly, and his captivity became almost unendurable.

Hendon's arts all failed with the king—he could not be comforted; but a couple of women who were chained near him succeeded better. Under their gentle ministrations he found peace and learned a degree of patience. He was very grateful and came to love them dearly and to delight in the sweet and soothing influence of their presence. He asked them why they were in prison, and when they said they were Baptists, he smiled and inquired, "Is that a crime to be shut up for, in a prison? Now I grieve, for I shall lose ye—they will not keep ye long for such a little thing."

They did not answer, and something in their faces made him uneasy. He said eagerly, "You do not speak; be good to me and tell me—there will be no other punishment? Prithee tell me there is no fear of that."

They tried to change the topic, but his fears were aroused, and he pursued it, "Will they scourge thee? No, no, they would not be so cruel! Say they would not. Come, they *will* not, will they?"

The women betrayed confusion and distress, but there was no avoiding an answer, so one of them said in a voice choked with emotion, "Oh, thou'lt break our hearts, thou gentle spirit! God will help us to bear our—"

"It is a confession!" the king broke in. "Then they *will* scourge thee, the stonyhearted wretches! But oh, thou must not weep; I cannot bear it. Keep up thy courage; I shall come to my own in time to save thee from this bitter thing, and I will do it!"

When the king awoke in the morning, the women were gone.

"They are saved!" he said, joyfully; then added despondently, "but woe is me, for they were my comforters."

Each of them had left a shred of ribbon pinned to his clothing in token of remembrance. He said he would keep these things always and that soon he would seek out these dear good friends of his and take them under his protection.

Just then the jailer came in with some subordinates

and commanded that the prisoners be conducted to the jailyard. The king was overjoyed: it would be a blessed thing to see the blue sky and breathe the fresh air once more. He fretted and chafed at the slowness of the officers, but his turn came at last and he was released from his staple and ordered to follow the other prisoners, with Hendon.

The court, or quadrangle, was stone-paved and open to the sky. The prisoners entered it through a massive archway of masonry, and were placed in file, standing with their backs against the wall. A rope was stretched in front of them, and they were also guarded by their officers. It was a chill and lowering morning, and light snow which had fallen during the night whitened the great empty space and added to the general dismalness of its aspect. Now and then a wintry wind shivered through the place and sent the snow eddying hither and thither.

In the center of the court stood two women, chained to posts. A glance showed the king that these were his good friends. He shuddered and said to himself, "Alack, they are not gone free, as I had thought. To think that such as these should know the lash! In England! Aye, there's the shame of it—not in Heathenesse, but Christian England! They will be scourged; and I, whom they have comforted and kindly entreated, must look on and see the great wrong done; it is strange, so strange, that I, the very source of power in this broad realm, am helpless to protect them. But let these miscreants look well to themselves, for there is a day coming when I will require of them a heavy reckoning for this work. For every blow they strike now they shall feel a hundred then."

A great gate swung open and a crowd of citizens poured in. They flocked around the two women and hid them from the king's view. A clergyman entered and passed through the crowd, and he also was hidden. The king now heard talking back and forth as if questions were being asked and answered, but he could not make out what was said. Next there was a deal of bustle and preparation, and much passing and repassing of officials through that part of the crowd that stood on the further side of the women; and whilst this proceeded a deep hush gradually fell upon the people.

Now, by command, the masses parted and fell aside, and the king saw a spectacle that froze the marrow in his bones. Fagots had been piled about the two women, and a kneeling man was lighting them!

The women bowed their heads and covered their faces with their hands; the yellow flames began to climb upward among the snapping and crackling fagots, and wreaths of blue smoke to stream away on the wind; the clergyman lifted his hands and began a prayer; just then two young girls came flying through the great gate uttering piercing screams and threw themselves upon the women at the stake. Instantly they were torn away by officers, and one of them was kept in a tight grip, but the other broke loose, saying she would die with her mother; and before she could be stopped she had flung her arms about her mother's neck again. She was torn away once more, and with her gown on fire. Two of three men held her, and the burning portion of her gown was snatched off and thrown flaming aside, she struggling all the while to free herself, and saying she would be alone in the world now, and begging to be allowed to die with her mother. Both the girls screamed continually and fought for freedom, but suddenly this tumult was drowned under a volley of heart-piercing shrieks of mortal agony; the king glanced from the frantic girls to the stake, then turned away and leaned his ashen face

*"For every blow they strike now they shall feel
a hundred then"*

against the wall, and looked no more. He said, "That which I have seen in that one little moment will never go out from my memory, but will abide there; and I shall see it all the days, and dream of it all the nights, till I die. Would God I had been blind!"

Hendon was watching the king. He said to himself with satisfaction, "His disorder mendeth, he hath changed, and groweth gentler. If he had followed his wont, he would have stormed at these varlets, and said he was king, and commanded that the women be turned loose unscathed. Soon his delusion will pass away and be forgotten, and his poor mind will be whole again. God speed the day!"

That same day several prisoners were brought in to remain overnight, who were being conveyed under guard to various places in the kingdom to undergo punishment for crimes committed. The king conversed with these—he had made it a point from the beginning to instruct himself for the kingly office by questioning prisoners whenever the opportunity offered—and the tale of their woes wrung his heart. One of them was a poor half-witted woman who had stolen a yard or two of cloth from a weaver; she was to be hanged for it. Another was a man accused of stealing a horse; he said the proof had failed, and he had imagined that he was safe from the halter; but no, he was hardly free before he was arraigned for killing a deer in the king's park; this was proved against him, and now he was on his way to the gallows. There was a tradesman's apprentice whose case particularly distressed the king; this youth said he found a hawk one evening that had escaped from its owner, and he took it home with him, imagining himself entitled to it; but the court convicted him of stealing it and sentenced him to death.

The king was furious over these inhumanities and

wanted Hendon to break jail and fly with him to Westminster so that he could mount his throne and hold out his scepter in mercy over these unfortunate people and save their lives. "Poor child," sighed Hendon. "These woeful tales have brought his malady upon him again; alack, but for this evil hap, he would have been well in a little time."

Among these prisoners was an old lawyer—a man with a strong face and a dauntless mien. Three years past he had written a pamphlet against the Lord Chancellor, accusing him of injustice, and had been punished for it by the loss of his ears in the pillory and degradation from the bar, and in addition had been fined £3,000 and sentenced to imprisonment for life. Lately he had repeated his offense; and in consequence was now under sentence to lose *what remained of his ears,* pay a fine of £5,000, be branded on both cheeks, and remain in prison for life.

"These be honorable scars," he said, and turned back his gray hair and showed the mutilated stubs of what had once been his ears.

The king's eye burned with passion. He said, "None believe in me; neither wilt thou. But no matter; within the compass of a month thou shalt be free; and more, the laws that have dishonored thee and shamed the English name shall be swept from the statute books. The world is made wrong; kings should go to school to their own laws at times, and so learn mercy."

28

The Sacrifice

Meantime Miles was growing sufficiently tired of confinement and inaction. But now his trial came on, to his great gratification, and he thought he could welcome any sentence provided a further imprisonment should not be a part of it. But he was mistaken about that. He was in a fine fury when he found himself described as a "sturdy vagabond" and sentenced to sit two hours in the pillory for bearing that character and for assaulting the master of Hendon Hall. His pretensions as to brothership with his prosecutor, and rightful heirship to the Hendon honors and estates, were left contemptuously unnoticed as being not even worth examination.

He raged and threatened on his way to punishment, but it did no good; he was snatched roughly along by the officers and got an occasional cuff besides for his unreverent conduct.

The king could not pierce through the rabble that swarmed behind, so he was obliged to follow in the rear, remote from his good friend and servant. The king had been nearly condemned to the stocks himself for being in such bad company, but had been let off with a lecture and a warning in consideration of his youth. When the crowd at last halted, he flitted feverishly from point to point around its outer rim hunting a place to get through, and at last, after a deal of difficulty and delay, succeeded. There sat his poor henchman in the degrading stocks, the sport and butt of a dirty mob—he the body servant of the king of England! Edward had heard the sentence pronounced, but he had not realized the half that it meant. His anger began to rise as the sense of this new indignity which had been put upon him sank home; it jumped to summer heat the next moment, when he saw an egg sail through the air and crush itself against Hendon's cheek, and heard the crowd roar its enjoyment of the episode. He sprang across the open circle and confronted the officer in charge, crying, "For shame! This is my servant; set him free! I am the—"

"Oh, peace!" exclaimed Hendon in a panic. "Thou'lt destroy thyself. Mind him not, officer, he is mad."

"Give thyself no trouble as to the matter of minding him, good man; I have small mind to mind him; but as to teaching him somewhat, to that I am well inclined." He turned to a subordinate and said, "Give the little fool a taste or two of the lash, to mend his manners."

"Half a dozen will better serve his turn," suggested Sir Hugh, who had ridden up a moment before to take a passing glance at the proceedings.

The king was seized. He did not even struggle, so paralyzed was he with the mere thought of the monstrous outrage that was proposed to be inflicted upon his sacred person. History was already defiled with the record of the scourging of an English king with whips; it was an intolerable reflection that he must furnish a duplicate of that shameful page. He was in the toils; there was no help for him: he must either take this punishment or beg for its remission. Hard conditions; he would take the stripes—a king might do that, but a king could not beg.

But meantime Miles Hendon was resolving the difficulty. "Let the child go," said he; "ye heartless dogs, do ye not see how young and frail he is? Let him go; I will take his lashes."

"Marry, a good thought, and thanks for it," said Sir Hugh, his face lighting with a sardonic satisfaction. "Let the little beggar go, and give this fellow a dozen in his place—an honest dozen, well laid on." The king was in the act of entering a fierce protest, but Sir Hugh silenced him with the potent remark, "Yes, speak up, do, and free thy mind; only, mark ye, that for each word you utter he shall get six strokes the more."

Hendon was removed from the stocks and his back laid bare, and whilst the lash was applied the poor little king turned away his face and allowed unroyal tears to channel his cheeks unchecked. "Ah, brave good heart," he said to himself, "this loyal deed shall never perish out of my memory. I will not forget it; and neither shall *they!*" he added with passion. Whilst he mused, his appreciation of Hendon's magnanimous conduct grew to greater and still greater dimensions in his mind, and so also did his gratefulness for it. Presently he said to himself, "Who saves his prince from wounds and possible death—and this he did for me—performs high service; but it is little—it is nothing, oh, less than nothing!—when 'tis weighed against the act of him who saves his prince from shame!"

Hendon made no outcry under the scourge, but bore the heavy blows with soldierly fortitude. This, together with his redeeming the boy by taking his stripes for him, compelled the respect of even that forlorn and degraded mob that was gathered there; and its gibes and hootings died away, and no sound remained but the sound of the falling blows. The stillness that pervaded the place when Hendon found himself once more in the stocks was in strong contrast with the insulting clamor which had prevailed there so little a while before. The king came softly to Hendon's side and whispered in his ear, "Kings cannot ennoble thee, thou good, great soul, for

One who is higher than kings hath done that for thee; but a king can confirm thy nobility to men." He picked up the scourge from the ground, touched Hendon's bleeding shoulders lightly with it, and whispered, "Edward of England dubs thee earl!"

Hendon was touched. The water welled to his eyes, yet at the same time the grisly humor of the situation and circumstances so undermined his gravity that it was all he could do to keep some sight of his inward mirth from showing outside. To be suddenly hoisted, naked and gory, from the common stocks to the Alpine altitude and splendor of an earldom seemed to him the last possibility in the line of the grotesque. He said to himself, "Now am I finely tinseled indeed! The specter knight of the Kingdom of Dreams and Shadows is become a specter earl! A dizzy flight for a callow wing! An' this go on, I shall presently be hung like a very maypole with fantastic gauds and make-believe honors. But I shall value them, all valueless as they are, for the love that doth bestow them. Better these poor mock dignities of mine, that come unasked from a clean hand and a right spirit, than real ones bought by servility from grudging and interested power."

The dreaded Sir Hugh wheeled his horse about, and as he spurred away, the living wall divided silently to let him pass, and as silently closed together again. And so remained; nobody went so far as to venture a remark in favor of the prisoner or in compliment to him, but no matter, the absence of abuse was a sufficient homage in itself. A latecomer who was not posted as to the present circumstances and who delivered a sneer at the "impostor" and was in the act of following it with a dead cat was promptly knocked down and kicked out, without any words, and then the deep quiet resumed sway once more.

29

To London

When Hendon's term of service in the stocks was finished, he was released and ordered to quit the region and come back no more. His sword was restored to him, and also his mule and his donkey. He mounted and rode off, followed by the king, the crowd opening with quiet respectfulness to let them pass, and then dispersing when they were gone.

Hendon was soon absorbed in thought. There were questions of high import to be answered. What should he do? Whither should he go? Powerful help must be found somewhere or he must relinquish his inheritance and remain under the imputation of being an impostor besides. Where could he hope to find this powerful help? Where, indeed! It was a knotty question. By and by a thought occurred to him which pointed to a possibility—the slenderest of slender possibilities, certainly, but still worth considering, for lack of any other that promised anything at all. He remembered what old Andrews had said about the young king's goodness and his generous championship of the wronged and unfortunate. Why not go and try to get speech of him and beg for justice? Ah, yes, but could so fantastic a pauper get admission to the august presence of a monarch? Never mind; let that matter take care of itself; it

was a bridge that would not need to be crossed till he
should come to it. He was an old campaigner, and used
to inventing shifts and expedients; no doubt he would
be able to find a way. Yes, he would strike for the
capital. Maybe his father's old friend Sir Humphrey
Marlow would help him—"good old Sir Humphrey,
head lieutenant of the late king's kitchen, or stables, or
something"—Miles could not remember just what or
which. Now that he had something to turn his energies
to, a distinctly defined object to accomplish, the fog of
humiliation and depression which had settled down
upon his spirits lifted and blew away, and he raised his
head and looked about him. He was surprised to see
how far he had come; the village was away behind him.
The king was jogging along in his wake with his head
bowed, for he too was deep in plans and thinkings. A
sorrowful misgiving clouded Hendon's newborn cheer-
fulness: would the boy be willing to go again to a city
where, during all his brief life, he had never known
anything but ill usage and pinching want? But the
question must be asked; it could not be avoided; so
Hendon reined up and called out, "I had forgotten to
inquire whither we are bound. Thy commands, my
liege!"

"To London!"

Hendon moved on again, mightily contented with the
answer, but astounded at it too.

The whole journey was made without an adventure of
importance. But it ended with one. About ten o'clock
on the night of the nineteenth of February, they stepped
upon London Bridge in the midst of a writhing, struggling jam of howling and hurrahing people whose
beer-jolly faces stood out strongly in the glare from
manifold torches; and at that instant the decaying head
of some former duke or other grandee tumbled down

between them, striking Hendon on the elbow and then bounding off among the hurrying confusion of feet. So evanescent and unstable are men's works in this world! The late good king is but three weeks dead and three days in his grave, and already the adornments which he took such pains to select from prominent people for his noble bridge are falling. A citizen stumbled over that head and drove his own head into the back of somebody in front of him, who turned and knocked down the first person that came handy, and was promptly laid out himself by that person's friend. It was the right ripe time for a free fight, for the festivities of the morrow— Coronation Day—were already beginning; everybody was full of strong drink and patriotism; within five minutes the free fight was occupying a good deal of ground; within ten or twelve it covered an acre or so and was become a riot. By this time Hendon and the king were hopelessly separated from each other and lost in the rush and turmoil of the roaring masses of humanity. And so we leave them.

30

Tom's Progress

Whilst the true king wandered about the land poorly clad, poorly fed, cuffed and derided by tramps one while, herding with thieves and murderers in a jail another, and called idiot and impostor by all impartially, the mock king, Tom Canty, enjoyed a quite different experience.

When we saw him last, royalty was just beginning to have a bright side for him. This bright side went on brightening more and more every day; in a very little while it was become almost all sunshine and delightfulness. He lost his fears; his misgivings faded out and died; his embarrassments departed and gave place to an easy and confident bearing. He worked the whipping boy mine to ever-increasing profit.

He ordered my lady Elizabeth and my lady Jane Grey into his presence when he wanted to play or talk, and dismissed them when he was done with them, with the air of one familiarly accustomed to such performances. It no longer confused him to have these lofty personages kiss his hand at parting.

He came to enjoy being conducted to bed in state at night and dressed with intricate and solemn ceremony in the morning. It came to be a proud pleasure to march to dinner attended by a glittering procession of officers of state and gentlemen-at-arms; insomuch, indeed, that he doubled his guard of gentlemen-at-arms and made them a hundred. He liked to hear the bugles sounding down the long corridors and the distant voices responding, "Way for the king!"

He even learned to enjoy sitting in throned state in council and seeming to be something more than the Lord Protector's mouthpiece. He liked to receive great ambassadors and their gorgeous trains and listen to the affectionate messages they brought from illustrious monarchs who called him "brother." O happy Tom Canty, late of Offal Court!

He enjoyed his splendid clothes and ordered more; he found his four hundred servants too few for his proper grandeur and trebled them. The adulation of salaaming courtiers came to be sweet music to his ears. He remained kind and gentle and a sturdy and determined champion of all that were oppressed, and he made tireless war upon unjust laws; yet upon occasion, being offended, he could turn upon an earl, or even a duke, and give him a look that would make him tremble. Once, when his royal "sister," the grimly holy lady Mary, set herself to reason with him against the wisdom of his course in pardoning so many people who would otherwise be jailed, or hanged, or burned, and reminded him that their august late father's prisons had sometimes contained as high as sixty thousand convicts at one time and that during his admirable reign he had delivered seventy-two thousand thieves and robbers over to death by the executioner, * the boy was filled with generous indignation and commanded her to go to her closet, and beseech God to take away the stone that was in her breast and give her a human heart.

Did Tom Canty never feel troubled about the poor little rightful prince, who had treated him so kindly and flown out with such hot zeal to avenge him upon the

* Hume's *England*.

insolent sentinel at the palace gate? Yes; his first royal days and nights were pretty well sprinkled with painful thoughts about the lost prince, and with sincere longings for his return, and happy restoration to his native rights and splendors. But as time wore on, and the prince did not come, Tom's mind became more and more occupied with his new and enchanting experiences, and by little and little the vanished monarch faded almost out of his thoughts; and finally, when he did intrude upon them at intervals, he was become an unwelcome specter, for he made Tom feel guilty and ashamed.

Tom's poor mother and sisters traveled the same road out of his mind. At first he pined for them, sorrowed for them, longed to see them, but later the thought of their coming some day in their rags and dirt, and betraying him with their kisses, and pulling him down from his lofty place, and dragging him back to penury and degradation and the slums made him shudder. At last they ceased to trouble his thoughts almost wholly. And he was content, even glad; for whenever their mournful and accusing faces did rise before him now, they made him feel more despicable than the worms that crawl.

At midnight of the nineteenth of February Tom Canty was sinking to sleep in his rich bed in the palace, guarded by his loyal vassals and surrounded by the pomps of royalty, a happy boy, for tomorrow was the day appointed for his solemn crowning as king of England. At that same hour Edward, the true king, hungry and thirsty, soiled and draggled, worn with travel, and clothed in rags and shreds—his share of the results of the riot—was wedged in among a crowd of people who were watching with deep interest hurrying gangs of workmen who streamed in and out of Westminster Abbey, busy as ants: they were making the last preparation for the royal coronation.

31

The Recognition Procession

When Tom Canty awoke the next morning, the air was heavy with a thunderous murmur; all the distances were charged with it. It was music to him, for it meant that the English world was out in its strength to give loyal welcome to the great day.

Presently Tom found himself once more the chief figure in a wonderful floating pageant on the Thames, for by ancient custom the "recognition procession" through London must start from the Tower, and he was bound thither.

When he arrived there, the sides of the venerable fortress seemed suddenly rent in a thousand places, and from every rent leaped a red tongue of flame and a white gush of smoke; a deafening explosion followed, which drowned the shoutings of the multitude and made the ground tremble; the flame jets, the smoke, and the explosions were repeated over and over again with marvelous celerity, so that in a few moments the old Tower disappeared in the vast fog of its own smoke, all but the very top of the tall pile called the White Tower: this, with its banners, stood out above the dense bank of vapor as a mountain peak projects above a cloud rack.

Tom Canty, splendidly arrayed, mounted a prancing war steed, whose rich trappings almost reached to the ground; his "uncle" the Lord Protector Somerset, similarly mounted, took place in his rear; the king's guard formed in single ranks on either side, clad in burnished armor; after the Protector followed a seemingly interminable procession of resplendent nobles attended by their vassals; after these came the Lord Mayor and the aldermanic body, in crimson-velvet robes and with their gold chains across their breasts; and after these the officers and members of all the guilds of London, in rich raiment and bearing the showy banners of the several corporations. Also in the procession, as a special guard of honor through the city, was the Ancient and Honorable Artillery Company, an organization already three hundred years old at that time, and the only military body in England possessing the privilege (which it still possesses in our day) of holding itself independent of the commands of Parliament. It was a brilliant spectacle, and was hailed with acclamations all along the line as it took its stately way through the packed multitudes of citizens. The chronicler says, "The king, as he entered the city, was received by the people with prayers, welcomings, cries, and tender words, and all signs which argue an earnest love of subjects toward their sovereign; and the king, by holding up his glad countenance to such as stood afar off, and most tender language to those that stood nigh his Grace, showed himself no less thankful to receive the people's goodwill than they to offer it. To all that wished him well, he gave thanks. To such as bade 'God save his Grace,' he said in return, 'God save you all!' and added that he thanked them with all his heart. Wonderfully transported were the people with the loving answers and gestures of their king."

In Fenchurch Street a "fair child, in costly apparel,"

stood on a stage to welcome his Majesty to the city. The last verse of his greeting was in these words:

Welcome, O king, as much as hearts can think;
Welcome again, as much as tongue can tell;
Welcome to joyous tongues, and hearts that will
not shrink:
God thee preserve, we pray, and wish thee
ever well.

The people burst forth in a glad shout, repeating with one voice what the child had said. Tom Canty gazed abroad over the surging sea of eager faces, and his heart swelled with exultation and he felt that the one thing worth living for in this world was to be a king, and a nation's idol. Presently he caught sight, at a distance, of a couple of his ragged Offal Court comrades—one of them the Lord High Admiral in his late mimic court, the other the First Lord of the Bedchamber in the same pretentious fiction; and his pride swelled higher than ever. Oh, if they could only recognize him now! What unspeakable glory it would be if they could recognize him and realize that the derided mock king of the slums and back alleys was become a real king, with illustrious dukes and princes for his humble menials and the English world at his feet! But he had to deny himself and choke down his desire, for such a recognition might cost more than it would come to; so he turned away his head and left the two soiled lads to go on with their shoutings and glad adulations, unsuspicious of whom it was they were lavishing them upon.

Every now and then rose the cry, "A largess! A largess!" and Tom responded by scattering a handful of bright new coins for the multitude to scramble for.

The chronicler says, "At the upper end of Grace-church Street, before the sign of the Eagle, the city had erected a gorgeous arch, beneath which was a stage which stretched from one side of the street to the other. This was a historical pageant, representing the king's immediate progenitors. There sat Elizabeth of York in the midst of an immense white rose whose petals formed elaborate furbelows around her; by her side was Henry VII, issuing out of a vast red rose, disposed in the same manner; the hands of the royal pair were locked together, and the wedding ring ostentatiously displayed. From the red and white roses proceeded a stem which reached up to a second stage, occupied by Henry VIII, issuing from a red-and-white rose, with the effigy of the new king's mother, Jane Seymour, represented by his side. One branch sprang from this pair, which mounted to a third stage, where sat the effigy of Edward VI himself, enthroned in royal majesty; and the whole pageant was framed with wreaths of roses, red and white."

This quaint and gaudy spectacle so wrought upon the rejoicing people that their acclamations utterly smothered the small voice of the child whose business it was to explain the thing in eulogistic rhymes. But Tom Canty was not sorry, for this loyal uproar was sweeter music to him than any poetry, no matter what its quality might be. Whithersoever Tom turned his happy young face, the people recognized the exactness of his effigy's likeness to himself, the flesh and blood counterpart, and new whirlwinds of applause burst forth.

The great pageant moved on, and still on, under one triumphal arch after another, and past a bewildering succession of spectacular and symbolical tableaux, each of which typified and exalted some virtue, or talent, or merit of the little king's. "Throughout the whole of Cheapside, from every penthouse and window, hung banners and streamers; and the richest carpets, stuffs, and cloth of gold tapestried the streets—specimens of the great wealth of the stores within; and the splendor of this thoroughfare was equaled in the other streets, and in some even surpassed."

"And all these wonders and these marvels are to welcome me—me!" murmured Tom Canty.

The mock king's cheeks were flushed with excitement, his eyes were flashing, his senses swam in a delirium of pleasure. At this point, just as he was raising his hand to fling another rich largess, he caught sight of a pale, astounded face which was strained forward out of the second rank of the crowd, its intense eyes riveted upon him. A sickening consternation struck through him; he recognized his mother! And up flew his hand, palm outward, before his eyes—that old involuntary gesture born of a forgotten episode and perpetuated by habit. In an instant more she had torn her way out of the press, and past the guards, and was at his side. She embraced his leg, she covered it with kisses, she cried, "O my child, my darling!" lifting toward him a face that was transfigured with joy and love. The same instant an officer of the king's guard snatched her away with a curse and sent her reeling back whence she came with a vigorous impulse from his strong arm. The words "I do not know you, woman!" were falling from Tom Canty's lips when this piteous thing occurred, but it smote him to the heart to see her treated so; and as she turned for a last glimpse of him, whilst the crowd was swallowing her from his sight, she seemed so wounded, so brokenhearted, that a shame fell upon him which consumed his pride to ashes and withered his stolen royalty. His grandeurs were stricken valueless; they seemed to fall away from him like rotten rags.

The procession moved on, and still on, through ever-augmenting splendors and ever-augmenting tempests of welcome, but to Tom Canty they were as if they had not been. He neither saw nor heard. Royalty had lost its grace and sweetness; its pomps were become a reproach. Remorse was eating his heart out. He said, "Would God I were free of my captivity!"

He had unconsciously dropped back into the phraseology of the first days of his compulsory greatness.

The shining pageant still went winding like a radiant and interminable serpent down the crooked lanes of the quaint old city, and through the huzzahing hosts; but still the king rode with bowed head and vacant eyes, seeing only his mother's face and that wounded look in it.

"Largess!" The cry fell upon an unheeding ear.

"Long live Edward of England!" It seemed as if the earth shook with the explosion, but there was no response from the king. He heard it only as one hears the thunder of the surf when it is blown to the ear out of a great distance, for it was smothered under another sound which was still nearer, in his own breast, in his accusing conscience—a voice which kept repeating those shameful words, "I do not know you, woman!"

The words smote upon the king's soul as the strokes of a funeral bell smite upon the soul of a surviving friend when they remind him of secret treacheries suffered at his hands by him that is gone.

New glories were unfolded at every turning; new wonders, new marvels, sprung into view; the pent clamors of waiting batteries were released; new raptures poured from the throats of the waiting multitudes; but the king gave no sign, and the accusing voice that went moaning through his comfortless breast was all the sound he heard.

By and by the gladness in the faces of the populace changed a little and became touched with a something

"I do not know you, woman!"

like solicitude or anxiety; an abatement in the volume of applause was observable too. The Lord Protector was quick to notice these things; he was as quick to detect the cause. He spurred to the king's side, bent low in his saddle, uncovered, and said, "My liege, it is an ill time for dreaming. The people observe thy downcast head, thy clouded mien, and they take it for an omen. Be advised; unveil the sun of royalty and let it shine upon these boding vapors and disperse them. Lift up thy face and smile upon the people."

So saying, the duke scattered a handful of coins to right and left, then retired to his place. The mock king did mechanically as he had been bidden. His smile had no heart in it, but few eyes were near enough or sharp enough to detect that. The noddings of his plumed head as he saluted his subjects were full of grace and graciousness; the largess which he delivered from his hand was royally liberal, so the people's anxiety vanished and the acclamations burst forth again in as mighty a volume as before.

Still once more, a little before the progress was ended, the duke was obliged to ride forward and make remonstrance. He whispered, "O dread sovereign! Shake off these fatal humors; the eyes of the world are upon thee." Then he added with sharp annoyance, "Perdition catch that crazy pauper! 'Twas she that hath disturbed your Highness."

The gorgeous figure turned a lusterless eye upon the duke and said in a dead voice, "She was my mother!"

"My God!" groaned the Protector as he reigned his horse backward to his post. "The omen was pregnant with prophecy. He is gone mad again!"

32

Coronation Day

Let us go backward a few hours and place ourselves in Westminster Abbey at four o'clock in the morning of this memorable Coronation Day. We are not without company, for although it is still night, we find the torchlighted galleries already filling up with people who are well content to sit still and wait seven or eight hours till the time shall come for them to see what they may not hope to see twice in their lives—the coronation of a king. Yes, London and Westminster have been astir ever since the warning guns boomed at three o'clock, and already crowds of untitled rich folk who have bought the privilege of trying to find sitting room in the galleries are flocking in at the entrances reserved for their sort.

The hours drag along tediously enough. All stir has ceased for some time, for every gallery has long ago been packed. We may sit now and look and think at our leisure. We have glimpses, here and there and yonder, through the dim cathedral twilight, of portions of many galleries and balconies wedged full with people, the other portions of these galleries and balconies being cut off from sight by intervening pillars and architectural projections. We have in view the whole of the great north transept—empty and waiting for England's privileged ones. We see also the ample area or platform, carpeted with rich stuffs, whereon the throne stands. The throne occupies the center of the platform, and is raised above it upon an elevation of four steps. Within the seat of the throne is enclosed a rough, flat rock—the stone of Scone—which many generations of Scottish kings sat on to be crowned, and so it in time became holy enough to answer a like purpose for English monarchs. Both the throne and its footstool are covered with cloth of gold.

Stillness reigns, the torches blink dully, the time drags heavily. But at last the lagging daylight asserts itself, the torches are extinguished, and a mellow radiance suffuses the great spaces. All features of the noble building are distinct now, but soft and dreamy, for the sun is lightly veiled with clouds.

At seven o'clock the first break in the drowsy monotony occurs, for on the stroke of this hour the first peeress enters the transept, clothed like Solomon for splendor, and is conducted to her appointed place by an official clad in satins and velvets, whilst a duplicate of him gathers up the lady's long train, follows after, and when the lady is seated, arranges the train across her lap for her. He then places her footstool according to her desire, after which he puts her coronet where it will be convenient to her hand when the time for the simultaneous coroneting of the nobles shall arrive.

By this time the peeresses are flowing in in a glittering stream, and the satin-clad officials are flitting and glinting everywhere, seating them and making them comfortable. The scene is animated enough now. There is stir and life, and shifting color everywhere. After a time, quiet reigns again, for the peeresses are all come and are all in their places—a solid acre, or such a matter, of human flowers, resplendent in variegated colors and frosted like a Milky Way with diamonds. There are all ages here: brown, wrinkled, white-haired dowagers who are able to go back, and still back, down the stream of time and recall the crowning of Richard III and the troublous days of that old forgotten age; and there are handsome middle-aged dames; and lovely and gracious young matrons; and gentle and beautiful young girls with beaming eyes and fresh complexions who may possibly put on their jeweled coronets awkwardly when the great time comes, for the matter will be new to them and their excitement will be a sore hindrance. Still, this may not happen, for the hair of all these ladies has been arranged with a special view to the swift and successful lodging of the crown in its place when the signal comes.

We have seen that this massed array of peeresses is sown thick with diamonds, and we also see that it is a marvelous spectacle, but now we are about to be astonished in earnest. About nine the clouds suddenly break away and a shaft of sunshine cleaves the mellow atmosphere and drifts slowly along the ranks of ladies, and every rank it touches flames into a dazzling splendor of many-colored fires, and we tingle to our fingertips with the electric thrill that is shot through us by the surprise and the beauty of the spectacle! Presently a special envoy from some distant corner of the Orient, marching with the general body of foreign ambassadors, crosses this bar of sunshine, and we catch our breath, the glory that streams and flashes and palpitates about him is so overpowering, for he is crusted from head to heel with gems, and his slightest movement showers a dancing radiance all around him.

Let us change the tense for convenience. The time drifted along—one hour—two hours—two hours and a half; then the deep booming of artillery told that the king and his grand procession had arrived at last, so the waiting multitude rejoiced. All knew that a further delay must follow, for the king must be prepared and robed for the solemn ceremony; but this delay would be pleasantly occupied by the assembling of the peers of the realm in their stately robes. These were conducted ceremoniously to their seats and their coronets placed conveniently at hand; and meanwhile the multitude in the galleries were alive with interest, for most of them were beholding for the first time dukes, earls, and barons, whose names had been historical for five hundred years. When all were finally seated, the spectacle from the galleries and all coigns of vantage was complete—a gorgeous one to look upon and to remember.

Now the robed and mitered great heads of the church and their attendants filed in upon the platform and took their appointed places; these were followed by the Lord Protector and other great officials, and these again by a steel-clad detachment of the guard.

There was a waiting pause; then, at a signal, a triumphant peal of music burst forth, and Tom Canty, clothed in a long robe of cloth of gold, appeared at a door and stepped upon the platform. The entire multitude rose, and the ceremony of the Recognition ensued.

Then a noble anthem swept the Abbey with its rich waves of sound; and thus heralded and welcomed, Tom Canty was conducted to the throne. The ancient ceremonies went on with impressive solemnity, whilst the audience gazed; and as they drew nearer and nearer to completion, Tom Canty grew pale, and still paler, and a deep and steadily deepening woe and despondency settled down upon his spirits and upon his remorseful heart.

At last the final act was at hand. The Archbishop of Canterbury lifted up the crown of England from its cushion and held it out over the trembling mock king's head. In the same instant a rainbow radiance flashed along the spacious transept, for with one impulse every individual in the great concourse of nobles lifted a coronet and poised it over his or her head—and paused in that attitude.

A deep hush pervaded the Abbey. At this impressive moment a startling apparition intruded upon the scene—an apparition observed by none in the absorbed multitude until it suddenly appeared, moving up the great central aisle. It was a boy, bareheaded, ill-shod, and clothed in coarse plebeian garments that were falling to rags. He raised his hand with a solemnity which ill comported with his soiled and sorry aspect and delivered this note of warning, "I forbid you to set the crown of England upon that forfeited head. *I* am the king!"

In an instant several indignant hands were laid upon the boy; but in the same instant Tom Canty, in his regal vestments, made a swift step forward and cried out in a ringing voice, "Loose him and forbear! He *is* the king!"

A sort of panic of astonishment swept the assemblage, and they partly rose in their places and stared in a bewildered way at one another and at the chief figures in this scene, like persons who wondered whether they were awake and in their senses or asleep and dreaming. The Lord Protector was as amazed as the rest, but quickly recovered himself and exclaimed in a voice of authority, "Mind not his Majesty, his malady is upon him again; seize the vagabond!"

He would have been obeyed, but the mock king stamped his foot and cried out, "On your peril! Touch him not; he is the king!"

The hands were withheld; a paralysis fell upon the house; no one moved, no one spoke; indeed no one knew how to act or what to say in so strange and surprising an emergency. While all minds were struggling to right themselves, the boy still moved steadily forward, with high port and confident mien; he had never halted from the beginning; and while the tangled minds still floundered helplessly, he stepped upon the platform, and the mock king ran with a glad face to meet him and fell on his knees before him and said, "Oh, my lord the king, let poor Tom Canty be first to swear fealty to thee and say, 'Put on thy crown and enter into thine own again!' "

The Lord Protector's eye fell sternly upon the newcomer's face, but straightway the sternness vanished away and gave place to an expression of wondering surprise. This thing happened also to the other great officers. They glanced at each other and retreated a step by a common and unconscious impulse. The thought in each mind was the same: "What a strange resemblance!"

The Lord Protector reflected a moment or two in perplexity; then he said with grave respectfulness, "By your favor, sir, I desire to ask certain questions—"

"I will answer them, my lord."

The duke asked him many questions about the court, the late king, the prince, the princesses; the boy answered them correctly and without hesitating. He described the rooms of state in the palace, the late king's apartments, and those of the Prince of Wales.

It was strange, it was wonderful; yes, it was unaccountable—so all said that heard it. The tide was beginning to turn, and Tom Canty's hopes to run high, when the Lord Protector shook his head and said, "It is true it is most wonderful, but it is no more than our lord the king likewise can do." This remark and this reference to himself as still the king saddened Tom Canty, and he felt his hopes crumbling from under him. "These are not *proofs*," added the Protector.

The tide was turning very fast now, very fast indeed,

but in the wrong direction; it was leaving poor Tom Canty stranded on the throne and sweeping the other out to sea. The Lord Protector communed with himself—shook his head—the thought forced itself upon him, "It is perilous to the state and to us all to entertain so fateful a riddle as this; it could divide the nation and undermine the throne." He turned and said, "Sir Thomas, arrest this—No, hold!" His face lighted, and he confronted the ragged candidate with this question, "Where lieth the Great Seal? Answer me this truly, and the riddle is unriddled, for only he that was Prince of Wales *can* so answer! On so trivial a thing hang a throne and a dynasty!"

It was a lucky thought, a happy thought. That it was so considered by the great officials was manifested by the silent applause that shot from eye to eye around their circle in the form of bright, approving glances. Yes, none but the true prince could dissolve the stubborn mystery of the vanished Great Seal; this forlorn little impostor had been taught his lesson well, but here his teachings must fail, for his teacher himself could not answer *that* question—ah, very good, very good indeed; now we shall be rid of this troublesome and perilous business in short order! And so they nodded invisibly, and smiled inwardly with satisfaction, and looked to see this foolish lad stricken with a palsy of guilty confusion. How surprised they were, then, to see nothing of the sort happen—how they marveled to hear him answer up promptly, in a confident and untroubled voice, and say, "There is nought in this riddle that is difficult." Then, without so much as a by-your-leave to anybody, he turned and gave this command, with the easy manner of one accustomed to doing such things: "My lord St. John, go you to my private cabinet in the palace—for none knoweth the place better than you—and, close

down to the floor, in the left corner remotest from the
door that opens from the antechamber, you shall find in
the wall a brazen nailhead; press upon it and a little
jewel closet will fly open which not even you do know
of—no, nor any soul else in all the world but me and the
trusty artisan that did contrive it for me. The first thing
that falleth under your eye will be the Great Seal; fetch
it hither."

All the company wondered at this speech, and wondered still more to see the little mendicant pick out this
peer without hesitancy or apparent fear of mistake, and
call him by name with such a placidly convincing air of
having known him all his life. The peer was almost
surprised into obeying. He even made a movement as if
to go, but quickly recovered his tranquil attitude and
confessed his blunder with a blush. Tom Canty turned
upon him and said sharply, "Why dost thou hesitate?
Hast not heard the king's command? Go!"

The lord St. John made a deep obeisance—and it was
observed that it was a significantly cautious and noncom-
mittal one, it not being delivered at either of the kings,
but at the neutral ground about halfway between the
two—and took his leave.

Now began a movement of the gorgeous particles of
that official group which was slow, scarcely perceptible,
and yet steady and persistent—a movement such as is
observed in a kaleidoscope that is turned slowly,
whereby the components of one splendid cluster fall
away and join themselves to another; a movement which
little by little, in the present case, dissolved the glittering
crowd that stood about Tom Canty and clustered it
together again in the neighborhood of the newcomer.
Tom Canty stood almost alone. Now ensued a brief
season of deep suspense and waiting, during which even
the few fainthearts still remaining near Tom Canty

gradually scraped together courage enough to glide, one by one, over to the majority. So at last Tom Canty, in his royal robes and jewels, stood wholly alone and isolated from the world, a conspicuous figure occupying an eloquent vacancy.

Now the lord St. John was seen returning. As he advanced up the mid-aisle the interest was so intense that the low murmur of conversation in the great assemblage died out and was succeeded by a profound hush, a breathless stillness, through which his footfalls pulsed with a dull and distant sound. Every eye was fastened upon him as he moved along. He reached the platform, paused a moment, then moved toward Tom Canty with a deep obeisance and said, "Sire, the Seal is not there!"

A mob does not melt away from the presence of a plague patient with more haste than the band of pallid and terrified courtiers melted away from the presence of the shabby little claimant of the crown. In a moment he stood all alone, without friend or supporter, a target upon which was concentrated a bitter fire of scornful and angry looks.

The Lord Protector called out fiercely, "Cast the beggar into the street and scourge him through the town; the paltry knave is worth no more consideration!"

Officers of the guard sprang forward to obey, but Tom Canty waved them off and said, "Back! Whoso touches him perils his life!"

The Lord Protector was perplexed in the last degree. He said to the lord St. John, "Searched you well? But it boots not to ask that. It doth seem passing strange. Little things, trifles, slip out of one's ken, and one does not think it matter for surprise; but how a so bulky thing as the Seal of England can vanish away and no man be able to get track of it again—a massy golden disk—"

Tom Canty, with beaming eyes, sprang forward and shouted, "Hold, that is enough. Was it round? And thick? And had it letters and devices graved upon it? Yes? Oh, *now* I know what this Great Seal is that there's been such worry and pother about! An' ye had described it to me, ye could have had it three weeks ago. Right well I know where it lies, but it was not I that put it there—first."

"Who, then, my liege?" asked the Lord Protector.

"He that stands there—the rightful king of England. And he shall tell you himself where it lies; then you will believe he knew it of his own knowledge. Bethink thee, my king—spur thy memory—it was the last, the very *last* thing thou didst that day before thou didst rush forth from the palace, clothed in my rags, to punish the soldier that insulted me."

A silence ensued, undisturbed by a movement or a whisper, and all eyes were fixed upon the newcomer, who stood, with bent head and corrugated brow, groping in his memory among a thronging multitude of valueless recollections for one single little elusive fact, which, found, would seat him upon a throne—unfound, would leave him as he was, for good and all, a pauper and an outcast. Moment after moment passed—the moments built themselves into minutes—still the boy struggled silently on, and gave no sign. But at last he heaved a sigh, shook his head slowly, and said with a trembling lip and in a despondent voice, "I call the scene back—all of it—but the Seal hath no place in it." He paused, then looked up and said with gentle dignity, "My lords and gentlemen, if ye will rob your rightful sovereign of his own for lack of this evidence which he is not able to furnish, I may not stay ye, being powerless. But—"

"Oh, folly, Oh, madness, my king!" cried Tom Canty

in a panic. "Wait! Think! Do not give up! The cause is not lost! Nor *shall* be, neither! List to what I say—follow every word; I am going to bring that morning back again, every hap just as it happened. We talked; I told you of my sisters, Nan and Bet—ah, yes, you remember that; and about mine old grandam, and the rough games of the lads of Offal Court—yes, you remember these things also; very well, follow me still; you shall recall everything. You gave me food and drink, and did with princely courtesy send away the servants so that my low breeding might not shame me before them—ah, yes, this also you remember."

As Tom checked off his details, and the other boy nodded his head in recognition of them, the great audience and the officials stared in puzzled wonderment; the tale sounded like true history, yet how could this impossible conjunction between a prince and a beggar boy have come about? Never was a company of people so perplexed, so interested, and so stupefied before.

"For a jest, my prince, we did exchange garments. Then we stood before a mirror; and so alike were we that both said it seemed as if there had been no change made—yes, you remember that. Then you noticed that the soldier had hurt my hand. Look! Here it is; I cannot yet even write with it, the fingers are so stiff. At this your Highness sprang up, vowing vengeance upon that soldier, and ran toward the door; you passed a table; that thing you call the Seal lay on that table; you snatched it up and looked eagerly about, as if for a place to hide it; your eye caught sight of—"

"There, 'tis sufficient! And the dear God be thanked!" exclaimed the ragged claimant in a mighty excitement. "Go, my good St. John; in an armpiece of the Milanese armor that hangs on the wall thou'lt find the Seal!"

"Right, my king! Right!" cried Tom Canty, *"Now* the scepter of England is thine own; and it were better for him that would dispute it that he had been born dumb! Go, my lord St. John; give thy feet wings!"

The whole assemblage was on its feet now and well nigh out of its mind with uneasiness, apprehension, and consuming excitement. On the floor and on the platform a deafening buzz of frantic conversation burst forth, and for some time nobody knew anything or heard anything or was interested in anything but what his neighbor was shouting into his ear or he was shouting into his neighbor's ear. Time—nobody knew how much of it—swept by unheeded and unnoted. At last a sudden hush fell upon the house, and in the same moment St. John appeared upon the platform and held the Great Seal aloft in his hand. Then such a shout went up!

"Long live the true king!"

For five minutes the air quaked with shouts and the crash of musical instruments, and was white with a storm of waving handkerchiefs; and through it all a ragged lad, the most conspicuous figure in England, stood flushed and happy and proud in the center of the spacious platform with the great vassals of the kingdom kneeling around him.

Then all rose, and Tom Canty cried out, "Now, O my king, take these regal garments back and give poor Tom, thy servant, his shreds and remnants again."

The Lord Protector spoke up, "Let the small varlet be stripped and flung into the Tower."

But the new king, the true king, said, "I will not have it so. But for him I had not got my crown again; none shall lay a hand upon him to harm him. And as for thee, my good uncle, my Lord Protector, this conduct of thine is not grateful toward this poor lad, for I hear he hath made thee a duke"—the Protector blushed—"yet he was not a king; wherefore, what is thy fine title worth now? Tomorrow you shall sue to me, *through him,* for its confirmation, else no duke, but a simple earl, shalt thou remain."

Under this rebuke his grace the Duke of Somerset retired a little from the front for the moment. The king turned to Tom and said kindly, "My poor boy, how was it that you could remember where I hid the Seal when I could not remember it myself?"

"Ah, my king, that was easy, since I used it divers days."

"Used it, yet could not explain where it was?"

"I did not know it was *that* they wanted. They did not describe it, your Majesty."

"Then how used you it?"

The red blood began to steal up into Tom's cheeks, and he dropped his eyes and was silent.

"Speak up, good lad, and fear nothing," said the king. "How used you the Great Seal of England?"

Tom stammered a moment in a pathetic confusion, then got it out, "To crack nuts with!"

Poor child, the avalanche of laughter that greeted this nearly swept him off his feet. But if a doubt remained in any mind that Tom Canty was not the king of England and familiar with the august appurtenances of royalty, this reply disposed of it utterly.

Meantime the sumptuous robe of state had been removed from Tom's shoulders to the king's, whose rags were effectually hidden from sight under it. Then the coronation ceremonies were resumed; the true king was anointed and the crown set upon his head, whilst cannon thundered the news to the city, and all London seemed to rock with applause.

33

Edward as King

Miles Hendon was picturesque enough before he got into the riot on London Bridge; he was more so when he got out of it. He had but little money when he got in, none at all when he got out. The pickpockets had stripped him of his last farthing.

But no matter, so he found his boy. Being a soldier, he did not go at his task in a random way, but set to work first of all to arrange his campaign.

What would the boy naturally do? Where would he naturally go? Well, argued Miles, he would naturally go to his former haunts, for that is the instinct of unsound minds when homeless and forsaken, as well as of sound ones. Whereabouts were his former haunts? His rags, taken together with the low villain who seemed to know him and who even claimed to be his father, indicated that his home was in one or another of the poorest and meanest districts of London. Would the search for him be difficult or long? No, it was likely to be easy and brief. He would not hunt for the boy, he would hunt for a crowd; in the center of a big crowd or a little one, sooner or later, he should find his poor little friend, sure; and the mangy mob would be entertaining itself with pestering and aggravating the boy, who would be proclaiming himself king, as usual. Then Miles

Hendon would cripple some of those people, and carry off his little ward, and comfort and cheer him with loving words, and the two would never be separated any more.

So Miles started on his quest. Hour after hour he tramped through back alleys and squalid streets seeking groups and crowds, and finding no end of them, but never any sign of the boy. This greatly surprised him but did not discourage him. To his notion there was nothing the matter with his plan of campaign; the only miscalculation about it was that the campaign was becoming a lengthy one, whereas he had expected it to be short.

When daylight arrived at last, he had made many a mile and canvassed many a crowd, but the only result was that he was tolerably tired, rather hungry, and very sleepy. He wanted some breakfast, but there was no way to get it. To beg for it did not occur to him; as to pawning his sword, he would as soon have thought of parting with his honor; he could spare some of his clothes—yes, but one could as easily find a customer for a disease as for such clothes.

At noon he was still tramping—among the rabble which followed after the royal procession now, for he argued that this regal display would attract his little lunatic powerfully. He followed the pageant through all its devious windings about London and all the way to Westminster and the Abbey. He drifted here and there amongst the multitudes that were massed in the vicinity for a weary long time, baffled and perplexed, and finally wandered off thinking and trying to contrive some way to better his plan of campaign. By and by, when he came to himself out of his musings, he discovered that the town was far behind him and that the day was growing old. He was near the river and in the country;

it was a region of fine rural seats—not the sort of district to welcome clothes like his.

It was not at all cold, so he stretched himself on the ground in the lee of a hedge to rest and think. Drowsiness presently began to settle upon his senses; the faint and far-off boom of cannon was wafted to his ear, and he said to himself, "The new king is crowned," and straightway fell asleep. He had not slept or rested before for more than thirty hours. He did not wake again until near the middle of the next morning.

He got up lame, stiff, and half famished, washed himself in the river, stayed his stomach with a pint or two of water, and trudged off toward Westminster grumbling at himself for having wasted so much time. Hunger helped him to a new plan now; he would try to get speech with old Sir Humphrey Marlow and borrow a few marks, and—but that was enough of a plan for the present; it would be time enough to enlarge it when this first stage should be accomplished.

Toward eleven o'clock he approached the palace; and although a host of showy people were about him, moving in the same direction, he was not inconspicuous—his costume took care of that. He watched these people's faces narrowly, hoping to find a charitable one whose possessor might be willing to carry his name to the old lieutenant; as to trying to get into the palace himself, that was simply out of the question.

Presently our whipping boy passed him, then wheeled about and scanned his figure well, saying to himself, "An' that is not the very vagabond his Majesty is in such a worry about, then am I an ass—though belike I was that before. He answereth the description to a rag; that God should make two such would be to cheapen miracles by wasteful repetition. I would I could contrive an excuse to speak with him."

Miles Hendon saved him the trouble, for he turned about then as a man generally will when somebody mesmerizes him by gazing hard at him from behind; and observing a strong interest in the boy's eyes, he stepped toward him and said, "You have just come out from the palace; do you belong there?"

"Yes, your worship."

"Know you Sir Humphrey Marlow?"

The boy started and said to himself, "Lord! Mine old departed father!" Then he answered aloud, "Right well, your worship."

"Good; is he within?"

"Yes," said the boy; and added to himself, "Within his grave."

"Might I crave your favor to carry my name to him and say I beg to say a word in his ear?"

"I will dispatch the business right willingly, fair sir."

"Then say Miles Hendon, son of Sir Richard, is here without; I shall be greatly bounden to you, my good lad."

The boy looked disappointed; "The king did not name him so," he said to himself, "but it mattereth not; this is his twin brother and can give his Majesty news of t'other Sir-Odds-and-Ends, I warrant." So he said to Miles, "Step in there a moment, good sir, and wait till I bring you word."

Hendon retired to the place indicated; it was a recess sunk in the palace wall, with a stone bench in it—a shelter for sentinels in bad weather. He had hardly seated himself when some halberdiers in charge of an officer passed by. The officer saw him, halted his men, and commanded Hendon to come forth. He obeyed, and was promptly arrested as a suspicious character prowling within the precincts of the palace. Things began to look ugly. Poor Miles was going to explain, but the officer roughly silenced him and ordered his men to disarm him and search him.

"God of his mercy grant that they find somewhat," said poor Miles; "I have searched enow and failed, yet is my need greater than theirs."

Nothing was found but a document. The officer tore it open, and Hendon smiled when he recognized the "pothooks" made by his lost little friend that black day at Hendon Hall. The officer's face grew dark as he read the English paragraph, and Miles blenched to the opposite color as he listened.

"Another new claimant of the crown!" cried the officer. "Verily they breed like rabbits today. Seize the rascal, men, and see ye keep him fast whilst I convey this precious paper within and send it to the king."

He hurried away, leaving the prisoner in the grip of the halberdiers.

"Now is my evil luck ended at last," muttered Hendon, "for I shall dangle at a rope's end for a certainty, by reason of that bit of writing. And what will become of my poor lad! Ah, only the good God knoweth."

By and by he saw the officer coming again in a great hurry, so he plucked his courage together, purposing to meet his trouble as became a man. The officer ordered the men to loose the prisoner and return his sword to him, then bowed respectfully and said, "Please you sir, to follow me."

Hendon followed, saying to himself, "An' I were not traveling to death and judgment, and so must needs economize in sin, I would throttle this knave for his mock courtesy."

The two traversed a populous court and arrived at the grand entrance of the palace, where the officer, with another bow, delivered Hendon into the hands of a gorgeous official, who received him with profound respect and led him forward through a great hall lined on both sides with rows of splendid flunkies (who made reverential obeisance as the two passed along, but fell into death throes of silent laughter at our stately scarecrow the moment his back was turned) and up a broad staircase, among flocks of fine folk, and finally conducted him into a vast room, clove a passage for him through the assembled nobility of England, then made a bow, reminded him to take his hat off, and left him standing in the middle of the room, a mark for all eyes, for plenty of indignant frowns, and for a sufficiency of amused and derisive smiles.

Miles Hendon was entirely bewildered. There sat the young king under a canopy of state five steps away, with his head bent down and aside, speaking with a sort of human bird of paradise—a duke, maybe; Hendon observed to himself that it was hard enough to be sentenced to death in the full vigor of life without having this peculiarly public humiliation added. He wished the king would hurry about it; some of the gaudy people nearby were becoming offensive. At this moment the king raised his head slightly and Hendon caught a good view of his face. The sight nearly took his breath away! He stood gazing at the fair young face like one transfixed, then presently ejaculated, "Lo, the lord of the Kingdom of Dreams and Shadows on his throne!"

He muttered some broken sentences, still gazing and marveling, then turned his eyes around and about, scanning the gorgeous throng and the splendid saloon, murmuring, "But these are *real*—verily these are *real*— surely it is not a dream."

He stared at the king again and thought, "*Is* it a dream? Or *is* he the veritable sovereign of England, and not the friendless poor Tom o' Bedlam I took him for? Who shall solve me this riddle?"

A sudden idea flashed in his eye, and he strode to the wall, gathered up a chair, brought it back, planted it on the floor, and sat down in it!

A buzz of indignation broke out, a rough hand was laid upon him, and a voice exclaimed, "Up, thou mannerless clown! Wouldst sit in the presence of the king?"

The disturbance attracted his Majesty's attention, who stretched forth his hand and cried out, "Touch him not; it is his right!"

The throng fell back, stupefied. The king went on, "Learn ye all, ladies, lords and gentlemen, that this is my trusty and well-beloved servant Miles Hendon, who interposed his good sword and saved his prince from bodily harm and possible death; and for this he is a knight, by the king's voice. Also learn that for a higher service, in that he saved his sovereign stripes and shame, taking these upon himself, he is a peer of England, Earl of Kent, and shall have gold and lands meet for the dignity. More—the privilege which he hath just exercised is his by royal grant, for we have ordained that the chiefs of his line shall have and hold the right to sit in the presence of the Majesty of England henceforth, age after age, so long as the crown shall endure. Molest him not."

Two persons who, through delay, had only arrived from the country during this morning and had now been in this room only five minutes stood listening to these words and looking at the king, then at the scarecrow, then at the king again, in a sort of torpid bewilderment. These were Sir Hugh and the lady Edith. But the new earl did not see them. He was still staring at the monarch in a dazed way and muttering, "Oh, body o' me! *This* my pauper! This my lunatic! This is he whom *I* would show what grandeur was in my house of seventy rooms and seven and twenty servants! This is he who had never known aught but rags for raiment, kicks for comfort, and offal for diet! This is he whom *I* adopted and would make respectable! Would God I had a bag to hide my head in!"

Then his manners suddenly came back to him, and he dropped upon his knees, with his hands between the king's and swore allegiance and did homage for his lands and titles. Then he rose and stood respectfully aside, a mark still for all eyes—and much envy too.

Now the king discovered Sir Hugh and spoke out with wrathful voice and kindling eye, "Strip this robber of his false show and stolen estates and put him under lock and key till I have need of him."

The late Sir Hugh was led away.

There was a stir at the other end of the room now; the assemblage fell apart, and Tom Canty, quaintly but richly clothed, marched down between these living walls, preceded by an usher. He knelt before the king, who said, "I have learned the story of these past few weeks and am well pleased with thee. Thou has governed the realm with right royal gentleness and mercy. Thou hast found thy mother and thy sisters again? Good; they shall be cared for, and thy father shall hang if thou desire it and the law consent. Know, all ye that hear my voice, that from this day they that abide in the shelter of Christ's Hospital and share the king's bounty shall have their minds and hearts fed, as well as their baser parts; and this boy shall dwell there, and hold the chief place in its honorable body of governors during life. And for that he hath been a king, it is meet that other than common observance shall be his due; wherefore, note this his dress of state, for by it

he shall be known, and none shall copy it; and whereso-
ever he shall come, it shall remind the people that he
hath been royal in his time, and none shall deny him his
due of reverence or fail to give him salutation.   He hath
the throne's protection, he hath the Crown's support, he
shall be known and called by the honorable title of the
King's Ward."

The proud and happy Tom Canty rose and kissed the
king's hand, and was conducted from the presence.   He
did not waste any time, but flew to his mother to tell her
and Nan and Bet all about it and get them to help him
enjoy the great news.

CONCLUSION

Justice and Retribution

When the mysteries were all cleared up, it came out by confession of Hugh Hendon that his wife had repudiated Miles by his command that day at Hendon Hall—a command assisted and supported by the perfectly trustworthy promise that if she did not deny that he was Miles Hendon and stand firmly to it, he would have her life; whereupon she said take it, she did not value it—and she would not repudiate Miles; then the husband said he would spare her life but have Miles assassinated! This was a different matter, so she gave her word and kept it.

Hugh was not prosecuted for his threats or for stealing his brother's estates and title because the wife and brother would not testify against him, and the former would not have been allowed to do it even if she had wanted to. Hugh deserted his wife and went over to the Continent, where he presently died; and by and by the Earl of Kent married his relict. There were grand times and rejoicings at Hendon village when the couple paid their first visit to the Hall.

Tom Canty's father was never heard of again.

The king sought out the farmer who had been

branded and sold as a slave, and reclaimed him from his
evil life with the Ruffler's gang, and put him in the way
of a comfortable livelihood.

He also took that old lawyer out of prison and
remitted his fine.   He provided good homes for the
daughters of the two Baptist women whom he saw
burned at the stake, and roundly punished the official
who laid the undeserved stripes upon Miles Hendon's
back.

He saved from the gallows the boy who had captured
the stray falcon, and also the woman who had stolen a
remnant of cloth from a weaver; but he was too late to
save the man who had been convicted of killing a deer in
the royal forest.

He showed favor to the justice who had pitied him
when he was supposed to have stolen a pig, and he had
the gratification of seeing him grow in the public esteem
and become a great and honored man.

As long as the king lived he was fond of telling the
story of his adventures, all through, from the hour that
the sentinel cuffed him away from the palace gate till the
final midnight when he deftly mixed himself into a gang
of hurrying workmen and so slipped into the Abbey and
climbed up and hid himself in the Confessor's tomb, and
then slept so long next day that he came within one of
missing the coronation altogether.   He said that the
frequent rehearsing of the precious lesson kept him
strong in his purpose to make its teachings yield benefits
to his people; and so, whilst his life was spared he should
continue to tell the story, and thus keep its sorrowful
spectacles fresh in his memory and the springs of pity
replenished in his heart.

Miles Hendon and Tom Canty were favorites of the
king all through his brief reign, and his sincere
mourners when he died.   The good Earl of Kent had too

much sense to abuse his peculiar privilege, but he exercised it twice after the instance we have seen of it before he was called from the world—once at the accession of Queen Mary, and once at the accession of Queen Elizabeth. A descendant of his exercised it at the accession of James I. Before this one's son chose to use the privilege, near a quarter of a century had elapsed, and the "privilege of the Kents" had faded out of most people's memories; so when the Kent of that day appeared before Charles I and his court and sat down in the sovereign's presence to assert and perpetuate the right of his house, there was a fine stir indeed! But the matter was soon explained, and the right confirmed. The last earl of the line fell in the wars of the commonwealth fighting for the king, and the odd privilege ended with him.

Tom Canty lived to be a very old man, a handsome, white-haired old fellow of grave and benignant aspect. As long as he lasted he was honored; and he was also reverenced, for his striking and peculiar costume kept the people reminded that "in time he had been royal"; so wherever he appeared the crowd fell apart, making way for him and whispering, one to another, "Doff thy hat, it is the King's Ward!" And so they saluted and got his kindly smile in return, and they valued it too, for his was an honorable history.

Yes, King Edward VI lived only a few years, poor boy, but he lived them worthily. More than once when some great dignitary, some gilded vassal of the crown, made argument against his leniency and urged that some law which he was bent upon amending was gentle enough for its purpose and wrought no suffering or oppression which anyone need mightily mind, the young king turned the mournful eloquence of his great compassionate eyes upon him and answered, "What dost *thou* know of suffering and oppression?   I and my people know, but not thou."

The reign of Edward VI was a singularly merciful one for those harsh times.   Now that we are taking leave of him, let us try to keep this in our minds, to his credit.